MALORY'S KNIGHTS *of* ALBION

The SAVAGE KNIGHT

PAUL LEWIS

Abaddon
Books

WWW.ABADDONBOOKS.COM

The SAVAGE KNIGHT

DODINAL WENT ON the offensive, lunging forward as two of the creatures came at him, swinging the sword with such brutal force that the blade sliced clean through them both. The rest turned tail and fled, regrouping half a dozen strides away, crouching on all fours, hissing and spitting in fury.

A sudden weight on his back nearly knocked him off balance, and he felt sharp claws digging into his shoulders. Shifting the sword to his left hand, he reached back with his right and grabbed the creature by the throat, squeezing hard. It thrashed wildly, fangs piercing his skin, and he squeezed harder until he'd crushed its windpipe. The creature went limp, and Dodinal hurled its lifeless body into the trees.

He strode relentlessly towards the horde, blind anger giving him strength, the stink of their blood driving him on. There was no room in his head for conscious thought, or in his heart for compassion. Maybe half of them were dead, but he wanted them *all* dead, would not stop until he had cut the life from every last one of them.

And then the earth shook...

WWW.ABADDONBOOKS.COM

An Abaddon Books™ Publication
www.abaddonbooks.com
abaddon@rebellion.co.uk

First published in 2011 by Abaddon Books™, Rebellion Publishing
Limited, Riverside House, Osney Mead, Oxford, OX2 0ES, UK.

10 9 8 7 6 5 4 3 2 1

Editor-in-Chief: Jonathan Oliver
Desk Editor: David Moore
Cover art: Pye Parr
Design: Simon Parr & Luke Preece
Creative Director and CEO: Jason Kingsley
Chief Technical Officer: Chris Kingsley
Malory's Knights of Albion created by
David Moore and Jason Kingsley

UK ISBN: 978-1-907992-33-9
US ISBN: 978-1-907992-34-6

Printed in the US

To Sue and Jack, with love.

ACKNOWLEDGEMENTS

THANKS TO EVERYONE at Abaddon, particularly David Moore for his razor-sharp editing; thanks also to my family; and Steve Lockley, Paul Meloy, Keith Rees, Bob Lock, Steve Savile and Lee Russ for friendship, kind words and encouragement (and beers).

INTRODUCTION

FOUND IN A church vestry in 2006, the Salisbury Manuscript (British Library MS Add. 1138) is the only existing copy of *The Second Book of King Arthur and His Noble Knights*. Apparently a sequel to Thomas Malory's *Le Morte D'Arthur*, the best-known and most influential version of the story of King Arthur and his Round Table, the *Second Book* has caused enormous controversy throughout the academic world.

Following negotiations with the manuscript's owner, Abaddon Books won the rights to modernise and publish the stories for the mainstream market in early 2010. *The Savage Knight* is the second title to be released to the public.

Some of this book is also taken from the *Lesser Dodinal*, the second book of the Hereford Fragment (Hereford Cathedral Library MS 1701.E).

For more information about the Salisbury Manuscript and the Hereford Fragment, this translation, and themes and notes from this story, see the Appendices at the rear of this book.

ONE

IT WAS WINTER. A white cloak obscured the land. Trees rose from the snow, reaching for the grey sky. Nothing stirred, as if the world itself were hibernating. Through this silent, brooding forest, a tall man strode with effortless grace, not once losing his footing on the ice-crusted snow, nor in the tangled undergrowth it concealed.

His pace suggested he had walked this way many times before and knew the route instinctively. In truth he was a stranger here, this knight, yet the frozen woodland felt more like home to him than Camelot ever had. His name was Dodinal. Sir Dodinal the Savage[1] they called him. With affection, yes, but with good reason. He only fought when he had to, but when he had to, he fought like a wild man.

The sun, a watery smudge barely visible through the clouds, would soon slip behind the distant hills of the borderlands. Dodinal would have to stop before the forest turned dark and find shelter for the night, when the air became so cold it could lull a man to sleep and steal his breath while he slept. Not yet, though; enough daylight remained for another hour of walking, maybe two. With no destination, he had no need to

[1] *Le Sauvage*, a title he shares in various sources with Sir Balin and Sir Balan. Literally "wild" or "untamed," its usually interpreted in Arthurian texts as referring to a fondness for hunting, rather than to the knight's temperament; Malory appears to be suggesting both interpretations. See Appendix II for more on Sir Dodinal.

concern himself with direction. All that mattered was that he remain on the move, until he found what he had been searching for these long months.

He closed his eyes and cast around, seeking other life. The trees were like tiny dim lights. A crow appeared to him as a small, bright glow, which cried harshly and sent a clump of snow to the ground as it clattered away from a branch overhead, disgruntled by this stranger's presence in its realm. There were no other living creatures anywhere nearby. Dodinal had the forest to himself.

When he opened his eyes he saw a child standing a dozen or so paces ahead of him, utterly still, as if fear or the elements had frozen him into place. A boy of perhaps eight or nine years, with hair the colour of night. He stared at Dodinal with unblinking eyes.

He wore a tunic, leggings and boots, all too big for him. He would have been a comical sight, were it not for the weather. Although the snow was light after the morning's heavy fall, the air was bitter enough to hurt the lungs. The child's flimsy clothes would soon be the death of him.

"Are you lost?" the knight asked softly, not wanting to startle him. The boy said nothing. "It's all right. I won't hurt you."

He might as well have been talking to himself, for all the reaction his words provoked. The boy's gaze did not waver. His eyes were a remarkably vivid blue. Wondering if perhaps he was blind or deaf, or both, Dodinal took a tentative step towards him. Quest or no quest, he could not leave a child alone in the forest with night fast approaching, to abandon him would be to condemn him to death.

With luck, the child's home would be close by and easily found, or Dodinal would have to find shelter for them both until dawn. The prospect made him uncomfortable and slightly apprehensive. He had no experience of children, and not the faintest idea of how to deal with them.

He ran his fingers through his beard, long and tangled after his months of travelling, while he considered what to do. The boy could not or would not speak. Dodinal had no choice but to search for his village or farmstead. Surely the child had not wandered too far, or else he would have been a frozen corpse by now. There would be signs to look out and listen for; spirals of wood smoke, the sounds of people. There was a good chance the boy's kin were already looking for him, unless they were working too hard to have noticed he was gone.

"Come on, then," Dodinal said with a weary sigh. "Let's get you home before night falls and the cold does for both of us."

Again, the boy gave no sign of having understood a word the knight had said. Dodinal would have to follow the tracks the youngster had made before snow could obscure them. First, though, he had to get close enough to see them in the dying grey light.

The boy suddenly cocked his head as if he were listening to something far away; yet Dodinal, for all his keen senses, could hear nothing other than the soft patter of snowflakes on branches and the gentle creak of the trees as the breeze sighed through them. The birds had abandoned this place, the crow the last to leave. Even in winter, the silence felt wrong.

Dodinal edged closer, anxious not to appear to be a threat, imagining how he would look to a lost child: tall and broad and wild, with a shield held by its strap over one shoulder, a leather pack slung over the other and a sword in its scabbard at his side.

Then he heard it, a faint howl, then another, and a third. He looked at the boy with surprise; the child had felt the wolves' distant presence before he had. Now the knight could sense them: three faint lights like small fires, moving swiftly through the forest, heading their way.

That gave him no real cause for concern. Wolves did not attack men, especially a man such as Dodinal. He was more worried about the impending night. "We should go," he said, wanting to pick up the boy's tracks and get him home, with enough daylight left for Dodinal to continue on his journey through the borderlands.

To his relief the child nodded, turned and walked away.

Dodinal followed. He saw the tracks. The boy was heading back the way he came. Maybe the sound of the wolves had unnerved him enough to want to return to his people. Dodinal could not bring himself to let the child make the journey alone. He had to be certain the youngster was safe. Hungry wolves might consider a child easier prey than a man.

He could feel them drawing closer, their life lights growing brighter as they raced through the forest. Dodinal wished them good hunting. Game had been unusually scarce for days, in a way the weather alone could not explain. The supply of dried meat he had brought with him from Camelot was dwindling fast. He had not eaten fresh food for two days, when he had succeeded in trapping a hare. With luck, the boy's people would be sufficiently grateful to offer his saviour a warm meal.

The wolves drew nearer, heading directly towards them. Dodinal frowned, reaching for his sword. Wolves rarely attacked men, but that did not mean they never did. Starvation could make them desperate and dangerous. He could defend himself. Defending a helpless child at the same time would not be easy. The boy was entirely oblivious to danger, or else he would not have been wandering alone in the forest.

He could hear them now, their panting breath, the crunch of their paws as they pushed relentlessly through the snow. Dodinal grabbed the boy and lifted him effortlessly onto a branch high enough to be out of their reach. "Don't move," he commanded. The lad said nothing, just stared at him with those startling blue eyes.

Dodinal dropped his shoulder, and the shield slid down his arm. He let it fall to the ground. It was heavy, and he needed speed and agility. For the same reason, he unfastened the gold brooch on his cloak and threw it on top of the shield. He held the cloak up to the boy, who wrapped it around his shivering body. Finally, he shrugged off the leather pack and quickly tied it to the branch by its strap. Then he drew the sword and crouched in readiness.

Three shadows bounded through the gloom. Dodinal moved to intercept them, not wanting to be standing still when they struck. The wolves separated, so that one came at him from either side, and the third disappeared. Dodinal felt rather than saw it loop around him to attack from behind.

With a roar that echoed around the forest, Dodinal ran at the wolf to his right. He swung the sword the moment the animal was in reach, making a deep cut along its side. The wolf yelped in shock and pain. Blood sprayed as Dodinal swung the sword again, this time feeling a jolt of metal hitting bone. The animal staggered and fell, writhing in agony. Blood gushed from the stump of one of its hind legs, darkening the snow.

A red mist descended and he barely felt the second wolf barrel into him, almost knocking him off his feet. He regained his balance just in time as it jumped up at him, front paws slamming into his chest. Its scrabbling claws tore through his tunic and undershirt, digging into his chest, and its jaws snapped inches from his face. Foetid breath washed over him. Dodinal grabbed it by the throat and shoved its head away an instant before the jaws could close on him.

Its strength was ferocious, threatening to push him over. Dodinal forced it away from him and then rammed the point of the sword into its belly.

The wolf yelped, its movements becoming frantic as it tried to break free. Dodinal's muscles strained to maintain his grip on its throat. Hot blood gushed over his hand as he drove the sword deeper and pulled it down sharply. The animal went rigid, and Dodinal let it go to join the steaming heap of its spilled guts on the forest floor.

Before he could catch his breath, the third wolf pounced. Dodinal heard the thump of its paws from behind and threw himself out of the way; jaws that would have seized and crushed his leg instead clacked shut on air. He rolled on the ground and immediately leapt to his feet, crouching, sword held at the ready, his other arm outstretched for balance. For a moment his eyes met those of the wolf, seeing only madness. They had not been starving, these beasts.

The wolf snarled and lunged at him. Dodinal stood his ground, holding the sword with both hands at waist height. He sidestepped at the last moment, opening up a wound in its flank with the edge of his blade.

Now Dodinal hoisted the sword and prepared to strike, but the wolf moved with a speed that belied its injury. Before Dodinal could react, it spun around and lunged at him. Pain flared in his right leg and the wolf bounded away, well out of reach of the blade. The red mist that had overtaken him died, and he felt his heartbeat subside.

Dodinal, eyes fixed on the beast, reached down and tentatively felt his thigh, grimacing as his fingers touched torn cloth and ripped flesh. The wound was deep and would doubtless become infected from the wolf's bite if it were not properly cleaned. He could put his weight on the leg, but he could not afford any more carelessness. This animal was cunning, despite the madness that clouded its senses. Even now it was pacing at a safe distance, teeth bared, a deep growl rumbling in its throat as it watched him intently for any sign of weakness.

There was little time to lose. The forest had grown noticeably darker. Before long, the temperature would fall so low that Dodinal would be overcome by the cold, if the wolf did not get to him first. Climbing a tree would put him beyond the beast's reach but would not protect him from the elements. He needed shelter, a place to light a fire. And he could not make a shelter with the wolf on his back.

He roared and charged. The wolf ceased pacing and bared its teeth. Pain lanced through his leg with every step he took and he felt blood run freely into his boot. Dodinal needed strength. He needed *rage*. He reached down and pressed his hand hard against the wound. The pain was unspeakable, but he relished it, and the red mist fell again.

The wolf, startled by his sudden aggression, took a moment to react as Dodinal struck out with the sword, ramming it deep into the animal's shoulder. It yelped and snapped its teeth at him, ripping his sleeve but not puncturing the skin, as he pulled the blade free. Now the wolf took the offensive, hurling itself at him, trying to get at his injured leg, only to be repelled by his precise sword strikes. Its body pierced and slashed, still it persisted, bloodlust overruling its wits.

Soon, however, the punishment it had taken began to tell. The wolf's movements slowed and it backed away, still snarling. Dodinal did not hesitate. He raised the sword and lunged, swinging the blade around and down before the wolf could move. It died without a sound, save that of its severed head striking the forest floor.

Dodinal staggered from the corpse, and his legs buckled. He pushed the tip of his sword into the ground and leaned on it for support, clutching the hilt with both hands to prevent himself from collapsing. His lungs ached for air, which was cold enough to hurt when he gasped it down. He knew he had to get moving, and quickly, before his fingers became too numb to fashion a shelter and light a fire.

With a groan, he looked around to regain his bearings. The light had dimmed, so it took him several seconds to find the tree in whose branches he had left the boy. There was no sensing him in the near-darkness, for Dodinal was attuned to nature, not to man. Using the sword as a makeshift support, Dodinal limped over to the tree, feeling the wound stretch and tear. "It's all right," he called as he approached. The boy regarded him with that same implacable gaze. "The wolves are dead. You're safe now."

Dodinal reached up to retrieve his cloak from the boy, tugging it around him gratefully and using the brooch to close it. He would share it once he could, but for now he needed its warmth. With the heat of battle dissipating inside him, the way was open for ice to steal into his blood and that would be fatal. For the boy, too. Without Dodinal there to help him find his way home, he would be dead in no time. He was suddenly wracked by shivers, and had to wait for them to subside so he could speak without his teeth rattling.

"You will have to jump down."

The child did not move.

Dodinal grew impatient. Were all children so stupid or was there something wrong with this one? "My leg... I cannot take your weight. Do you understand?"

Now the child nodded. He looked down. The blank expression had gone and there was anxiety on his face.

"It's not much of a drop," Dodinal encouraged. "Hang down from the branch and then let go."

To his relief, the boy obeyed, gripping the branch and lowering himself until his arms were fully outstretched. Then he dropped, barely stumbling as his feet hit the ground. Without so much as a backward glance he began to walk away. Dodinal shook his head, unsure whether he was bemused or angry by the boy's complete lack of gratitude or concern. Perhaps that was how all children behaved.

Hopefully the boy was heading home, rather than just wandering through the wood. Dodinal shrugged and collected his pack and shield, ready to follow. He needed warmth and shelter, and food in his belly. He had some of the dried meat left but not enough to satisfy his hunger after seeing off the wolves. Besides, if the boy's home was not far away, he could reserve the last of his supplies for another day when he might have greater need of them. While he did not know how long his quest would last, he sensed it would not be over for some time yet.

He tore a strip from his tunic and bound the wound, grimacing as he tightened and tied it, then he set off after the boy. Within a few steps he knew he would not get far. He could barely walk, even with the sword taking some of his weight, and the boy was already pulling away from him. The bite was burning, perhaps infected by whatever sickness had driven the wolves mad. Dodinal saw a fallen branch and picked it up, sliding the sword into its sheath. The branch made a better crutch. Grunting in pain, he set off again.

At least he could still make out the boy's tracks, although for how much longer was impossible to predict. Stars were already out, winking through the few gaps between the snow clouds. Dodinal had no choice but to keep going, to force his way through the pain and hope he would reach safety before the blood loss overcame him. He pulled the cloak's hood over his head to conserve as much of his body heat as possible, and drove himself on through the darkening woodland. Only then did he realise there were no life-lights to be found, now that those of the wolves had been extinguished. Man and boy aside, this entire stretch of forest was deserted.

This was unknown in his experience, even for winter. Game had been plentiful for weeks. Not once had he gone hungry since leaving Camelot. Yet in the last few days he had encountered only a hare, which had ended up skinned and roasted over a fire, and a few squirrels that had eluded him. There had been crows aplenty, but they were not to his taste and offered too little meat to make it worth the effort of snaring them, and now even the birds had gone. It was very strange. In all his thirty-some years he had never known anything like it.

Clouds gathered, obscuring the stars, and the sky grew blacker yet. Even if the wound had not hampered him, Dodinal would have been forced to slow anyway, to make out the scuffed snow the child had left in his wake. Making the task harder yet was his growing desire to sleep, as the cold drained warmth and strength from his body. Sleep was the cure for all ills, he'd heard it said, but not here and not now; if he gave in and slept, he would not wake up again. But it was hard, so hard, to keep going, to force one leg to move and then the other, over and over until he could think of nothing else. The snow came down hard and the wind picked up, blowing stinging white flakes into his face and blinding him. Dodinal's head was light. He had given up all hope of following the child now. It was all he could do to stay on his feet and stumble through the deepening shadows.

Just when he thought he could not take another step, he saw lights in the distance. Real lights, not life-lights, burning bright in the darkness. Torches, he realised, moving through the trees ahead of him. A hound barked excitedly, as if it had picked up a familiar scent. Now Dodinal could hear voices, too, calling out, the wind devouring the words. When he tried to call back, his voice was a croak in his throat. The lights began to spin, the world spinning with them. He staggered and fell. Then there was nothing but darkness.

TWO

THE BOY LAY buried under a pile of furs and tried to sleep.[2] When he had ventured out with his father in search of game, it had been colder than he imagined possible. They had hunted together since the boy was small, but this time, the icy air had brought tears to his eyes and had driven him back indoors, leaving his father to hunt alone.

Now he was warm and snug, with a full belly and furs heaped on top of him. A blanket hung from the ceiling, separating his pallet from the rest of the hut. Beyond it, the fire burned brightly, popping and snapping and throwing dancing shadows on the walls. Between the furs and the fire and his father's hound curled at his feet, the boy wondered if he had imagined the cold after all.

But while he was comfortable and his eyelids drooped, he could not sleep. Perhaps it was the low murmur of his parents' voices that kept him awake. They would not take to their bed for a while yet. He smiled a drowsy smile and closed his eyes.

He must have drifted off, for when he opened them again the hut was in darkness, the fire a subdued glow behind the blanket. For a moment the boy wondered what had woken him. Then he heard the clamour of many voices raised outside.

Seconds later there came a curse and a thump as his father threw his boots to the floor and pulled them on, followed by a

[2]The bulk of this chapter, and parts of chapters 4, 7 and 9, are drawn from the *Lesser Dodinal* rather than the *Second Book*; see Appendix I.

fast rustling as he put on his outer garments. The boy's mother started to speak, but his father hushed her.

He raised himself up on one elbow, a thrill of excitement surging through him. Something was happening. He thought he smelled smoke. A fire? It was only when he heard the unmistakeable rasp of a blade being drawn from its sheath that he felt the first stirrings of fear. Why would his father need his sword if someone's hut was on fire? Before he could call out to ask what was happening, footsteps clumped across the floor and the door opened, letting in a freezing blast of air that the boy felt despite the furs. "Stay here," his father commanded. "If the worst happens, take the boy and hide in the woods. Whatever you do, don't let them take you."

"Be careful," his mother replied, sounding strained. "Come back to me."

"I will. Remember what I said. And you be careful too."

With that the door slammed shut. For a moment there was silence inside the hut, and then the sound of quiet weeping. The boy could stand it no longer. He pushed the furs away and got up.

The fire had burned low and his father had been in too much of a hurry to feed more wood to the flames. The air was cold enough to make him shiver. The hound was gone; his father must have taken it with him. Pushing past the blanket, he crept across the floor towards his parents' bed, not sure if he would be in trouble for getting up at such a late hour, but desperately needing to be with his mother. He had never heard her cry before and did not like how it made him feel, empty and helpless.

A board creaked beneath his feet and the crying stopped.

"Dodinal? Is that you?"

He stepped closer until he could see her in the low light, sitting upright on the edge of her pallet, hands pressed to her face.

"What's wrong, mother?"

For a moment she did not answer, but then she held out her arms.

Dodinal ran into them, the bad feeling going away as she held him close. "What's happening?" His face was pressed into her chest, so the words sounded muffled.

"Nothing you need to worry about. Everything will be fine."

The shouting grew closer. There were other sounds, too, reverberating through the night: metal clashing on metal, dogs barking and yelping, the roar and crackle of great fires burning. Tendrils of smoke snaked under the door, making the boy cough. His mother held him tight. Then she pushed him away and abruptly stood. "We have to go."

"Why? What's happening?" He knew he had already asked but had not had an answer. "Why is there so much smoke?"

"No time for explanations," his mother snapped as she wrapped her cloak around her. "Get your boots and put a second shirt on. Oh, and don't forget your cloak. Quickly, Dodinal!"

He went back to his pallet, dragged his boots and a shirt from under the furs and hastily pulled them on. He could hear his mother pacing anxiously. The moment he was dressed, she grabbed him by the hand and squatted down so she could look him directly in the eyes. "You have to be brave."

Her voice trembled. Dodinal's throat tightened. He was sad, and scared. His world had been ripped apart in an instant. Whatever was happening, it must be very bad. It sounded like fighting. But that was impossible. Why would there be fighting here?

"I will," he said.

His mother hugged him briefly. "Just move quickly and do everything I tell you, understand?"

Dodinal nodded, not trusting himself to speak.

"That's good." His mother somehow managed a smile. "My big, brave boy. Now we must go."

She hesitated momentarily before taking a deep breath, pulling open the door and hurrying out, pulling him closely behind her. Dodinal blinked, trying to make sense of what he saw. Most of the village was in flames. Thick clouds of smoke boiled into the night sky and swirled between the huts. Sparks flew everywhere. People were running around. Dodinal saw a man stagger about like someone who'd had too much to drink. He fell to the ground and lay still. Others were already down, their bodies broken and twisted. Firelight flashed from naked blades. Screams of pain and roars of anger rent the air, as did the maddened baying of hounds. It was like the ground had swallowed up the world and sent it to hell.

His mother pulled at him impatiently. They ran from the village, away from the fighting, heading for the woods. It was bitterly cold, but his cloak kept the worst of it away, and exertion did the rest. At least he and his mother would be safe. There were places to hide if you knew where to look for them, and Dodinal knew them all. He had loved wandering through the forest for as long as he could remember, especially in the spring when the trees burst into life after slumbering all winter. He had never once got lost. If his mother did not know the way, Dodinal would guide her. He would keep her from harm.

They were a stone's throw away from the sanctuary of the wildwood when his mother cried out and stumbled, her hand pulling from his as she fell headlong to the ground. Dodinal reached down to help her up but she whimpered in pain when she tried to stand. He heard deep voices, drawing closer, lending fresh urgency to his attempt to lift her. There was no way of knowing whether they belonged to his people or those who had attacked the village. He could not take a chance; better to run from a friend than linger to be killed by an enemy. "Please," he implored. "You have to get up. Just a few steps more and we'll be in the woods. They'll never find us."

His mother pushed him away. "Go on without me."

"No!" His vision blurred. There was a burning in his throat that had nothing to do with the smoke. "I'll never leave you."

She squeezed his fingers hard enough to make him wince. "I don't care about anything other than you, son. Go. I'll find you."

Before Dodinal had chance to respond his mother's eyes widened in sudden terror and he was struck a blow to the head, hard enough to knock him senseless.

When he came to, he was in a heap on the ground, face pressed into the cold earth. A ringing filled his ears and he shook his head to clear them. For a moment he was too dazed to know what had happened. Then he remembered being hit, and scrambled to his feet, looking around wildly.

A man twice as tall as Dodinal had taken hold of his mother. He had one arm wrapped around her waist and his free hand clamped over her mouth to smother her screams. He was dragging her away from the forest, towards the village. She struggled to break free, but the man was too strong. Without pausing to think, Dodinal ran at him, grabbed one of his legs and sunk his teeth into it.

The man kicked out, roaring words in a guttural language the boy did not understand. Dodinal held on with all his strength and bit down again. Blood filled his mouth. Yelling, the man struggled to shake him off and keep hold of this mother at the same time. Then he released his grip on her waist to bring his fist down hard on Dodinal's head.

It hurt, but the boy stubbornly refused to let go. A second blow came, this one harder than the first. White light exploded behind his eyes, and his fingers loosened. Had he not let go, the third blow would have knocked him out cold. He tumbled to the earth and felt a gust of air as the man's fist missed him by inches.

Dodinal rolled away and jumped to his feet, wiping his eyes and trying to ignore the pounding in his skull. He tensed, expecting another blow, but the man was not interested in Dodinal, only in his mother. Furious, the boy charged at him again. This time the man was ready and swatted him away like a troublesome fly. The back of his hand smacked into Dodinal's face and blood erupted from the boy's nose. This time it took him longer to get to his feet. When he did, his legs trembled so violently he feared he would collapse.

Yet he would not give up. Again and again he ran at the man. Each time he was halted brutally in his tracks. One of his eyes closed up. Blood from a cut to his forehead mixed with the blood streaming from his nose until his face and tunic were soaked crimson.

All the while, his mother's struggles and muffled screaming drove him on. Finally the man finally tired of the boy's relentless onslaughts, threw his captive to the ground and kicked her hard in the stomach to silence her and prevent her from escaping, then drew his sword.

Dodinal's gaze flicked between the blade and his mother's groaning, writhing form. The man tossed the sword from one hand to the other, showing off, his mouth splitting into a gap-toothed grin behind his filthy beard. He was close enough for Dodinal to see the soot and blood that smeared his face. He was huge, a man-mountain.

Dodinal's sole hope of survival was to dash for the forest. Emotions tore him up. He loved his mother, and every part of him cried out to stay there, but he would be no use to her dead. If he could escape and lay low until the invaders moved on, he could find help and go looking for her.

The man-mountain raised the sword, and Dodinal whirled around and ran, sprinting as fast as his unsteady legs and heaving chest would allow. His feet slapped across the hard earth. Trees loomed out of the darkness, almost close enough to touch. Something whistled past his ear and an axe thudded into an oak immediately ahead of him.

Knowing how close he had come to having his head taken off spurred him on. As desperate as he was to look back at his mother, he had to watch his step to avoid tripping. The countless hours he had spent in the woods saved him, for he ran at a pace and with a sure-footedness that his pursuer found hard to keep up with.

Even when the trees closed around him he knew he was still not safe. He had to get deeper into the forest, to one of his secret hiding places. Dodinal plunged headlong into the darkness, avoiding being snared by brambles or slipping on the leafy mulch.

There was a rustle and a loud thud from behind him, and a grunt of pain. The man must have tripped. He sounded closer than Dodinal had thought.

He drove on, pushing himself hard. The sky was clear and the winter winds had torn the leaves from the branches, but the trees were so closely packed together that moonlight and stars were not enough to show the way. He knew these woods, and the warrior did not.

Dodinal had another advantage. He could see the trees even in the dark. Their life lights were everywhere; dim, like candles in distant windows. He remembered the first time he saw them. He had been very little and had thought they were fireflies, until he reached out for one and his hand scraped against cold, hard bark. When he had told his parents, they had made him swear never to speak of it to anyone. People would think he was slow in the head. So it became his secret, the lights he could see in the trees and the beasts of the wild.

He headed deep into the forest, moving with barely a sound. An echoing voice called out, taunts or threats perhaps, but it soon faded and then was gone. He was alone. Alone and cold and sick with hurt and misery. All he could see was his mother's face, her eyes blazing fiercely as she struggled to break free from the man's grip.

Don't let them take you. She hadn't let them take her, Dodinal had. He should have done more to help, should have run back to the village, not away from it, should have... should have...

No! It didn't matter what he should have done or what he had had failed to do. None of it would have made any difference. He could not have protected his mother. Going back to the village would only have got him killed, he was sure of it.

The certainty did not make him feel better.

He found a path and followed it. When it forked, he continued right for a while and then stepped from it to trudge through the tangle of undergrowth. Eventually, he came to an oak, ancient and massive, its life flickering and failing, with a split in its trunk barely wide enough for the boy to squeeze through. Inside it was hollow, the floor littered with dried leaves, small bones and mice droppings. Filthy, but at least it offered some shelter from the cold. Dodinal wrapped his cloak tightly around him and sat with his back pressed against the wood, hugging himself and trying in vain to stem the rising tears.

He cried until he felt empty, as hollow as the tree.

A long time later, he slept.

WHEN HE AWOKE he was in the hut again, flat on his back on a scratchy straw mattress, looking up at the rafters. Grey light crept in through the smoke hole in the roof. The fire crackled steadily in its pit. Otherwise there was silence.

Dodinal frowned in groggy confusion. Had it all just been a bad dream, a nightmare so vivid it had felt real?

He raised his hands. They were the hands of a grown man, not a boy, etched with scars and with skin chafed from months of exposure.

It had been a memory, not a dream.

He remembered something else. Something far more recent. The boy in the forest, the wolves. His hand reached down to his right thigh and brushed against a thick wad of cloth. The wound throbbed but was nothing like as painful as it had been.

Still, he knew he was far from well. Every bone and muscle ached as if he had been beaten. He was burning with fever and reeked of sour sweat. It could have been worse. In the woods he had been certain he was going to die. Someone had obviously tended to him, but he had no idea who. He had no recollection of being brought here.

Wherever *here* was.

Exhaustion washed over him. He could not even lift his head. Just before he drifted back to sleep, he heard a rustle of movement and shuffling feet next to where he lay, and through half-closed eyes saw the boy from the woods staring down at him.

Then he surrendered to weariness and slept the dreamless sleep of the dead.

THREE

Dodinal awoke to darkness. He had slept all day, if not days. Certainly he felt better than the last time he was conscious, when the boy had regarded him with those startling blue eyes. Now that seemed no more real than a dream. The fever had broken and the strength had returned to his limbs. But when he tried to sit up he had to bite on his lip to stop himself crying out. It seemed the wound in his leg was far from healed.

"Keep still," a woman's voice ordered. Firm hands pushed him down. He did not resist, sinking back into the rough, uneven mattress with a low groan.

He caught glimpses of the woman as she rearranged the furs he had disturbed attempting to get up. Questions crowded his mind, but he could not voice them. His throat burned as if he had swallowed an ember. He craned his neck to get a proper look at her, but she was busy tending to him and there was too little light to see clearly by.

"Try that again and you'll make it worse," she chided, but not unkindly. Her voice had a musical lilt to it. He had heard such accents before on his travels along the Welsh border but it seemed to him that hers was perhaps sweeter than most. "You're on the mend, but you have a long way to go yet."

When she was done she stood over him, then crouched down to take a closer look. Dodinal regarded her in return. Her hair was raven, her face thin, with high cheekbones and eyes of cornflower blue. She was, he concluded, rather beautiful.

"Y-you," he croaked. He licked his parched lips and tried again but his throat was too tight. *You're the boy's mother,* was what he wanted to say. The woman nodded, either anticipating the question or merely offering a gesture of reassurance. Then she reached out and took one of his hands in both of hers. Her skin was soft and cool. A tingle ran down Dodinal's spine; it had been a long time since he last felt a woman's touch.

"Try not to speak. You were badly hurt. The fever has broken but it will have left you weak. Lay still. I will bring you something to drink."

She left him. Dodinal closed his eyes. He cast his senses beyond the walls that enclosed him, seeing hounds and a pair each of oxen, sheep, pigs and chickens.[3] Dodinal wondered how many people lived here, and how long they could survive if the storm did not lift soon.

The feast of Christmas was months past and Candlemas had been and gone. Spring should have arrived weeks ago. Dodinal had set out from Camelot in late winter, expecting the weather to have improved before he reached the borderlands, but he had been wrong. He could hear the wind gusting outside, and feel it rattle the walls.

The woman returned holding a steaming beaker. Dodinal's nose wrinkled at the foul smell. Worse than gone-off meat. When she raised it to his lips, his stomach rebelled. He shook his head firmly.

"Drink," she said. "You've been drinking it for the last three days, only you weren't aware of it. Took me long enough to spoon it into your mouth as well. Come on, it'll do you good."

He hesitated, certain that anything that gave off such a noxious stench could do him nothing but harm, but the pain radiating from his mauled leg eventually convinced him it

---

[3]Small medieval villages often slaughtered most of their animals in November, drying and salting the meat for the cold months, to save on grain. Breeding pairs were kept in barns over the winter.

might be wise to do as he were told. He nodded reluctantly, and the woman pressed the beaker to his mouth and tilted it. Dodinal almost gagged as the warm liquid flowed over his lips. It tasted like water drawn from a stagnant pond that animals had wallowed and pissed in.

He had to fight back the urge to retch up every mouthful he swallowed. "Are you trying to poison me?" he gasped, once he had forced the last of it down. The words rasped painfully in his throat. Yet no sooner had he spoken than a warmth spread out from his belly, banishing the aches and pains from his body.

"Don't be such a baby. It was just a simple infusion, nothing in it that would hurt you. Meadowsweet and yarrow and comfrey. Some mugwort too, and agrimony. All good for healing."

Dodinal studied her, intrigued. It did not sound simple to him. "You're a healer?"

She shook her head. "Not really. I just... when I was a girl I used to watch my mother. I learned without realising it."

Dodinal sensed she was uncomfortable with the question.

She lowered her gaze and eased back the furs covering him. "Now I need to take a look at the wound. I think the worst of the infection has gone, but I have to be certain."

It was the knight's turn to feel discomfort. He tensed, not liking the idea of her hand on his thigh. He cleared his throat to object, but she shushed him. "It's a bit late to be embarrassed," she said. "Seeing as I've already washed the blood away, cleaned and stitched the wound and covered it with a poultice. *And* changed the poultice several times."

With a heavy sigh, Dodinal tried to relax. She was right, of course, although that did not make him feel any less mortified as her cool fingers began to untie the cloth that held the poultice in place. It was only then he realised the lightweight clothes he wore were not his own, which meant the woman had stripped and dressed him too.

He almost groaned aloud.

"You have a name?" she asked.

"Dodinal. And you?"

"Rhiannon."[4] He liked the way she said it, with the R rolling so that the name flowed like water from her lips.

"Dodinal. That's a strange name. Not from around here?"

"No," he answered softly, almost to himself. "No, I'm a long way from home. Where are my clothes? My belongings?"

"Your clothes were a mess. They are being cleaned and repaired. I don't know about any belongings. I've not seen anything, but I will ask later. Now keep still. This will hurt a little." She peeled the cloth away. Dodinal tensed, wincing. It hurt a great deal.

"Looks good," Rhiannon said, nodding. "The infection is completely clear. It was bad, already starting to putrefy. You were lucky they found you when they did, else you would not have lasted the night. If the infection hadn't got you, the cold would have. I've never known a winter like it."

"The boy. He's your son." It was a statement, not a question. The child was the image of his mother.

"Yes," she said, with a smile that was as much sadness as love. "Owain. My only child. He wandered off. Put on some of his grandfather's clothes when no one was looking and left. He's never done anything like it before. If you hadn't come along…" She broke off and quickly wiped her eyes with the back of her hand. "Well, Owain told me what you did. How you fought. You saved his life."

"And now you have saved mine," Dodinal answered, a little more gruffly than he had intended. He was a man who was never at ease listening to others when they spoke from the heart. Sometimes he wondered if that was because his own had died along with his parents. For years after that terrible night, all he had felt was hate, a seething rage that had consumed him

---

[4]"Ryannon" in the manuscript. In the *Mabinogion*, Rhiannon is the widow of Pwyll, and mother of the hero Pryderi; when Pryderi is born, the infant is lost by her ladies-in-waiting, and eventually recovered and restored to his mother by Teyrnon. References like these support the argument that Malory had access to the *Mabinogion*, or to an earlier source document, when he wrote the *Second Book*.

like wildfire. Even now, many years later, the hate smouldered deep within him. Perhaps these days he needed a little more provocation to bring forth the flames, but it was there all the same. "A life for a life. We're even."

She did not answer. Her fingers tenderly probed the skin around the wound. Dodinal flinched. He had not looked, but could picture the torn flesh and the bruising that surrounded it. He had been hurt many times, but always in battle; clean wounds that had healed quickly. This one was different. Perhaps it never would heal properly.

No matter. His quest would continue regardless.

"Where is the boy now?"

"Asleep. He scarcely left your side for three days. In the end I had to force him into bed. He was just about dead on his feet."

Dodinal remembered something else. "You say he told you what happened. Yet in the woods he made no sound, not even when the wolves attacked. I assumed he was incapable of speech."

"He speaks only to me. Owain is not like other children. They all think he's strange, and even though he's my son and I love him, I suppose in his way he is. Sometimes I wonder…"

"Yes?"

She hesitated. Then, brusquely: "Nothing. He has his health and that's all that matters. I'm going to put a fresh poultice on the wound. The infection has cleared, but the skin is still swollen. I have some already made up so I might as well use it."

Dodinal noted how deftly she steered the subject away from her son but did not pursue it. "Could you bring me some water?"

"Of course."

She took the empty beaker away, returning shortly with the water and a wooden bowl. The liquid was stale and tepid, but it tasted as sweet as Camelot's finest mead as it flowed down his parched throat.

The poultice was like warm mud as Rhiannon gently spread it over his skin. It stank to high heaven,[5] the reek even worse than

[5]Medieval poultices often included animal dung and other foul-smelling substances, in the belief that the odor would "drive away" illnesses.

the infusion he had drunk. While she worked on him, Dodinal looked around to try to gain a measure of his surroundings. The fire burned bright enough in its pit to show four walls around him and a thatched roof above his head. Snowflakes swirled in through the smoke-hole, melting in the rising heat. Beyond it lay nothing but darkness. He was not in the corner of a larger building, as he had supposed. Rhiannon and her son appeared to have the place to themselves.

He wanted to know the whereabouts of his clothes, his sword, his shield, his pack. But as he was going nowhere just yet, the questions were not pressing. They could wait until his throat had recovered.

Dodinal wondered about the boy's father, who was nowhere to be seen and whose name had not been mentioned. Again he decided against asking. It was none of his business and, besides, as soon as he was strong enough, he would be on his way. There was no reason for him to get involved in these people's affairs.

"There," Rhiannon said as she wrapped the cloth around his leg and tied it. "You should be back on your feet in a day or two."

He nodded. "Thank you."

"Idris has asked to see you, when you feel up to it."

"Idris?"

"Our *brehyrion*."[6]

"Brehe – ?"

Rhiannon smiled at the attempt. "In days long gone it meant 'chieftain,' if that is easier for you."

Dodinal nodded. Many of the settlements in the borderlands had been founded long ago by the fractured remnants of the great tribes that once ruled these lands. Some traditions remained. Land and leadership were handed down from father to son, their lineages long forgotten, lost in the mists of time.

Rhiannon said, "You don't remember him?"

"No. Should I?"

"It was Idris who found you in the woods. I'm not surprised you don't remember, you were far gone by the time they carried

[6] "Bregirran," in the manuscript. *Brehyrion* is Old Welsh for "chieftain."

you back here. The fever had taken hold. You called out several times while you slept."

"What did I say?"

"Nothing I could understand."

Dodinal was relieved to hear it. He did not want Rhiannon or her people to know who he was or why he was wandering the forest alone during the hardest winter in memory. He swallowed the last of the water. The burning in his throat had eased.

"So why does this Idris not come to see me?"

"Oh, he wanted to. But I told him he had to wait until you are strong enough to go to him. He always listens to me."

The mischievous smile that flitted across her face suggested a closer bond between Rhiannon and Idris than that of healer and chieftain. Perhaps he was the boy's father.

"I'll fetch more water," she said. "Are you hungry?"

He had not been, but no sooner had she asked than his stomach growled and saliva flooded his mouth. "Yes."

"Then I will bring you something to eat, too. The better rested you are, the sooner you will be up and about."

With that she was gone. Dodinal heard a door open, and an icy blast of wind made the fire gutter and dance before the door was slammed shut. There was nothing he could do other than stare at the ceiling and listen to the whistling of the wind as it found the gaps in the walls and insinuated itself under the thatched roof. The weather was showing no sign of improving.

He was alone with his thoughts for only a few minutes, before the door clattered open and Rhiannon hurried in, puffing in the cold. She held a cloth-covered wooden bowl with both hands and had to back into the door to close it against the raging gale.

The moment she stepped inside, Dodinal smelled the food. The aroma was far more pleasant than the foul infusion she had persuaded him to drink. His mouth watered and he licked his lips hungrily. He did not care what was in the bowl; he would eat it regardless.

"I've brought you some cawl." Another unfamiliar word. She

removed the cloth and handed him the bowl and spoon. "Here. We don't have much to share, but it's better than nothing."

Dodinal thanked her and set about eating. The cawl was a stew of meat and vegetables in a watery broth. The meat, cured and dried to last through winter, had softened somewhat during cooking but still required a lot of determined chewing. The vegetables were tender, so he ate them first to silence the grumbling in his belly. When they were gone he turned to the meat, chewing and chewing until he could swallow without choking, drinking the broth directly from the bowl to wash it down. Finally he was done. His stomach, while not full, had at least ceased its gurgling protests.

"I don't think I have ever seen anyone eat so fast."

Dodinal started. He had been so intent on devouring the meal that he had become oblivious to Rhiannon's presence.

"Forgive my lack of manners. I was ravenous."

"Of course you were." She took the bowl from him. "You haven't eaten for three days. I wish I could bring you more, but that was all we could spare. Food is scarce. Our men have been out, but there is no game to be found."

Dodinal nodded agreement. There was game aplenty further to the south, but no hunting party could endure these conditions to search for it. Even fit and rested, Dodinal might have struggled. The senses that attuned him to nature offered him no protection against the elements. As one at home in the forest, he was no stranger to extreme weather, but the snow had fallen and the freezing winds had blown for far longer than usual this year. It had become a challenge even for him. Had he not encountered the boy, he would still be wandering the forest, struggling from shelter to makeshift shelter, his supply of dried meat dwindling with no prey to supplement it. His odds for survival would have diminished with each passing day.

"I'll leave you now." Rhiannon gathered up the bowl and spoon, leaving the beaker at his side. "Seeing as the fever has broken, there is no longer a need for me to be here. I'll stay with Owain."

"Where is he?"

"With Idris. He hardly left your side. Slept now and then, but not for long, and wouldn't listen to me when I sent him to his bed. But he listens to his grandfather, which is why I took him there."

So Idris was either Rhiannon's father or her absent husband's.

It occurred to him that Rhiannon, too, would have had little sleep while she tended to him. No wonder her skin was so pale, her face so drawn. It was not just because her people were having to eke out the last of their food. "Thank you. For all you have done for me."

She waved his words away. "I'll put some more wood on the fire. It will burn until morning, and I will be back to tend to it then. Don't even think about getting up to do it yourself. I don't want those stitches pulling and coming undone, understand?"

Dodinal smiled at her persistence. "As long as you promise not to give me any more of that hellish infusion."

Her response was a look of mock indignation. "That hellish infusion, as you call it, helped break the fever."

"I think I preferred the fever."

"Yes, well, you certainly sound as if you're on the mend. I'll see you tomorrow."

Once she had gone, Dodinal sighed and stared up at the roof. For someone who was never fully at ease in the company of others he felt oddly alone. There was something about Rhiannon that intrigued him. Not her healing skills, although he was certainly grateful for them. Something else, something that remained stubbornly elusive.

Eventually he got it. Rhiannon had seemed entirely relaxed in his company. More often than not people found his very appearance intimidating. He was taller and broader than most men and he kept his hair and beard long and unkempt. He looked and fought like a savage, hence the nickname his fellow knights had given him. Dodinal frowned. Fellow knights? They had nothing in common, other than a title bestowed by King Arthur and a duty they had sworn to uphold.

Women and children, many men too, gave him a wide berth when they saw him restlessly prowling the halls and corridors of Camelot, even when he had left his sword in his chambers. Word had reached him that he had a reputation for sudden, unprovoked violence, but that was not true. He fought only in battle or in self-defence, and would never knowingly harm an innocent. But it was a reputation he was not inclined to dispel, as it meant people tended to leave him alone. Dodinal had never been one for small talk.

Rhiannon was different. Granted, he was weak from fever and unable to stand and so hardly presented a threat. That he had saved her son's life would also have helped. Even so, she had not once recoiled from him or flinched at the sight of his battle-scarred face. She had looked at him as if he were no different from any other man.

That felt strange. But not unpleasant.

They had something in common too. Their skills might be completely different but they were both derived from an understanding of the natural world. She had learned from her mother, he from his father.

Dodinal shifted uncomfortably on the mattress, wincing as the stitches tightened. He had not wanted complications, yet here he was, feeling the first stirrings of interest in a woman he hardly knew. That was not advisable. He resolved to leave the moment he could, weather be damned. The quest could not be abandoned.

And yet...

Sleep was a long time coming that night.

FOUR

THE FIRE WAS burning low by the time dawn approached, but Rhiannon returned early, ushering in the boy Owain, who held a bowl with both hands. She stamped her boots on the floor to shake off the snow and then took the bowl from her son. Their clothes and hair were flecked with white that melted into glistening dewdrops.

"Put some wood on the fire," she told Owain, before coming to Dodinal's side, helping to ease him into a sitting position before handing him the bowl. He thanked her. His stomach had felt empty for several hours, and its rumblings had kept him awake.

"Did you sleep well?" she asked.

He had not, but felt it impolite to say so. "Yes. Thank you." In the bowl were a few meagre pieces of dried meat, some bread and a handful of nuts and berries. Not much but, at a time when food was hard to come by, it was more than he had any right to expect.

After Rhiannon had left for the night, Dodinal had pushed himself up on one elbow to peer into the dimness around him. He could make out a square table and bench, a smaller pallet than the one he lay on and a dresser, jars and pots stacked on its shelves. There was no other furniture. Clearly these were not prosperous people.

The hut's austerity was a world away from the opulence of Camelot, but he knew which he preferred. Life may be an endless struggle here, but at least it was real. Sometimes Camelot seemed to be no more than an illusion, a dream from which he was constantly expecting to wake. Returning to nature had revived a strength he had forgotten he had possessed, and powers that civilisation had caused to lie dormant. He felt vibrant, alive, for the first time in years.

Soon the fire was blazing again, and Dodinal heard Rhiannon bustling around the hut. Looking up from the bowl, he watched her remove her cloak and hang it from a peg on the wall to dry. After that she undid Owain's and hung it alongside hers.

Then she sat at the bench, elbows resting on the table, waiting in silence for Dodinal to finish. Was this how they spent their days when the weather was too bad to be outdoors? Sitting around, saying and doing nothing? Time must stretch on forever.

As he ate, the knight became aware that the boy, sitting cross-legged by the fire, was studying him intently. Dodinal met his eyes.

"Hello."

He had not expected a response, and did not get one.

"We had a close call." Dodinal kept his tone light and friendly, though he could do nothing about the rasp of his voice. He felt he should at least make an effort. "Just as well your people came along when they did, eh?"

Again, he might just as well have been talking to himself.

"Does his silence bother you?" Rhiannon asked, as if the child was deaf as well as dumb. Dodinal considered this possibility, then dismissed it when he recalled Owain hearing the wolves in the wood before he had. Or perhaps there had been another sense at work, one that Dodinal was familiar with. Intriguing.

"Not at all. But I should imagine he will get very bored very quickly, sitting there like that."

"I won't let him stay here long. I don't think he believed you had made such a good recovery. Now he's seen it with his own eyes, he can go back to his grandfather in the Great Hall. There are other children there. He will be better off with them than here, even if…"

She did not finish the sentence; there was no need. Dodinal could guess what the other children thought of the boy. It must be hard on him, he thought, feeling an unexpected flicker of pity as he remembered his own troubled childhood. Twice now, these strangers had invoked emotions he thought he was no longer capable of feeling.

Dodinal ate the meat and bread, but only picked at the rest of it. Berries and nuts were for birds and squirrels. He craved a platter of hot roast beef, bloody in the middle, dripping with fat, with bread to mop up the juices and a flagon of ale to slake his thirst. While he was forever restless in Camelot, constantly yearning for the wilderness, at least he had never gone hungry. He had wanted for nothing. Arthur had seen to that.

But Camelot was a long way from here and he was grateful for what he was given. Owain continued to study him while he ate, his eyes following Dodinal's hand as it moved from the bowl to his mouth. While amused at first, he soon found it slightly disconcerting. There was plainly something odd about the boy.

Rhiannon must have sensed this, for she suddenly announced she was taking Owain back to his grandfather. "Now you've seen for yourself your friend is on the mend, you can leave him in peace," she told the boy as she wrapped his cloak around him and pulled on her own. "He still needs plenty of rest. Don't worry, you'll see him again." She turned to Dodinal. "I'll return soon."

The knight picked a shard of nut from between his teeth. "Don't feel as if you have to for my sake. Your place is with your son. You should spend your time with him, not with me."

"I will, but later. First I want to clean the wound, perhaps apply another poultice. You look much better this morning; it's obviously done you good. You might be up and about sooner than I thought."

That prospect alone was worth any amount of foul-smelling muck smeared on his leg. Only a day had passed since the fever broke, and already he felt like tearing out his hair with boredom and frustration. He felt his spirits lift at the thought of moving on.

Rhiannon was likeable and caring and there was something about the son, his oddness notwithstanding, that Dodinal found strangely beguiling. Perhaps it was because they were both outsiders. But they were not a good enough reason to stay. He was not a part of their lives and had no interest in becoming one.

When Rhiannon returned she brought his clothes, folded and carried in a neat bundle in her arms, with his boots balanced on top. "All mended, as I promised," she said as she stooped to place the pile at the end of the bed. That done, she took off her cloak and hung it up. "Not quite as good as new, but close."

"You did this?" Dodinal said admiringly. The ripped leggings had been expertly stitched, likewise the tear in the front of his tunic where the wolf had leapt on him.

"Not me," Rhiannon laughed. "There are women in the village who can work wonders with a needle and thread. Yes, I stitched your leg, that was straightforward enough. The rest I left to them."

Dodinal frowned. "And my belongings?"

"You mean your sword? Don't worry, it's safe with Idris. I would have brought it with me, but I already had enough to carry and the ground is icy underfoot. It could have been dangerous."

Dodinal nodded, placated for now. The sword was not just another weapon. "Very well. And my shield and pack?"

"I have not seen them and they have not been mentioned. You must have dropped them before Idris found you."

"Damn," he said softly. The shield he could live without, but losing the pack was a blow. It had contained the last of his store of dried meat, a hand axe to cut wood for shelter, some knives, and a flint and steel together with kindling to make fire, along with other oddments that had been of use. Without it, surviving the weather and wilderness would be an even greater struggle.

"I'm sorry," Rhiannon said. "But there's no chance of finding them, not now. The snow will have covered them and the tracks the men made bringing you here." She hesitated. "For a wandering wild man, your clothes are well made."

Her raised eyebrows asked a silent question that Dodinal did not answer. "You should turn around while I dress," he said instead.

She crossed her arms and tilted her head to one side. "You can wait until after I've left, or better yet, when you have fully recovered. Now keep still while I see how that leg is coming along."

Dodinal did as he was told. This time he felt no embarrassment as she uncovered the stitches and prodded the flesh around the wound. There was very little pain. "Very good," she said. "I don't see the need for another poultice. The swelling has almost entirely gone." Her voice turned serious. "Do you always heal this quickly?"

"Hard to say. I have never been mauled by a wolf before."

She ignored his attempt at levity. "There is something strange about you, Dodinal. You're not like any man I know."

"In what sense?"

"In every sense."

When Dodinal made no reply, she did not question him further. Instead she busied herself retying the cloth, brought him a beaker of water and made sure there was enough wood on the fire. "I'll leave you to rest. Sleep if you can. The shadows under your eyes tell me you are not yet fully recovered."

He felt a sudden need to talk. "Stay a while."

"That isn't possible," she said, with no hint of apology. "It was different when you were sick. Now you are awake, it wouldn't be right for me to be here alone with you."

So that was it. "Fair enough. The questions can wait."

"I will bring food later. Owain wants to see you again."

As she reached for her cloak Dodinal impulsively asked, "Where is the boy's father?"

The question stopped her in her tracks. In the charged moment of silence that followed, Dodinal regretted blurting it out; he hadn't wanted to cause offence. To his relief she smiled, a small, sad smile. "He died four years ago, when Owain was little."

"I'm sorry." It was the best he could manage.

"He was taken sick," Rhiannon continued unprompted, looking at Dodinal with eyes that saw only the past. "It was nothing at first: he complained of feeling tired, and we thought nothing of it. Then he lost his appetite. If you knew Elwyn like I did, you would have known then that something was wrong."

She sat on the bench and ran a hand through her hair. "The weight began to fall off him. So I gathered healing plants in the forest and persuaded him to eat them, which was no easy task. He was as big a baby as you."

Again came that fleeting smile, and in it, Dodinal saw the great love that husband and wife had shared.

"But it made no difference. As the weeks passed he became weaker and weaker until he could not stand on his feet unaided. Owain was four then. Old enough to know that his father was ill, but too young to understand his father was dying.

"He lay in his bed for weeks. He was the toughest of men, my Elwyn, but night after night, he would cry out with the pain of it. When the end came, the tears I wept were as much of gratitude as loss. I could not bear to see him suffer. Does that sound selfish to you?"

"Not at all," he said softly. "No man deserves to die that way, let alone a brave man like your husband."

"Thank you," she said, getting up from the bench. "Now perhaps you can understand why I will always be in your debt for saving Owain. Without him, I would have no reason to live. And I suspect it's also why he is so desperate to be around you all the time."

"Because I remind him of his father?" To his surprise, Dodinal found the idea did not sit uneasily. After all these years, he still could not think of his own father without an aching sadness.

"Because he needs someone to look up to."

Uneasy, Dodinal cleared his throat. "Then he would be better off looking up to others. I am hardly a shining example."

"Oh, I think you are. You just haven't realised it yet."

She turned abruptly and took her cloak from the peg, a clear indication there was nothing further to be said on the matter. "Now, remember what I told you. Try to sleep if you can. I'll bring whatever food can be spared, when it is ready."

Time passed maddeningly slowly once she had left. Dodinal tried to sleep, but the tumbling thoughts in his head kept him awake. Finally he could tolerate it no longer; despite Rhiannon's admonitions, he pushed the furs away and set about getting to his feet.

He did so slowly and carefully, using the wall for support, not wanting to risk tearing the stitches that bound the wound shut. Even then it was not easy. When he was finally standing, dizziness overcame him and he had to wait for it to pass.

Once his head was clear, he tested his right leg, putting as much weight on it as he dared. Satisfied it would not collapse under him, he took a few tentative steps past the fire. A pot of simmering water was suspended from an iron tripod over it, and a smaller pot stood in the ashes at the edge, containing what looked like the muddy remnants of the poultice. He shuffled across to the door, overwhelmed by an impulsive desire to see, feel and smell the outside world.

The wind threatened to tear the door from his grasp. It buffeted him, making his hair and beard dance. Cold cut through the light clothes he wore, and which he now suspected had belonged to poor doomed Elwyn. Snow blew into his eyes, concealing much of what lay beyond the doorway. Through the swirling haze he could see the Great Hall, directly ahead of him across a square. Tiers of smaller huts stood to his left and right. Behind them, tall shapes that could have been trees, but whose lives he couldn't sense, rose into the sky. The rest of the world was lost in a tumult of white.

He leaned against the door frame and stared out, seeing not this village but another, or what remained of it. The smoke rising from the roofs of these huts became the smoke that had risen from the smouldering remnants of the village of his childhood.

With nothing to distract him, the memories of that dreadful night flooded back, as unstoppable as they were unwanted.

DODINAL DID NOT sleep, that first night alone in the forest. Through the long hours he sat inside the hollow tree, wrapped in his cloak, shivering from cold and grief and fear, tears leaving frozen trails down his cheeks. He could not get his mother's face out of his mind. He could still hear her groans of pain. He desperately needed to believe she was alive, his father too, but there was an unbearable heaviness in his heart because he knew they must be dead.

Eventually the sky lightened. As much as he wanted to stay here, where he was safe, he knew that to do so meant he would soon die from the cold. He felt sick, yet if he did not eat he would not have the strength to move. So he left the sanctuary of the oak and retraced his steps through the forest, moving slowly and quietly.

All he could hear was the sigh of a breeze through bare branches, the rustle of small creatures in the undergrowth, the harsh calling of crows overhead that sounded like the cries of restless spirits. He was alone.

Shivering, Dodinal pulled the cloak tighter and continued towards the village. He remained tense and alert as he ghosted through the trees, fearful his mother's attacker might have guessed he would return and was hiding in wait for him, as doubtful as it was that a mere boy was worth his time and trouble.

The trees thinned out. He smelled burning, yet there was no smoke to be seen. The fires must have burned themselves out.

Dodinal's mouth was dry, his hands were slick with sweat despite the cold morning air and his stomach was twisted into knots. He did not want to go any further; his mind screamed at him to turn and run until he had left the village far behind.

But he could not. There was nowhere to run to and no point in living if that meant spending the rest of his life alone. Slowly, braced to flee at the slightest sound, he emerged from the forest and stared in wide-eyed, open-mouthed horror at the devastation that confronted him.

The village had gone. What had once been huts were now smouldering, shapeless heaps of blackened wood. Dodinal staggered towards them as if in a daze. Bodies lay everywhere, not all of them intact: as he drew closer, what he had taken for fallen branches were revealed as severed limbs. He wanted to look away, yet found his eyes taking in every detail.

Carrion birds fussed over the corpses, too busy feasting to make any sound other than a rustle of feathers and the wet ripping noise of beaks tearing at flesh. They did not react as Dodinal passed them by.

Onwards he crept, stepping over the bodies, peering at their clothes and faces, trying not to look into their sightless eyes. Some he recognised, others were strangers. The invaders had not been inclined to bear their fallen away for burial.

Dodinal found his father, lying on his back and opened up from throat to groin. His guts had spilled out and lay in a coiled heap alongside him. One arm was pinned beneath his body, the other was outstretched, hand still clutching his sword.

For a moment Dodinal was unable to move for the shock. This could not possibly be his father, not the big man whose fiery temper was leavened by a dry humour, who would always indulge his son whenever Dodinal begged to go hunting with him. No, it could not be.

Yet there was no mistaking him.

Dodinal's eyes blurred with tears. His throat tightened until he was gasping for breath. The gasps became sobs and the strength left his legs, so he crumpled to his knees and stayed there, head down, tears falling from his eyes like rain until he could not cry any more. When he was done, he sat back on his heels and wiped his face dry with his cloak. His hand closed around his father's. He prised the fingers open and pulled the sword free. The blade was heavy, but he was determined to take it with him. His face momentarily convulsed. No, there would be no more tears. No more sadness. Nothing but hatred and a thirst for vengeance.

He could not bury his father. He lacked the tools and the strength to break the hard ground. Yet somehow that did not feel important. It was fitting that this man, who had passed on his love of the forest and his huntsman's skills to his son, should now provide food for the beasts of the wild. He would have liked that, Dodinal thought. It would have appealed to his sense of humour.

"Goodbye," he said softly. Then, remembering the words that had been spoken when his father's father had died, "Rest in peace."

A sense of foreboding filled him as he searched the rest of the village. Now he had seen his father dead, it was surely only a matter of time before he found his mother's body. But while he encountered the corpses of many women, and many children too, there was no sign of her.

Then, just when he was convinced there was no one left alive anywhere, he heard a muted groaning. He stood still until he heard the noise again; it had come from one of the huts, which was charred here and there, its roof partly collapsed, but was otherwise intact. Heart thumping, arms trembling with the strain of holding the sword, he walked slowly towards it. The door was not quite closed, but Dodinal could see only darkness inside. Using the tip of the blade, he eased the door open. A soft patter made him look down. A pool of blood that had gathered in the doorway dripped steadily to the ground.

Dodinal was too scared to go inside, afraid of what he might find, until he heard the low groaning again. Someone was alive in there. He had to help them. Taking a few deep breaths to steady his nerves, he stepped cautiously through the doorway.

What he saw next would stay in his memory forever.

A woman was seated on the floor with her back against the wall. Her head lolled. Her clothes were soaked crimson, and blood had sprayed from the deep slash across her throat and splattered the wall. He thought he recognised her, but it was difficult to be sure. Dodinal had never spent much time with the villagers or their children, preferring to be out hunting with his father. He knew they considered him strange. It had never bothered him.

A baby was sprawled like a discarded toy on the ground by her feet. Dodinal could not bring himself to look at it too closely. The dark puddle around its body told him more than he wanted to know.

As his eyes adjusted to the gloom he saw the woman had a long knife in one hand, its blade stained. She must have died fighting off those who had threatened her and her baby. Dodinal swallowed heavily. If they were both dead, who had he heard groaning?

He spun around and let out a startled yell. A man was curled up on the floor, arms around his midriff. Dodinal's first thought was that it was yet another corpse. Then the man shuddered and a low groan escaped his lips. Dodinal took a hesitant step towards him. Then he took a step back, unsure of what to do.

The man raised his head to look at him. His face was crisscrossed with bloody slashes and his right eye socket was a ragged, empty mess. He reached out with one hand. Two of the fingers had been lopped off at the middle joint. He must have been left for dead when his wife and child had been slaughtered. Despite his own loss, Dodinal could have wept for him.

The man mumbled something Dodinal could not hear; he eased forward until he was closer but still out of reach. He did not want those bloody stumps touching him.

"Say it again," he whispered, dry-mouthed.

The man coughed wetly and blood-flecked spittle sprayed from his lips. This time when he spoke, Dodinal heard him clearly but still could not understand a word. The man spoke the same harsh, guttural language as the giant who had taken Dodinal's mother.

The man called out again, and Dodinal scrambled away from him. The raider began to use his ruined hand to drag himself along the floor, leaving a broad smear of blood in his wake. Dodinal backed up to the door and made ready to run.

Before he could he saw his mother's face again, heard her agonised cries, remembered his father's body and the coil of guts that had spilled from it. A terrible anger rose within him, and he bellowed with raw fury. A red mist descended over his eyes, and when it cleared, he was on his knees outside the hut. He had dropped the sword. It was on the ground beside him. The blade's entire length was slick with gore. Dodinal stared numbly at his hands. They were stained red, his clothes too.

He stood and walked on unsteady legs to the doorway. Even before he reached it he could see that what had been a slow drip of blood was now a torrent. Breathing deeply, he peered inside the hut, glimpsed the glistening mess of flesh, bone and offal scattered across the floor and was immediately and violently sick.

Turning quickly away, he slumped to the ground and was sick again and again, heaving when there was nothing left inside him until his stomach felt like it was being turned inside out. He could only lie there helpless, groaning and retching, until the spasms had passed.

Then he stood and wiped his mouth. Memories flashed through his head like snatches of a nightmare that remained on waking: the man reaching out for him, the sword slashing down, blood spurting, a severed hand spinning as it fell to the floor. The blade rising and then falling. A scarlet rain filling the air...

Dodinal gagged and swallowed the searing bile that rose in his throat. He had never drawn a man's blood before; today, he had not merely drawn it but sprayed it liberally around the hut. He had chopped head and limbs from the body and hacked the torso to pieces, using a sword that was almost too heavy for him to lift. He had not been able to control himself. It was as if someone else had inhabited his body, someone wickedly strong and utterly without pity.

Dodinal was scared and shocked by his display of unrestrained violence. He was also strangely exhilarated.

As soon as he had recovered, he continued to look for his mother. Though he searched until darkness forced him to seek shelter for the night, he never found her. Often, in the lonely years that followed, he would reflect that never knowing her fate was a worse and more enduring agony than the certainty of her death.

THE KNIGHT LEANED against the doorway, gazing out across the deserted village. A long time had passed since then. His life had altered in a way he could never have foreseen, but in some ways it remained the same. He had been alone then, and he was alone now, and he imagined he would ever be so. Only one thing had changed: as a youth he had lusted only for vengeance, and now all he wanted was peace.

He did not think that was too much to ask for.

Dodinal sighed and closed the door.

No, not too much to ask for. Yet it eluded him.

Suddenly feeling the cold, he lowered himself to the mattress and pulled the furs over him. There he lay, eyes open, dwelling on his past while he waited for Rhiannon to return.

FIVE

THE NEXT MORNING he felt strong enough to leave the hut and decided it was time he met the chieftain Idris. Rhiannon made no secret of her displeasure, arguing he needed more rest. But Dodinal's mind was made up; he had rested long enough.

She had arrived with a bowl containing more of the nuts and berries that her people currently broke their fast with.

"Your chieftain will think I lack courtesy if I do not pay my respects, now I am recovered," Dodinal said around the mouthful of squirrel food he was reluctantly chewing. His stomach rumbled. Rhiannon had brought him more cawl the previous day, along with some flat bread, but nothing since. "All the more so because he was courteous enough to allow me to recover in peace."

"It was not so much courtesy as common sense." Rhiannon stood over him with folded arms and a stern look on her face. "He knew that disturbing you before you were ready to see him could hamper your recovery. And I would have had more work to do."

"Ah," Dodinal grinned. "No doubt you set him straight on that. So it was not so much common sense as his fear of you."

Rhiannon gave him a withering, thin-lipped glare. "Next time you can stitch your own leg." But she flashed a smile that vanished as quickly as it had appeared. She was not angry, and even seemed pleased at how swiftly he was healing. Of course, that might only be because she wanted him out of her hut as quickly as good manners allowed, yet he believed she was proud of her healing abilities, for all her reluctance to speak of them.

"I'll tell Idris you will call on him," Rhiannon said.

Dodinal raised an eyebrow. "Is that necessary? I mean only to pay him my regards and thank him for sharing his food."

"He will have none of that, mark my words. Owain is his only grandson and the old man dotes on him. I suspect he would have wanted you to take longer to get well. He tries not to show it, but he is enjoying having Owain spend more time with him than usual. Like me, he will be forever in your debt."

Her words made him uneasy. It was not in his character to draw attention to himself.

"I only did what any man would have done."

"I know many men who would have left him to his fate. As I have already said, I do not believe you are like other men."

"All men are the same," he countered.

"No, they are not. Now finish your food. I will tell Idris you are ready to meet him so he can get prepared."

Prepared? A greeting, a handshake, perhaps a few words of friendship were all that needed to pass between the two men. Unless these villagers had customs he was unfamiliar with. No matter. He would find out soon enough. "I'll dress while you are gone."

"You need to wash first," she answered. "You stink."

"And you are too kind."

Rhiannon smiled as she went over to the fire and took the pot outside to fill it with snow, then set it over the flames. She took an old blanket and a misshapen nugget of soap from the dresser. "This will clear away the worst of the stench."

It was obvious she was teasing him. Then again, he thought, sniffing at his chest and armpits, perhaps not. He had become so used to his own ripe scent while wandering the wintry wilderness that he had not really noticed it until now.

The moment Rhiannon had gone, he stripped and washed away the grime, revealing rubbed-raw flesh beneath. The water that pooled at his feet was dark and scummy, and steamed in the heat of the fire. Once he was as clean as he thought he could be, he used the cloth to dry before pulling on his clothes. It felt good to be in them again. It would feel even better to have his sword at his side.

When Rhiannon returned, she had her son with her, the boy giving Dodinal the same silent look as before. Then he knelt on the floor and reached under his tunic, pulling out a small pouch that hung from his neck by a leather strap. He emptied its contents into his hand, far more interested in them than in Dodinal.

"He seems less pleased to see me," Dodinal observed.

Rhiannon watched the boy affectionately. "He knows you are well now, that's why. He was worried you might die."

The knight said nothing. How strange to think that someone should fear his death when he himself did not.

"You smell much better," she said, smiling. "But you still look like a wild man. Sit here."

Dodinal obeyed. There was no point arguing. He sat on the bench while she took a wooden comb from the dresser and attacked his hair; it felt like it was being torn out by the roots. "Keep still," she chided. "Anyone would swear you were a child."

Finally she was done. His scalp tingled, yet when Rhiannon started on his beard the pain in his head paled into insignificance. He reached up but she slapped his hand away. "I wouldn't be surprised to find wildlife in here. Do you want to be presented to Idris harbouring mice?"

Dodinal gritted his teeth and said nothing, not even when Rhiannon produced a small knife and cut away at his hair and beard until clumps of it were scattered on the floor at his feet.

"There," she said finally, taking a step back and scrutinising the results. "You look almost civilised."

"Thank you," Dodinal said dryly, rubbing his aching chin.

"Now I'll take you to Idris and the village elders."

"Elders?" Dodinal was immediately wary. He had anticipated sharing a few words and perhaps some food with the chieftain, and him alone. More people meant more questions. As there were some answers he would not be inclined to share, it could become awkward.

"His best hunters, his closest friends. You'll like them, man of the wild that you are. But be mindful of his son." Rhiannon's mouth curled down. "Gerwyn is a difficult one. He insisted that two of his friends should be on the council too. To speak for the young as well as the old, or so he said. He was just causing trouble as always."

"He won't give me any trouble, I'm sure."

"I'm sure, too. You're twice his size. Don't worry; Idris tolerates him but keeps him under control. I'm sure you will have much to discuss. Come back when you're done. You can stay here for as long as you want. I'll remain in the Great Hall with Owain."

"No, please. I have caused enough disruption. You stay here with the boy. I will sleep in the hall, if Idris will have me."

"He will not. You are an honoured guest. You deserve a place of your own. Those were his words." Her eyes sparkled in the firelight as she handed Dodinal his cloak. "And I'm sure they were honestly spoken. But by coincidence, it also means he can have Owain stay with him a little while longer."

"Some coincidence," Dodinal agreed.

They went out into the howling white world. Rhiannon kept pace with the knight who moved slowly and carefully, feeling a twinge in his thigh as he walked. The snowstorm was so ferocious that, even in daylight, he struggled to take in his surroundings.

As they headed towards the Great Hall, hunched over and with their hoods up to escape the worst of the wind, he could see the tall shapes he had taken for trees were the remains of a palisade. It would have been a stout defence at the time it was built, but years of neglect had taken their toll. There were gaps Dodinal could walk through. With Arthur having stemmed the Saxon tide, there would have been no pressing need to keep it in good repair.

They scurried past smaller huts, maybe two score all told. The gale flattened the smoke columns that rose from their roof holes before tearing them to shreds. He imagined villagers huddled behind the doors, wondering how long this weather and their food could last, emerging only to share meagre communal meals in the Great Hall, where they would talk to while away the long, empty hours.

Squinting against the blizzard, Dodinal could see a barn, inside which a pair of oxen and two sheep stood listlessly, while two chickens paced around and pecked at the floor. Next to the barn was a small sty and Dodinal sensed two pigs curled up together for warmth.

By the time they reached their destination, a long rectangular building, the knight's face and fingers were numb with cold. Rhiannon went in first, pulling the heavy door open and holding it until Dodinal had followed her through. Then she let the door slam shut behind her and the bellowing wind was immediately muted.

Dodinal took stock of his surroundings.

A great fire burned in its pit at the near end of the hut; a mastiff stretched out asleep before it, legs twitching as it pursued whatever dream-prey it had scented. Several smaller fires burned further down the hut, either for cooking or heat. Smoke was drawn through the roof-holes but enough remained inside to sting his eyes. Before him was a table, longer than it was wide, with benches running along both sides and a chair at each end.

On the walls were mounted trophies – deer, boar and bear – the heads gazing down at the room with glassy, unseeing eyes. Skins had been hung roughly halfway along the hall. Presumably the area beyond them was where the chieftain and his family slept.

A dozen men watched him in silence from the benches, most of them older than Dodinal. A younger man with a mane of dark curly hair sat in the chair closest to the knight. At the opposite end from him was seated a stout, older man, his chair high-backed and ornate. It was he who broke the silence, rising and making for Dodinal, one hand outstretched, a grin across his face.

"So this is the man who saved my grandson's life," he boomed, taking Dodinal's hand in his to shake it vigorously, and clapping him repeatedly and forcibly on his shoulder. "It is good to finally meet you!"

Dodinal turned helplessly to Rhiannon.

"Our friend is a man of few words," she obliged. "And he is not comfortable with grand gestures of thanks. Not when he believes he only did what any man would have done."

"Nonsense," Idris exclaimed. The chieftain's voice was loud enough to rattle the walls, or so it seemed to Dodinal. "I know of no other man who could have fought off three ravenous wolves and then walk almost all the way here with half his leg bitten off!"

There was a low murmur of laughter from around the table.

"It did not seem that bad at the time," Dodinal mumbled, trying to ignore the way the men stared at him with friendly, curious expressions. All save the curly-haired man who sat in the chair near to Dodinal, who was, presumably, Gerwyn. He held Dodinal with a surly and defiant gaze. Could it be that he was intimidated by Dodinal and was determined not to show it? Maybe he was just looking for trouble, as Rhiannon had warned.

His father was powerfully built, with a broad chest and a creased, leathery face that spoke of years of exposure to the elements. His hair and beard were as white as snow but his brown eyes were clear and bright. His accent, like Rhiannon's, was rich and mellifluous. It was said the Welsh were a nation of poets, but Dodinal knew they were dangerous too. Perhaps that was why he felt comfortable in their presence.

"This is Dodinal." The chieftain addressed the room once Rhiannon had left them. "My grandson's saviour, as you will have heard. For that reason alone, if no other, he is now kin. One of us."

Idris took him by the arm and guided him around the table, calling out the names of the men as they passed: Emlyn, Tomos, Rhydian, Elfed, Hywel and so forth, the names all unfamiliar to Dodinal's ears. The men either nodded or murmured a greeting in return. Introductions done, the old man indicated the high-backed chair. "Be seated." Dodinal shook his head and made to squat at the end of the bench – it was the chieftain's chair and he had no right to take it – but Idris was insistent. "I would consider it an honour."

Dodinal reluctantly took the seat. Idris settled on the bench. "Gerwyn, fetch our guest some food and drink."

Gerwyn made no effort to rise. "Why? So we can sit here, watching him eat while we slowly starve?"

"It is tradition to offer hospitality to guests," Idris answered, his tone reasonable. "True, we are not blessed with as much food as we would like, but we will prevail. We always do. It has not reached such a low point that we can be excused for forgetting our manners."

"If this weather persists we will have nothing left," Gerwyn protested angrily. "We can barely feed ourselves, let alone strangers."

Idris banged his fist on the table, the crash echoing around the hall. When he spoke it was with a voice like iron. "Remember your place. You are the not the *brehyrion*, but his son. When I ask you to do something, I do not expect defiance."

Dodinal quickly revised his opinion. On the surface, Idris was calm and benevolent: beneath, he was as hard as the frozen earth.

Not wanting to be the cause of a row between father and son, Dodinal spoke up. "Though I thank you for your kindness, there is no need for food or drink. Rhiannon has taken care of me. And," he added, looking pointedly at Gerwyn, "I do not intend to be a burden. As soon as the storm eases I will leave. I have matters to attend to."

The words did not satisfy Gerwyn. He slouched in his chair, arms folded, looking meaningfully at two younger men sat near him. So similar were their features that they had to be brothers. It was clear they would back Gerwyn in a fight. Not that it would come to that, with Idris there to crack unruly heads together.

"Tell me," the chieftain said amicably, all smiles again, as if no harsh words had been exchanged. "What brings a man to such a godforsaken wilderness as this?"

Dodinal shrugged. He had lost count of how many times he had been asked the same question since embarking upon his quest. He always gave the same answer. "I am a traveller, a wanderer. I drift from place to place, looking for work to pay for food and shelter. Women and song, too, if I am lucky enough to find them."

The older men laughed, although Gerwyn and his friends did not. Dodinal would have to keep an eye on them if the weather forced him to stay longer. He knew trouble when he saw it.

"I see." Idris studied him closely. "For a wanderer and a drifter, you certainly possess very fine clothes. The women who stitched them for you told me they had never seen such fine workmanship."

It was true. While Dodinal could not see the men's boots under the table, he doubted they were made from soft leather and lined with fur. Their shirts were of the roughest of cloth, while his were of fine linen.

"I work hard and have few needs, so I can afford to buy the best of what I require. Cheaper garments would fall apart quickly, and would not protect me from the elements."

"And your sword?"

Dodinal sat up a little straighter. "It belonged to my father. When he died it was passed on to me." That too was a lie; Arthur had presented it to him. "Speaking of which, I would be grateful if you would return it to me."

"My father offers you hospitality and this is how you repay him?" Gerwyn spat. "By demanding your sword? You will happily take the last of our food and drink, yet you have so little trust in us?"

Gerwyn seemed determined to maintain hostilities no matter what. Perhaps there was already tension between father and son; Gerwyn could be using Dodinal to provoke the old man.

"One more word from you, you little whelp, and you'll be picking out your teeth from your beard," Idris warned. With studied slowness, he turned away from his son to face Dodinal. "Of course you can have it returned. Oh, and Rhiannon tells me you lost some of your belongings. That is unfortunate. If I can replace anything when you are ready to leave, I will gladly do so."

Gerwyn muttered something derogatory under his breath. Other than giving him a contemptuous look, Idris did not rise to the bait.

"Having said that," the chieftain added, "you are welcome to stay as long as you want."

"You're very kind. But, as I have mentioned, I have matters to attend to. I will be on my way as soon as the weather improves."

"Where are you heading?" Idris asked. There was something about his tone of voice that put Dodinal on his guard. "Camelot?"

"No. My travels take me north."

"But you *have* been there." It was not a question. "I can think of no other place where such fine clothes as yours could be bought."

"Yes, I have been there." Better to tell a half-truth than a lie. There was less danger of being caught.

"Did you see Arthur?"

"What if he did?" Gerwyn demanded. "Arthur has done nothing for us. They are not starving in Camelot, are they, Dodinal?"

"No. But then I am not in Camelot. And I am starving, too."

Idris roared with laughter and thumped him on the back. "Well answered. But that's enough talk for now. I am not brave enough to incur the wrath of my daughter-in-law. This man was badly hurt. He needs to rest." He turned to Dodinal. "Come. I will walk with you."

"No reason for us both to be out in the cold."

"Except if you fall and open the wound it will be me who needs stitching after Rhiannon gets her hands on me."

"A fair point," Dodinal conceded. "But before we go, I would ask again for my sword. Despite what your son thinks, it is not about lack of trust. The sword is of great personal value."

"I understand," Idris said, solemn for once. "I, too, have lost someone close. The possessions they leave behind take on a greater importance than they ever had while they lived."

With that he strode off into the depths of the Great Hall, disappearing past the hanging skins, returning moments later with Dodinal's sword belt in one hand and a spear in the other. Dodinal stood as the chieftain approached and gratefully took the belt from him and buckled it around his waist.

"A gift," the chieftain said, offering the spear. "I made it with my own hands. It served me well for many years."

"Idris, there is no need. You have done more than enough to repay me already."

"I am too old to hunt now, and I would rather it be put to good use than be left to gather dust in the corner." The chieftain grinned and dug an elbow into Dodinal's ribs. "And you could use it as a walking stick until your leg mends."

Dodinal bid the gathered men good day. Gerwyn and his friends made no attempt to respond, but the others did, even though their farewells were immediately lost when Idris pushed open the door and the wind charged in. The two of them stepped into the furious storm.

Although it was only late morning, it was as dark as dusk. Wind made the trees creak like the bones of the dead. The snow rose as high as Dodinal's knees, making the going slow. He was thankful he had the spear for support. By the time they reached Rhiannon's hut, his heart was beating hard and he was drenched with sweat.

He stumbled through the door and made straight for the bench, where he sat down heavily, groaning with relief. He barely felt the spear slip from his frozen fingers or heard it rattle on the floor.

"Wouldn't listen to me, would you?" Rhiannon scolded, picking up the spear and leaning it against the wall. "Wouldn't wait."

Dodinal raised a weak hand. His teeth were too busy chattering to allow him to speak.

"Well, never mind. What's done is done. Get your cloak and boots off and put them by the fire to dry, before you catch your death. You too, Idris. Not even a mighty *brehyrion* is immune to sickness."

Both men obeyed without question. Rhiannon took their sodden cloaks from them and hung them to dry, heaping fresh logs on the fire until the flames were roaring. Then she pressed a beaker into Dodinal's hand and gave another to Idris.

"Drink," she commanded.

He sniffed it cautiously. The infusion smelled herby and sweet. He drank it quickly, relishing its warmth in his belly. His skin tingled and he fought to keep his eyes open; although he had been awake for just a few hours, he felt like sleeping again. His leg ached. It was not as well healed as he'd thought. He *should* have listened to her.

Owain ran over and threw his arms around Idris. The old man grabbed him in a bear hug and lifted him up, growling like a wild animal as the boy wriggled helplessly in his arms. Dodinal watched them with a wistful smile on his face. He envied them. It had been a long time since he had felt affection for anyone, or anyone for him.

"Come on, then," Idris said as he put him down, the boy tussle-haired and flushed. "Time to get you back to the Great Hall, I think. We'll call for the women to get the cooking pots on." He gave Rhiannon an anxious look. "Though for how much longer we'll be able to do so is another matter. Hardly any of our stored food remains."

The hearty chieftain had gone. In his place was an ageing man struggling to conceal his fears for his people.

"The weather will turn soon," Rhiannon assured him, though she could have no way of knowing when the storm would break. It had already raged for longer than any Dodinal could remember.

"You're right," Idris said. "Of course it will. Dodinal, you are welcome to join us, although I understand if you would prefer to remain here alone to rest. You look like a man ready to drop."

Dodinal nodded gratefully. "I will stay. I would not want to embarrass myself by falling asleep at your table."

"Then rest for however long you need. We will arrange for food to be brought to you." Idris looked across at Rhiannon. "Take the boy and go on ahead. I will join you shortly."

She frowned as she listened to the wind rampage around the hut. "Do not tarry. The storm is blowing harder. Any worse and I fear the roofs will be torn off."

"Then all the more reason for you to go now. I will not be more than a few minutes behind you."

Mother and son left then, Idris tousling the boy's hair as he passed. The flames frantically swayed this way and that when Rhiannon opened the door, settling again once she had closed it behind her, leaving a flurry of snowflakes in her wake.

Idris stood and took his cloak off the peg Rhiannon had hung it on. "I will not keep you from your rest, Dodinal. But I want you to know I meant what I said. You are kin now. To lose my eldest son was bad enough. It tore a hole in my heart. But if I had lost my grandson, too ..." he broke off, visibly emotional.

"Your son does not regard me as kin," Dodinal answered lightly, in an attempt to brighten the mood.

Idris made a dismissive gesture. "Ignore Gerwyn. He is young and foolish. And a little disconcerted by you, I think. When he sees you he sees his older brother, whom he worshipped. That he was taken in such a cruel and meaningless way fills Gerwyn with anger. He hits out in every direction, not caring who he hurts."

"I understand."

"Yes, I believe you do. I know who you are, you see. I know *what* you are, Sir Dodinal. You talked, you know, in your fever."

Dodinal started to protest.

Idris raised a hand for silence. "I will not say a word. I asked if you had been to Camelot to give you the opportunity to tell the others, if you had been so inclined. You did not choose to tell them. I will honour that. You have my word."

Dodinal was too weary to add anything to that.

"Though why you are wandering this blasted wilderness and not staying warm and well fed in Camelot is beyond me," Idris said.

"I am on a quest," Dodinal answered without thinking, startling himself by speaking the truth. He had spent so much time of late dwelling on his past that he had allowed his guard to slip.

"Seeking what?"

"Whatever I might find."

What else was he supposed to say? That all he sought was peace, an end to the violence and bloodshed that had dogged him since childhood? Even if finding it meant having to sacrifice his own life? Death held no fear for him, provided it was an honourable death rather than the kind of unjust and demeaning end that Elwyn had suffered. That would be the unkindest fate of all.

"Well," Idris said, making for door. "I wish you luck. But it seems to me that if a man does not know what he is looking for, he might not know when he has found it. Rest well. I hope we can talk of these matters further, when your strength has returned."

He paused and reached into a pocket. From it he took a sharpening stone, which he placed on the table. "A blunt blade is as dangerous as a sharp blade, but in a different way."

He left Dodinal to stare dolefully around the hut. What had Idris been trying to say? That Dodinal *had* found what he was looking for, yet his eyes were closed to the truth? Then again, maybe the chieftain had not been trying to say anything. It may have been offered as advice, nothing more.

Yet the doubts persisted. Dodinal had been so intent on moving on it had not occurred to him he might want to stay. Not just until the storm had abated. To put down roots and settle. Already it felt like he had friends here; Idris, Rhiannon, Owain. No doubt the men he had met in the Great Hall would offer their hands in friendship too. Even Gerwyn might come round eventually. Stranger things had happened.

Dodinal stood and began to pace, limping around the fire as he tried to bring order to his confusion. He had sought peace, and there could surely be no more peaceful a place than this.

It was hard, here. A bad winter was no mere inconvenience, as it would be in Camelot. It could mean the difference between survival and a lingering death.

Yet Dodinal would consider himself blessed if his future battles were waged only against the weather. While the urge to move on still pulled at him, that could be because it was all he had ever done. Could it really be that he had found what he was looking for after all?

Feeling torn in too many ways, he lowered himself to the mattress and pulled the furs over him, banishing the thoughts from his head. At the moment he had no choice but to stay. Only when the snow stopped and the thaw came would he know how he really felt.

SIX

THE NEXT MORNING, Rhiannon removed the stitches with the same small knife with which she had trimmed his hair and beard. Slowly and carefully she cut through each stitch in turn and eased the scraps of sinew from his skin. She worked with such deftness that Dodinal felt only the slightest discomfort.

"So you knew all along I was a knight," he said, glancing towards Owain, who was seated at the table fiddling with the contents of the pouch he carried with him everywhere. A sharp pain made him question the wisdom of speaking when Rhiannon's attention was focused on not cutting him.

"Not my fault if you couldn't keep quiet about it," she said, angling his leg towards to the fire so she had better light to work by.

"I *was* delirious at the time."

"I had to tell Idris. You almost died. If you had, what then? Should we bury your body and do nothing or send men to tell the King? Only a chieftain could make such a decision."

"Fortunately for me, he is keeping it to himself. Otherwise every man, woman and child in the village would know what I am."

"Would that be such a burden to bear? You would have brought some excitement into their lives at a hard and fearful time. Besides –" She abruptly broke off, chewing her lip.

"Besides what?"

"Oh, it's nothing. But Idris never does or says anything without good reason. I think he wants you to stay."

Dodinal grunted sceptically. "Why, so he can worry about having another empty belly to fill?"

Rhiannon put the knife down before placing a cloth over the wound and binding it. "The storm will not last forever, and neither will Idris. He grows older by the day. This long winter, the dwindling food; it all weighs heavily on his mind. He worries what will happen to his people after he has gone."

"He is strong. He will be around for years yet."

"Perhaps, perhaps not. He has said nothing of this to me or anyone else, but I believe Idris sees you as his successor."

Dodinal laughed. He couldn't help it. The notion was so ridiculous he could not take it seriously. "And you think Gerwyn will accept that? He has not exactly welcomed me with open arms, and that's *without* any foolish talk of my becoming chieftain."

"Gerwyn is no leader, though he would never admit it. He is too headstrong and lazy. Elwyn, he would have been a great leader. That is why his death was such a terrible loss. Not just for me and for Owain, but for all of us. When he died, there were many who felt our future died with him. But now you are here, we have reason to hope." She paused. "As long as you want to stay, of course."

Dodinal did not know what to say. The silence between them felt awkward, so he glanced at Owain and said, "What's in that pouch of his that keeps him so occupied?"

"Why don't you ask him?"

"I would, but he won't answer."

"You never know. He's getting used to having you around."

Dodinal got awkwardly to his feet, gently brushing her away when she tried to help him. Once he was standing he put his weight on his leg. It felt good. Rhiannon had done well for him. His limp was scarcely noticeable as he made his way to the table. Owain must have heard him approach, but did not look round. Dodinal, familiar now with the boy's strange ways, was not offended.

"What have you got there?" He squinted to see the random collection the child had spread out on the table: a ring, a brooch to fasten a cloak, a flint and steel tied with string to a few twists of bark kindling, a few old coins, possibly Roman though he could not be certain in the firelight. Dodinal reached out to pick one of them up, hesitated and stooped so his head was level with Owain. "May I?"

The boy nodded. Dodinal examined the coin. Definitely Roman. Worthless, of course, and in other circumstances unlikely to interest a child. Dodinal replaced it on the table and picked up the ring, noticing how the boy's eyes followed his every movement. It was a plain silver band, lustreless and of little or no value.

"They belonged to his father," Rhiannon explained.

Dodinal put the ring back and, without thinking, ruffled the child's hair, just as Idris had done. A smile appeared on Owain's face, making him seem like any other boy of his age. Dodinal felt a surge of affection. Damn this place and these people. They were starting to get to him in ways he had not been prepared for, slipping stealthily through the defences he had put up many years ago.

Later that day, left alone again, he ventured outside. The sky was dark grey and the snow still fell but the wind, though bitingly cold, was slightly less vicious. Using the spear for support, Dodinal walked around the hut to see if his leg would hold up in these conditions. It did. Heartened, he moved deeper into the village. As he passed by one of the huts its door opened and a pinch-faced young woman looked out. She saw him, and her eyes widened and she slammed the door shut. Dodinal shook his head and laughed quietly to himself.

So much for making friends.

He made his way past a roofed wood store, then past the Great Hall towards the palisade that defined the village boundary.

Several posts were missing, and many of those still standing were crooked, riddled with rot. It was just as well the land was at peace. Dodinal stepped beyond the open gates, which hung crookedly on wooden hinges, and onto the frozen earth between the fence and the forest where the villagers grew their crops.

He closed his eyes and cast out. There was no wildlife within reach of his senses. Had something driven the beasts and birds away? What could do such a thing? No great predator, or else he would have sensed it. A forest fire, then, or some similar calamity? There was no other explanation.

He cast north and his senses brushed against... *something*. Not a life-light. Rather it was as if his mind had encountered the opposite; a great and terrible darkness. Dodinal had never known its like before. While he could not even guess what it was, it felt ancient and warped, so unnatural that his senses recoiled. He shuddered, feeling suddenly cold inside, despite the warmth of his cloak.

He returned through the broken gate, and from there to Rhiannon's hut. Other than the crump of his feet through the frozen crust of snow the silence was absolute.

Once indoors he warmed his hands by the fire and picked at the remains of the stew Rhiannon had brought earlier. He had not felt hungry then and did not feel hungry now, as if the slender pickings of the past few days had shrunk his appetite along with his belly. He had grown soft in Camelot, but wandering the wilderness had made him lean again. Now his ribs and cheekbones appeared as sharp as blades.

He yawned, out of boredom rather than tiredness. He needed a distraction. But what? Unlike Owain he could not occupy his mind with a few trinkets. But that gave him an idea. He went back out long enough to find what he wanted in the wood store, then returned to the hut and found Rhiannon's knife.

When she visited that evening, Dodinal was pleased to see she had brought Owain with her. "I have something for you," he said to the boy. He knelt before him and held out his hand. Resting on his palm was a small wooden carving of a wolf. "Go on, take it. Unlike the wolves we encountered, this one will not bite. But I hope it will remind you of me and our adventure in the forest."

After glancing uncertainly at his mother and receiving a nod of encouragement, Owain reached out and took it. He peered at it and gave Dodinal another of his rare smiles, then threw his arms around the knight and hugged him briefly before scurrying over to the table. Taking out the pouch, he emptied its contents onto the tabletop and set the wooden wolf down amongst them.

"That was nice," Rhiannon said. "Very thoughtful."

Dodinal busied himself with tending to the fire.

During the days that followed, he fell into the habit of walking around the village every morning and afternoon. Each time he left his sword in the hut; he had no need of it and it was something of an encumbrance. The worst of the storm had passed. Although the sky was laden with slate-coloured clouds there was only the occasional flurry of snow. Yet there was no respite from winter; the air remained bitterly cold, the ground icy beneath its thick covering of white.

One afternoon he went again to the cleared area beyond the palisade. Reluctantly he cast his mind northwards. There was nothing. He began to make his way back up to the village, feeling relieved.

As he reached the broken palisade, Gerwyn stepped through one of the gaps, one hand on the sword in his belt. Dodinal reached for his own and silently cursed its absence.

"Best you go back the way you came, traveller," Gerwyn spat. "We have barely enough food to feed ourselves."

"I thank you for your advice," Dodinal responded pleasantly. "But I have no intention of going anywhere for now."

Gerwyn glanced back. Dodinal followed his gaze. Gerwyn's two friends, the brothers who had sided with him in the Great Hall, waited on the other side of the fence. They, too, were armed, and glared at Dodinal with unconcealed animosity. If it came down to a fight it would be three men against one. But of course he could not allow it to come to that. In the heat of combat he might lose control.

He could disarm them. Yes, they carried swords, but it was unlikely they would have had much cause to use them. Dodinal, though unarmed, was battle-hardened and had brute strength to call upon. He might have to break the odd bone or blacken a few eyes, but at least these three would still be breathing when it was over.

He drew himself up to his full height. A flicker of unease crossed Gerwyn's face when he realised he had to crane his neck to meet Dodinal's eyes; his head was roughly level with Dodinal's chest.

"If you want me to leave, then I will leave. But not until I have said farewell to Rhiannon and your father."

"There's no need for that. Just go while you still have the chance." For all the bravado of his words there was uncertainty in the younger man's tone, the subtlest hint of a tremor.

"Not without my sword. I will fetch it and then leave."

Dodinal laced his fingers together and, stretching his arms out, flexed them until the joints popped, shockingly loud in the stillness of the late afternoon.

Gerwyn took a step back towards the fence. His friends backed away a little, too, sharing nervous glances.

As they edged away, so Dodinal stepped towards them. Gerwyn's back came up against the palisade and he looked around until he located the gap and hurried through it. Dodinal continued his slow advance until he was inside the village with them.

"Well, here we are. Now, my friends, if you will kindly step aside, I will fetch my sword and the spear your father so generously gave me and pay my respects to him before leaving."

Gerwyn looked a little desperately at his friends, and they looked back helplessly at him. They would be torn between anger, frustration and fear; wanting to take Dodinal on yet sensing they were no match for him, as much as their youthful pride was loathe to admit it.

Finally Gerwyn's shoulders slumped. "Stay, if you want. I no longer care. But remember, each morsel of food that passes your lips is denied the women and children of this village. I trust that rests easy on your conscience... assuming you have one."

He spat on the ground and stalked off towards the Great Hall, his two friends falling in behind him without a word.

Dodinal relaxed. He had avoided bloodshed, which was good, but now he had given Gerwyn even more of a reason to hate him, by facing him down in front of his friends. Dodinal would have to watch his back. There was no telling what the chieftain's son might do.

He looked up into the turbulent sky. When all was said and done, Gerwyn had spoken the truth. He was a burden on these people. He could not leave until the thaw came, yet to stay meant depriving them of food that was rightfully theirs.

There was only one answer. He hurried back to Rhiannon's hut.

He would take to his bed early. Tomorrow he would be up with the dawn.

SEVEN

THE SKY WAS dark, but streaked with light to the east. A wind had picked up during the night, driving the clouds away and sending the temperature plummeting. Dodinal hesitated by the broken gates long enough to tighten his cloak and pull the hood over his head. The sword hung in its scabbard from his belt, and he clutched the spear that Idris had gifted him in his right hand. One way or another, he would put it to use before he returned. With one last look at the cluster of huts he headed out of the village.

A sense of belonging swept over him when he entered the forest. He had spent most of his life with branches overhead, heavy with leaves in the summer and starkly bare in the cold months. Yet as he progressed south through the woodland, the snow-white ground dappled with shadows, he was overwhelmed by a strangely terrible feeling. Something was indistinctly wrong in the forest. It was utterly still, and that should not be. There was not so much as the raucous call of a scavenger crow to break the silence.

At least here, the snow was thinner on the ground. Dodinal made swift progress. Soon the sun rose, revealing a brilliant blue sky. It was bitterly cold, but he kept warm by moving steadily, not once stopping to rest. He had no need to, now he was fully recovered. Even if he had, there was no comfort to be found in the frozen wilderness, and he lacked the means to make a fire. And as he pressed on, the ghosts of another forest and another time came back to haunt him.

THE BOY DODINAL could not bring himself to spend his nights among the dead in the ruins of his village. His hut was among those damaged but still standing, and he returned to it to gather what belongings he could carry. His vision blurred as he stepped inside, and a chasm opened in his chest. Everyone he loved was gone. His life had turned from one of uncaring innocence to one of unbearable misery within a matter of hours. Dodinal bit down on his lip to stop himself crying.

There would be no more tears, not ever again.

He put the sword on the table and collected anything he thought he could use, piling it onto a fur that he tied into a bundle and slung over his shoulder. Then he picked up the sword and went back into the forest, hastening to the hollow tree that had become his home. He dumped the bundle inside it before returning to the hut for more furs and his mattress, which he dragged behind him to the oak.

Not daring to light a fire inside the hollow, he gathered branches and used his father's flint and steel to start one just outside it. While he was worried the smoke could attract unwanted attention, he had no choice; without the fire's warmth he would not survive another night.

He filled his stomach with some of the meat and fruit he had salvaged and sat wrapped in his cloak close to the fire until his eyelids grew heavy. Then he crawled inside the tree and slept on his mattress with furs heaped on top of him, just as he always had.

This was how his days and nights passed. Each time he ran out of food he would return to the village and scavenge what he could, returning to the tree to eat by the fire until darkness fell and he slept. He would try not to look at the dead, whose bones the scavengers and carrion birds had by now almost picked clean.

Finally, when there was no more food, Dodinal set a snare the way his father had done. Having searched for and found hare tracks he broke off a sturdy yet flexible branch and sharpened both ends, driving each end deep into the ground on either side of the tracks to form an arch. From it he hung a length of gut whose end he tied into a noose. Once a hare's head passed through the noose it would tighten around its neck, killing it.

That evening, dozing before the fire, he saw a small light move through the darkness. Through closed eyes he followed the hare's progress as it loped along the track where he had set the snare, and was then snuffed out.

Dodinal ate well that night.

Days passed, then months. Remembering everything his father had taught him, he grew into an accomplished hunter. His gifts meant he always knew where to find game, and his presence did not disturb it. It was as if the animals saw him as one of their own, a creature of the wild. When summer arrived and a putrid stench arose from the village he knew it was time to move on. He could not live inside a tree forever. Besides, he was growing at such a rapid rate it was becoming a squeeze getting in and out of the hollow. This did not worry him. He had all summer to find somewhere else.

He had to make one last journey home, to find clothes, as those he wore were becoming too small for him. So foul was the smell that he was forced to cut off a strip from his cloak to bind around his nose and mouth. The tracks of scavengers covered the ground and flies picked their way leisurely across the bony corpses. Dodinal changed his old clothes for some of his father's and fled for the trees, never to return.

From that day he wandered the forest, sleeping under stars and hunting whenever he was hungry. He learned which plants could be eaten safely and which would make him sick. Each year when the leaves changed colour and fell, he would fashion a shelter roomy enough to light a fire in and there he would spend the winter.

As he grew taller and stronger, he found work in the settlements and farmsteads he encountered on his travels.

Ploughing, sowing, harvesting... he laboured for food or for clothing, which was quickly worn through.

And so his time passed, uncomplicated and untroubled, until the day came when he heard the sound of fighting.

THE KNIGHT SNAPPED out of his reverie. There was a deer close by. Its life did not burn brightly; the animal was either injured or sick. That made no difference to Dodinal, for meat was meat and his mouth watered at the thought of it.

He stole through the trees, closing on his prey. It was a large roe buck, moving away but slowly enough for Dodinal to be confident it had not caught his scent. It had been attacked by some predator, leaving one of its hind legs lame.

Dodinal raised the spear to his shoulder, ready to strike the moment he was close enough. If he threw it from this distance, he could easily miss and the deer would be gone in the blink of an eye. It could outrun him, bad leg or not. He might not get another chance to track game for a long time.

It stopped to lower its head, nosing through the snow in search of food. Dodinal crept up behind it until it was almost close enough to touch, but as soundlessly as he moved, the deer somehow sensed him; it suddenly lifted its head and looked around, startled. Before it could run from him, Dodinal lunged forward and rammed the point of the blade deep into its shoulder, driving it towards its heart.

The deer bucked violently. The spear was torn from Dodinal's hands as it bolted, racing through the forest with an almost comically lopsided gait. He followed at a slow pace. There was no reason to hurry. The deer was dead but did not yet know it.

Sure enough, he found its body after a few minutes. He wrenched the spear from its side and wiped the blade clean in the snow. Idris would doubtless be pleased to hear the weapon that had served him so well for many years could still put meat on his table.

Butchery done, he picked up the gutted carcass, hoisted it over his shoulder and set off for the village. The deer was heavy, but Dodinal was strong and tireless, all the more so with the prospect of fresh meat that night spurring him on. As long as his luck and the weather held he would be back by late afternoon.

EIGHT

THE GREAT HALL was uncomfortably hot, as much from the mass of bodies that had gathered inside to celebrate as from the fires that burned day and night. Smoke made his eyes sting, and it was difficult to hear anything above the excited chatter of voices as the villagers welcomed the stroke of good fortune that had come their way after so many months of hardship.

The venison had been spit-roasted and stripped from the bone before being shared out between them. There was not much to go around, but Dodinal heard no complaints. Every last scrap of meat had been devoured but the air was still rich with the smell of it.

The chieftain's great hound lay contentedly near the fire, front paws outstretched as it chewed and crunched on a bone. The rest of the deer carcass would be boiled into a broth, its skin fashioned into clothes, stitched together with its sinew. Nothing went to waste here.

Dodinal had again been given pride of place in the chieftain's chair at the head of the table. Idris, Rhiannon and Owain sat nearest to him on the benches. Gerwyn was there too, sulking in his chair. It did not escape Dodinal's notice that the younger man's lips and chin were glistening with grease; he might resent Dodinal eating the village's food but had no problem with the village eating his.

Neither had Dodinal's gift softened his disdain. Gerwyn would not speak directly to him, and scowled whenever Dodinal spoke. There was no doubt he was still fuming at being humiliated in front of his friends. Dodinal did not care. He had friends of his own now.

It was starting to feel like home.

Villagers gathered around the table or sat with their backs against the walls, basking in the heat of the fires, laughing as they picked meat from their teeth. At first they had been nervous in Dodinal's presence, but as the evening wore on and ale had flowed, they had slowly relaxed around him. Many even thanked him for what he had done. The children regarded him with outright reverence. A few adults plucked up the courage to ask questions, but Idris shooed them away. Looking around the hut, Dodinal was in good spirits. He had helped to lift these people's hearts, for a while. Tomorrow they would return to their relentless struggle. Spring had still not arrived

"So, then," Idris bellowed, leaning forward as though his voice was not already loud enough to ring in Dodinal's ears. "When will you hunt next, my friend? Now we have the taste of fresh meat in our mouths, we hunger for more. Oh, and next time I will come with you. Between us we can carry more than you can manage alone."

Dodinal's expression was doubtful. "There is still little game to be found. I was lucky. The deer was lame. We might have to travel days, weeks possibly, before we find more."

"Then we travel for weeks or days."

"And if the storm returns?" Dodinal challenged. "No man could survive those conditions, not without fire and shelter. If we are caught in another blizzard, it would be the end of us."

"It could well be the end of us if we do nothing."

Idris was determined not to give up without a fight. Dodinal wondered what he could say to convince him to abandon the idea, when Rhiannon spoke up.

"You should listen to him." She was seated across from Idris, Owain at her side. The boy had his elbows on the table and rested his chin on his hands. He looked lost in his thoughts. "Remember how close he was to death when we found him? Dodinal is a man who has spent much of his life in the wilderness. He knows what he's talking about. If he has concerns, you would be wise to heed them."

"Siding with the stranger over your own *brehyrion*?" Gerwyn asked, his mouth curled into a sneer.

Rhiannon's blue eyes flashed. "Stop behaving like a child. It is not a question of siding with anyone. It's common sense."

"You're right, as always," Idris boomed, laughing with indulgent affection. "We have enough supplies to see us through the next few weeks and surely by then this bloody winter will be over."

His mood was more optimistic than it had been when he had walked Dodinal back to the hut.

"And if it isn't?" Gerwyn demanded.

Dodinal drained the last of his ale and put the beaker down on the table. "If it isn't, then I will go south alone. Better to risk the life of one man than the lives of many. If there is any game to be found in this forest, I will find it and bring it to you."

Gerwyn made a dismissive gesture and turned away.

They talked a while longer, and then, one by one, the villagers said their farewells and drifted off to their homes. It was dark. The air was already cruelly sharp. Everyone wanted to be wrapped up in furs around their fires before it got any colder.

Dodinal yawned. "I will take my leave. It has been a long day."

"You are welcome to stay." Idris placed a hand on Dodinal's arm. "Surely it must get lonely, spending so much time in that hut."

For a moment Dodinal was tempted. Then he shook his head. "Solitude suits some people, and I am one of them. I like to be alone with my thoughts." Realising that sounded as though he did not want *their* company, he quickly added: "And you would not like my snoring!"

As he got up from the chair he saw Owain gazing at him, head cocked, just as he had done before the wolves attacked. The hound dropped the bone and raised its head to look intently at the door. There was someone outside. The mastiff gathered itself and leapt to its feet, a growl rumbling in its throat.

"What's wrong with him?" Gerwyn asked, sounding more irritated than concerned.

Dodinal glanced at Idris and nodded towards the door, an unspoken thought passing between them. *Trouble.*

The knight had left both sword and spear in Rhiannon's hut, thinking he would have no need of them. It was too late to be concerned about that; he would have to make do with what he had.

"Stay here," he said. Idris started to protest, but Dodinal waved him silent. There were no wild beasts outside, he knew that much. Men, then. If there were intruders in the village, Dodinal would need to move quickly, without Idris getting in his way. Should the rage overwhelm him, he would not differentiate between friend and foe.

He moved swiftly to the door and pulled it open. The hound growled louder, snarling, but staying at Idris's side. Dodinal had encountered knights who were less disciplined.

He stood in the doorway and looked around. The sky was clear, the moon a polished coin. Stars glittered coldly. The village was a patchwork of silver and shadow. A faint voice called out from somewhere within the dense wall of trees beyond the palisade.

Dodinal glanced back into the hut towards Idris. "It could be trouble or nothing at all. I'll go and look. Give me fifteen minutes; if I have not returned by then, gather your best men and take arms."

"I will come with you," the chieftain offered.

"Stay here. I can move quickly and quietly. They will not even know I'm there. Don't worry, if I need your help I'll call for it."

"Be careful," Rhiannon said, and Dodinal nodded and stepped outside.

As ever, he was soundless as he drifted across the deserted village. Dodinal eased through the broken palisade and hurried across the clearing until the black maw of the forest devoured him. He heard the echoing voice again, this time near enough for him to be certain it was a man calling out. If these were intruders, they were not especially bright. Even a child would know to keep one's voice down while closing on a foe.

A twig snapped, unnaturally loud in the hushed woodland. Now Dodinal knew the man's exact location. But was he the vanguard of an invading force or just someone lost, blundering through the cold, dark forest in the hope of finding shelter?

Dodinal had not travelled far when he saw a man, short and stocky, staggering through the trees towards him. The moonlight was bright enough to show he was alone. The man called out. When Dodinal shouted back, he jumped in shock and stumbled to a halt.

"Stay where you are."

"Who are you?" the man asked, his voice shaking either with nerves or cold, or possibly both.

"I would ask that same question," Dodinal answered, stepping forward so the man could see him. The stranger took an involuntary step back, his arms flailing for balance.

"Are you alone?" the knight demanded.

"Yes, yes, I swear. Please, I intend no trouble."

"Then why are you here? It is hardly the place or the time of year for a midnight stroll."

"I am searching for the *brehyrion* Idris. My people sent me to find him and seek his help. Do you know where his village is? If so, I beg you, take me there. I have not rested since daybreak."

"Why do you need his help?"

The man clasped his hands together in supplication. "Please. I need to reach him while I still have the strength to walk."

"Are you armed?"

"Yes." The man approached Dodinal slowly. He withdrew his sword and dropped it to the ground, close to the knight's feet, before backing away. "There. Now, please, take me to Idris."

Dodinal stooped to pick up the sword. When he carefully ran his finger along its edge a thin red line appeared on his skin.

The blade had not been especially well made, but it *had* been kept sharp. The stocky man had been expecting trouble. "Very well." Dodinal sucked blood from his finger. "Stay ahead, where I can see you. I will tell you where to go."

"Thank you. You have no idea how important this is."

"Save your breath for Idris," the knight growled. The man nodded hurriedly and fell silent. He did not speak again until they arrived at the Great Hall. Dodinal opened the door and nodded him inside. As he stepped across the threshold, the man staggered and his legs gave way; Dodinal caught him before he collapsed.

"Who in God's name is this?" Idris demanded, leaping to his feet as Dodinal lowered the stranger to the bench. Gerwyn did not move from his chair, and watched proceedings unfold through half-closed eyes. By contrast, Owain was staring wide-eyed at the stranger. Dodinal was well used to that look.

The man gasped out a name, Ellis, but was too weak to say anything else. Rhiannon hurried away, returning with a beaker of warm ale. The man held it in his hands to heat them and then gulped down its contents, shivering as the brew drove the worst of the cold from his bones. Wiping the back of one hand across his lips he gasped: "Thank you."

Rhiannon nodded and returned to her seat.

"What brings you here?" Idris demanded. "Sneaking about in the night like a common thief?"

"We need your help," Ellis said. His voice was hoarse and his breathing ragged. Water trickled down his face and dripped onto his chest as the ice in his dark hair and beard melted in the heat. If he had not stumbled across the village, if his calls had not been answered, he would have perished before much longer. Now his skin, almost blue when Dodinal had helped him inside, bloomed a vivid red.

"What do you mean by *we*?" Idris was too much the good host for belligerence, but there was clear suspicion in his voice.

"I come from a village half a day's walk north of here."

Dodinal straightened, his interest piqued. He was still bothered by the memory of that troubling presence in the north.

"Your *brehyrion*?" Idris demanded.

"Madoc."

"I know him. A good man. You say you need our help. Explain."

Ellis fidgeted nervously. "Something has taken our children."

He looked at them and there was unmistakeable suffering in his eyes. "Two now. Vanished, as if they had never been there. Not one of mine, thank God, but my sister lost her only daughter." His voice caught and he struggled to continue. "We searched, but... nothing."

Rhiannon gently took the beaker from his unresisting hands and brought him more ale, and they waited in silence while he drank it. Even miserable Gerwyn seemed to have taken an interest, sitting up in his seat. Knowing him as he did, Dodinal suspected this was less out of concern for missing children than at the prospect of an intriguing tale.

He caught Rhiannon staring meaningfully at him. Owain could so easily have been lost that fateful night in the woods. Although the boy appeared none the worse for his encounter with the wolves, Dodinal felt this conversation was perhaps one he should not overhear. He need not have worried; when he looked down at Owain, the child had placed his head on his hands on the table and was asleep.

Once he had composed himself, Ellis told them his story. The first child to disappear was his sister's daughter, a beautiful blonde girl named Angharad. She had been playing with her friends in the woods at the edge of the village. It had been the summer of the previous year, when the days were long and heavy with heat.

The children had been taught not to stray too far, and dutifully returned home as dusk fell. Only then was it was discovered that Angharad was not with them. Men were quickly summoned and the forest searched in all directions until darkness defeated them. They returned the next morning, this time with hounds. There was no scent of the child to be found, nor of any predator.

"My sister harboured hopes that one day she would return," Ellis said, eyes seeing something far away. "It broke her. Madoc made the forest out of bounds to the children after that. We found no trace of wolves, but something *must* have happened, though we know not what. Children do not just blow away like smoke."

His tale continued. The months passed. Life moved on, until winter came and the food became scarce in Madoc's village, as it did in every settlement along the borderlands. Men hunted, but found no game. The struggle to survive pushed the tragedy of Angharad to the back of their minds. They had thought no more of it, until last night.

A frail and sickly boy named Wyn had been stricken by a coughing fit. His mother had sent him to the wood store, thinking the air would clear his lungs. Wyn had kissed her on the cheek and she had placed one hand on his face just before he left.

It was the last time anyone saw him.

"Was the snow still falling?" Dodinal asked.

"Yes. Very little, but it still lay deep on the ground."

"Were there tracks?"

A frown etched lines into Ellis's forehead. "Yes, but that's the strangest part. The boy's tracks were clear, leading from his hut to the store. Then there were other tracks. Strange tracks. They appeared as if out of nowhere in the woods, came into and out of the village. When they reached the forest again... nothing. They vanished."

Idris leaned forward. "They just stopped?"

"In the middle of a drift."

The old chieftain brought a meaty fist down on the table so hard, Dodinal half expected Owain to wake up. The boy, however, was too far gone to have heard or felt anything. "Impossible!"

"That's what we thought, too. But the proof was there before our eyes. Or, rather, it wasn't. The tracks were there and then they were gone. The snow all around was unbroken. Again, we searched for as long as we could, but we had no idea which way to look. The cold drove us back. By next morning the snow had filled in what tracks there had been. It was like the spirits had made off with him."

"Enough of that," Dodinal snapped. There was a rational explanation for everything. He had no time for those who blamed the gods or spirits for their tribulations. They were hiding from the truth: every death, every tragedy or misfortune in the world was down either to uncaring nature or to the cruelty of man.[7]

"I'm sorry," Ellis stammered. "But if you had been there and seen it with your own eyes then you would have felt the same way."

"Perhaps so," Dodinal said softly, reminding himself that the man had suffered personal tragedy as well as a hard and exhausting journey. "But you say you need our help. If you have searched and not found the boy, I fail to see what more we can do."

"Everyone believes whatever took Wyn, took Angharad as well, and they are scared it will happen again. They are afraid to leave their huts and will not let their children out of their sight. We need help to hunt down whatever took Angharad and the boy and put an end to it."

"But why us?" Idris asked. "I know Madoc and he knows me. We have shared stories and flagons of ale at the gatherings. We have respect for each other, but we're far from close."

Ellis shook his head. "It's not only you. He has sent a man to every village within a day's walk to seek their help. I would have been here hours ago, had I not lost my way. It was pure good fortune your..." – he eyed Dodinal nervously, not certain of the big man's status – "your friend here found me when he did."

Idris eyed him for a moment, chewing his lip. "Very well," he said. "We will help with the search. God knows, we have nothing else to occupy our time. We leave at first light."

[7]Clearly an extraordinary position for a medieval warrior to hold, especially in Malory's world of miracles. See Appendix II for a discussion of faith in the story.

Ellis looked ready to argue, to press the case for leaving there and then, but common sense prevailed. Any man who went out into the woods at this hour was as good as dead. Even in his anguish, he understood dead men were no good to anyone. "Thank you."

"You will stay here as my guest," Idris said. "We have little to share but what we have, we will share with you."

"I will go with you," said Dodinal. "I know the forest and can track better than any man. Believe me, that is no idle boast. If something out there *has* taken your children, I will find it."

Shortly afterwards he returned to Rhiannon's hut, where he tended to the fire all the while deep in thought.

He had come to believe he might have found peace, out here in the wilderness. He had come to hope there would finally be an end to the bloodshed that had been part of his life ever since he was a boy. Now he feared he had been wrong.

Before turning in, he sat at the table and used the stone Idris had given him to sharpen his sword and spear, running it along each blade in turn until they felt keen enough to cut the air itself. Something in his bones told him he would need them before long.

Sleep did not come easily that night. When it did, it was filled with such tormented dreams as to make him to cry out in despair.

NINE

THEY SET OUT at dawn, Ellis leading the way. With him were Dodinal and Idris and three of the chieftain's most trusted men. There was Emlyn, dark of hair and quick to smile, who had the surest aim. Then there was Hywel, dark also, a wiry man who rarely spoke but who was considered their most skilful tracker. And finally there was Elfed, a giant of a man whose blonde hair and beard set him apart from the others and who was said to have once wrestled a bear to the ground.

All three were younger than Idris but older than Dodinal. Each man held a spear, the weapon of a hunter. Their eyes were restless and vigilant, missing nothing. Dodinal carried the spear that Idris had given him, his sword sheathed at his side.

Idris had insisted on bringing his son. Why was anyone's guess. Gerwyn did not want to be there, and made his reluctance known by constantly scowling and muttering under his breath. He held back from the rest of the party as if to reinforce his displeasure. Dodinal grinned as understanding dawned; Idris was punishing him.

The sky, as before, was steel blue and cloudless. Though it was cold when they set out, the air grew noticeably warmer as the hours passed, though not so warm as to melt the snow that crunched under their feet as they walked. While there was still no game to be found, Dodinal felt renewed hope that spring was finally on its way.

They journeyed in silence, troubled by the story Ellis had told. Children, vanishing as if into the air. Stolen away, so Ellis had said, although Dodinal still harboured doubts. The borderlands were harsh and unforgiving. There were countless ways a man could lose his life, let alone a lost and helpless child. If ravines or rivers did not claim them, there were creatures that could. Dodinal knew that better than anyone.

They had travelled perhaps two hours and the men had drifted apart, following their own paths, certain now that the forest was devoid of any kind of threat. Idris caught up with Dodinal and cleared his throat. "The weather is improving. I suppose that means you will be leaving us once we are done."

As it was not a question, Dodinal chose not to answer. He had a feeling Idris would fill the silence, and he was right.

"As soon as the thaw comes, you'll have no reason to stay."

Dodinal shrugged. "Perhaps."

"You have doubts? I am surprised, sir knight. I would have thought you would be eager to be away on this quest of yours."

Dodinal raised his eyebrows at *sir knight,* but let it pass without comment. If Rhiannon was to be believed, and he had no reason to doubt her, Idris did not want him to leave. Yet the old chieftain was either too nervous or too proud to ask him to stay. Well, then. If he wanted to talk around the matter, so be it. Dodinal would do so too.

"I am in no hurry. The quest will be there whether I leave at the first sign of spring or wait 'til high summer."

"I see," Idris said. For a moment he seemed ready to say more, but then he bit his lip and turned away.

They walked in silence for a while after that. Dodinal watched Idris from the corner of his eye, suppressing a grin at the sight of the chieftain's mouth moving soundlessly, as though rehearsing the words he wanted to say. Finally Idris shook his head and gave up, perhaps having concluded it would be best to wait until such time as Dodinal announced he was leaving before trying to persuade him to stay.

For a moment, the knight was tempted to tell the old man the secrets he was keeping from him, the story of his life, although he had never before felt the need to share it with anyone. Idris had shown him nothing but courtesy and hospitality. If anyone deserved to hear Dodinal's tale, it was the white-haired chieftain.

Then again, he thought, remembering all that had happened to him since the Saxons had stolen his childhood, he would also reveal himself to be what he really was: a man with too much blood on his hands. A killer without mercy. Better to save his tale for another time, if at all. But still he remembered, and he let his mind drift...

ON A CLOUDLESS summer day in Dodinal's sixteenth year, he heard a distant commotion. With nothing else to occupy him, he went to investigate, moving through the forest until he was close enough to recognise the sounds of fighting.

As yet he could see nothing, as the battle was being fought on the other side of a wooded ridge ahead of him. His movements became more stealthy as he made his way closer; this was not his fight, and he had no desire to get involved.

Upon reaching the crest of the rise he pressed up against a tree for cover and peered around it. The ground before him fell away steeply, providing an uninterrupted view of the combat in the narrow valley below. Dodinal watched for a while, squinting against the flashes of light glinting off weapons and armour.

The melee was furious. There was no telling which side was winning. Bodies were strewn across the forest floor. Around them dozens of men, too many to count, hacked at each other with swords and axes, some blows blocked by shields or armour, others getting through to crush heads or tear through flesh and bone.

Dodinal grimaced as a man staggered away, mouth open wide in a scream that could not be heard above the clamour.

His hand was pressed against the ragged stump at his shoulder in a futile attempt to staunch the blood pumping from it.

His suffering was mercifully short-lived, for a moment later an axe blade sunk deep into his throat. His head snapped back, attached to the neck only by a flap of skin, and he took a few staggering steps forward before collapsing.

Another man, almost immediately below Dodinal, was holding off three aggressors, using his sword expertly to divert their blows and jab at them. He drew blood with every swing, yet failed to hurt them enough to bring them down. He was tall and wore fine armour. Dodinal could see, even from his vantage point, that his blade was of the highest quality. It glittered in the sunlight as he wielded it.

The tall man backed away from the three and they followed, circling him warily, prodding and testing with their swords, looking for a way through his stubborn defences but finding none.

Dodinal could not help but nod in admiration. He was no fighter, but he recognised skill when he saw it. What a shame this man would surely die, for the odds were not in his favour.

The stranger edged away until he had backed up into the steep slope. He came to a halt, unable to go any further. "Come on, then, you sons of Saxon whores!" he roared.

Saxons!

Dodinal had heard the name spoken many times on his travels, always with hatred and fear. It was the name given to the people who had attacked his village, who had slaughtered every man, woman and child there... who had killed his father and condemned his mother to an unknowable but doubtless terrible fate.

Fury boiled up inside him. He had been wrong to think this was not his battle. He had sworn vengeance after he found his father dead, and vengeance he would have.

With that, the same red mist that had engulfed him all those years ago descended on him again like a blood-soaked veil. With a bellow of unrestrained rage, he drew his sword and charged headlong down the slope, somehow keeping his footing as earth and stones shifted and tumbled down beneath him. The Saxons looked up, shock clear in their faces at the sight of the wild man bearing down on them at such a speed he could have been flying.

When it was over he rested on his haunches, heaving for breath. His hands were drenched with blood; his clothes were heavy with it. Everywhere he looked were bodies. Men moved around the fallen, checking for life. They slit the throats of their enemies[8] and delivered mercy blows to any of their own so badly injured as to be beyond hope. Those that could be saved, they lifted up and carried away.

Other men searched the bodies, gathering weapons which they piled up to be removed later. Clothing and valuables too; the former prized by an army on the move, the latter the spoils of victory.

Birds already feasted on the dead, plucking out eyes and thrusting their beaks into rent flesh to reach the soft organs within. The forest reeked of slaughter, the air ripe with the charnel stench of blood, and of faeces and urine where bowels and bladders had emptied in death. Dodinal rubbed at his eyes. It was almost as if he had been somehow sent back in time to his village, the day after the Saxon attack, although there were no huts to be seen and the slain were all men, there were no women and children.

Dodinal had not been injured, at least not seriously. Most if not all of the blood that soaked him had spilled from the veins of others. He looked down at his sword. With a soft cry of regret he saw that it was broken, the blade snapped off halfway along its length. In avenging his father's death, he had destroyed his last physical tie to him.

Then he felt a hand on his shoulder and looked up to find the tall man smiling down at him. "Are you hurt?" he asked as he helped Dodinal to his feet.

[8]Arthur's questionable chivalry is a recurring theme in both the *Morte* and the *Second Book*. From giving orders to have every newborn baby in the kingdom drowned, to his brutal conquest of Rome, to his pragmatic refusal to confront Lancelot over his conduct with Guinevere, Arthur strongly demonstrates Malory's anxieties about the impossibility of a truly chivalrous life.

Dodinal shook his head. He was still trembling from exertion and did not trust himself to speak.

"Good. And what is your name?" Dodinal told him, and he took his hand and shook it vigorously. "I am Arthur. And I owe you my life. I will never forget what you did here today."

Dodinal smiled with grim irony. Neither would he. Again it had felt as though someone else had taken control of his body, a stranger who was far stronger and more tireless than he, who could part heads from necks and limbs from torsos with little effort. Dodinal had no idea how many Saxons he had killed, but it was not enough, not now he had the scent of their blood in his nostrils.

There were men standing close by, tired and stained, but not involved in the gory salvage. Arthur called them to him. Once they had gathered around, he stood behind Dodinal with both hands on the young man's shoulders. "Remember this man's face. Remember his name. Were it not for Dodinal here, you would be drinking to your King's memory tonight.

"For one so young that he has not yet grown a beard, he wields a sword with a savagery I have never witnessed until this day. Truly, what he lacks in finesse he makes up for with brute strength!"

This provoked laughter, which sounded oddly out of place in the midst of so much carnage.

"Three Saxons felled before I had time to move," Arthur continued. "But was that enough? Far from it! A dozen or more have not lived to regret the day they encountered our savage young friend."

He introduced him to them: Sir Kay, Sir Bors, Sir Hector and others, names that meant nothing to him then, but would soon become as familiar to him as his own. They clapped him on the shoulder and praised him for his bravery. A shiver ran down Dodinal's spine.

Arthur took him aside and said, "Fight by my side."

For a moment Dodinal could not speak. He was still in shock from discovering he had saved a king's life. Perhaps he should have guessed? There was something about Arthur that commanded a man's attention; a presence about him that could not be denied.

"Fight?" he said. "Why, are you not done here?"

"Here, yes. But this is just one battle. I have fought many others before and I suspect I will fight many more to come. What I could do with an army of men such as you! Brave and ferocious and fearless. And this is no idle flattery. You fight like no other. What say you? Will you join me? Will you help me rid our land of the Saxons?"

Later Dodinal would come to suspect there had been a hint of idle flattery in Arthur's words after all. But, on hearing them, he did not hesitate. He had no one to care for and there was no one left alive who cared for him. While he would happily wander the forest for the rest of his life, there was no denying the exultant feeling that had surged through him when he realised what he was capable of. The sadness and anger that had festered inside him since that long-ago night had gone. Instead there was a fierce determination to finish what he had started; to vanquish the foreign invaders or die trying.

"I will fight with you." Dodinal raised the broken sword. "This belonged to my father. He died at a Saxon's hand. A thousand Saxons will die at mine before I am done."

Arthur clapped him on the shoulder. "Good. I will find you a sword your father would have been proud to see you wield. Clothes and armour too. Tonight we feast in your honour. My camp is not far from here; we have both seen more than enough death for one day."

As they walked away from the scene of slaughter, Dodinal let the sword fall from his fingers. It had served its purpose. He had no further need of it. One part of his life was over.

Another was about to begin.

Thereafter he had followed the King into battle after battle, using the old Roman roads to race from skirmish to skirmish on horseback, driving back the Saxons until that day on Mount Badon, when Arthur had masterminded a resounding victory that had finally brought peace to the kingdom. Dodinal, for his part in the rout of the invaders, had been knighted, an elevation he had neither asked for nor welcomed, but which he had found impossible to refuse.

He had been feted. Women had wanted him and he had taken more than his fair share of them, but his conquests had been empty, devoid of warmth or feeling. He made but a few friends, none of them close, their conversations bawdy, wine-fuelled reminiscences of the glory days when they had put the Saxons to the sword.

What he had been unable to bring himself to talk of, other than in the vaguest of terms, was the lives he had taken. Sometimes, when he slept, all he saw was the ravaged bodies of those who had fallen beneath the implacable ferocity of his vengeance.

So much blood, so much death; far too much death. Hundreds, some said thousands, had fallen before him. There were days when he could not get the stink of it out of his nostrils. Days when he tasted it in the food he ate and in the ale he quaffed.

Knights sought him out for single combat, to test their skills against his strength. He quickly learned to control his rage, and in doing so, he inevitably lost. At the same time he became a better swordsman, though he would never be the equal of his peers.

After Mount Badon, he had escaped to the forest and wept with relief, knowing that no man need die at his hand again for as long as peace prevailed. Yet even while Arthur ruled his kingdom with benevolent majesty, Dodinal became restless. Camelot, for all its glories, soon began to feel like a prison.

And so it was that he set out to wander the land in search of an end to his anguish. If it took his own death, then so be it. Dodinal was not afraid to die, as long as he died well. He left his armour in his chambers. A man travelled faster when he travelled lighter, and furs kept him warmer than cold metal.

Now he was starting to question whether salvation lay in life and not death. In Rhiannon he thought he had found it. Then had come Ellis with his stories of children being taken.

It seemed like the contentment Dodinal longed for had been snatched from him just as it came within reach.

Fate, it seemed, was not done with him yet.

Dodinal looked over his shoulder. Idris, Emlyn, Hywel and Elfed walked together a dozen or so paces behind him. He nodded at them and they returned the gesture solemnly. As for Gerwyn, the chieftain's son was making no effort to keep up. Dodinal watched him closely. The younger man was no stranger to the forest and moved with the confidence of a seasoned hunter. It was a shame he could not control the anger that festered within him.

Dodinal understood how that felt.

Gerwyn had lived in the shadow of an older brother who had been loved and respected by all, a man who would one day have followed in their father's footsteps, had it not been for the cruel whim of fate. Perhaps he knew, or suspected, that his father wanted Dodinal to become his successor. Were that the case, he need not bear a grudge. Dodinal had no desire to be anyone's leader; if he stayed it would be as a man without status. He'd had more than his fill of that.

They stopped to eat the nuts and berries they had brought with them. Idris sat with Dodinal on a fallen tree, while the other four men ate a short distance away. Gerwyn conspicuously sat on his own.

"You mentioned you knew the chieftain, Madoc, from the 'gatherings'," Dodinal said to Idris. "What did you mean by that?"

"At the start of every spring and every autumn, the villages from this region travel to a great clearing far from here." Idris raised his chin to indicate east. "We trade livestock and crops. We feast and get drunk. It is where young men find wives, and young women find husbands. It is where my son Elwyn met Rhiannon."

"I thought she was from your village."

Idris shook his head. "No, our young people find their partners elsewhere; it has always been so. We cannot have kin sleep with kin. Elwyn made the right choice, that is certain. Rhiannon's mother was a formidable woman too."

"I know she was a healer. Rhiannon learned from her."

"They reckon she was more than that. A seer, or so they said."

Dodinal remembered how Rhiannon had been reluctant to talk of her past. It seemed wrong to be asking about it when he refused to talk about his own. Still, he was curious. "Rhiannon too?"

"No. She is a gifted healer and a good mother. That is enough."

They continued on their way. It was past midday when Ellis, who had forged ahead of them in his eagerness to be home, stopped and raised his hand. "Not far now," he said when the others had caught up with him. "An hour, no more."

Dodinal looked around. Apart from the tracks they had made, the snow was unbroken. "Your people did not come even this far in the search for the missing boy?"

"They had no reason to," Ellis said sharply. "Remember what I said? There were no tracks anywhere. Whatever took Wyn could have gone in any direction. We only have so many men. We looked but could not search the entire forest, it was hopeless."

"No tracks." Gerwyn sneered his contempt. "I don't believe that. There is no creature walking this earth that does not leave tracks."

Ellis's face reddened. He looked ready to lunge at Gerwyn. Dodinal stepped forward and placed a hand gently on his shoulder before the man could do anything rash. Whatever the truth about the tracks, he had no reason to doubt the boy Wyn had been taken. It was understandable that feelings should be running high.

"Take us to your village," he said, in a tone that brooked no argument. "Once we have talked to your people, we can determine how best we can help."

Ellis seemed placated. He turned and led the way. Idris and the three hunters followed swiftly after him. Gerwyn gave

Dodinal a venomous look, but said nothing. He waited several seconds after the knight had walked off before following.

The trees thinned out. Soon the travellers emerged into a clearing, blinking against the sunlight. Ellis's village was a scattering of huts. One, noticeably larger than the rest, was presumably the home of the chieftain, Madoc. Nearby was a livestock pen, deserted and forlorn-looking. The village was smaller than Idris's, with only a waist-high fence to keep out any predators.

Ellis called out and a dozen men emerged from the largest hut, armed with spears and swords. Leading them was a bull of a man whose cropped dark hair and beard were flecked with grey. He stopped long enough to shake Ellis briskly by the hand before turning his attention to Idris.

"You answered my call," he said, grasping the chieftain by both shoulders. "I cannot thank you enough."

"You have nothing to thank me for, Madoc. This is a tragic time for sure. When we find the boy, or whatever took him, then I will accept your thanks. Until then, you owe me nothing."

"I cannot even offer you or your men much in the way of hospitality." Madoc stared grimly into the forest surrounding them. "No hunting here, not for months. The last of our livestock is gone, and we will struggle come the spring. If the new season ever shows itself."

"I understand. We have endured the same hardship. I have brought my finest trackers and hunters." Idris introduced Dodinal and the others in turn. "Whatever is to be found, they will find it."

Madoc's men had lined up behind him. There were no women or children to be seen.

"I appreciate your help, Idris. But even the finest tracker will be of little use to us; there is nothing to track."

"There is always something to track," Dodinal answered, eyes searching the surrounding ground for the merest hint of a trail. "I don't care whether it walks on four legs or two, it will leave a trace of where it has been. You just have to know where to look."

"Then look," Madoc challenged. "You will find nothing."

"We shall see."

Dodinal searched the forest floor intensely, Hywel joining him as he swept the area immediately beyond the village, the wiry tracker disappearing into the trees for a short while. When he returned, he shook his head. "Nothing, as far as I can tell," he said in his soft and lyrical voice. "The only tracks to be found are those we made on our way here. Either they have their story wrong or something very strange has happened."

"There's always an explanation," Dodinal assured him. "It is not always easy to find, but we *will* find it."

Madoc had watched their search with a resigned expression. "So, you admit defeat. Maybe now you will believe me. Whatever took Wyn left no tracks. It grieves me to say so, but we must assume the boy is dead. We cannot let whatever took him make off with any other children. Will you help us hunt it down and kill it?"

Idris raised his hands in a gesture of helplessness. "If we cannot find the boy, how can we hope to find whatever took him?"

"We will split into groups to search a wider area than before. Even with your men, there are not many of us, but it's all we have."

Dodinal looked at Ellis. "You told us that other men had been sent to other villages to seek their help. Where are they?"

"They cannot help us," Madoc said.

"Why not?" Idris demanded. "Surely they know we would help them if ever they had need of it."

"They have problems of their own."

"What problems?" The old chieftain was clearly annoyed.

Madoc hesitated. "They too have had children taken. They are too busy looking for them to help us find ours."

The men were shocked into silence. Even Gerwyn, who had followed the exchange with sneering disdain, seemed to perk up and take interest. "How were they taken?" he asked.

Madoc looked at him curiously, as if surprised the surly young man was capable of speech. "I don't know. Just as I don't know how our children were taken. I just know they were."

"Did the other villagers find any tracks?" Dodinal asked. He suspected he already knew the answer.

"Only tracks in and out of their villages. Strange tracks, like those we saw here before the snow filled them in. Then... nothing. It was as if something had come down from the sky and snatched the children, spiriting them away."

One of Madoc's men made a gesture to ward off evil. "It's the devil's work."

"There are no devils," Dodinal growled, and the man flinched at his fierce expression. "You can be sure of that. I have seen many terrible things, things you can count yourselves blessed you'll never see. But there are no devils. There are the creatures of the forest that kill to live or to defend their young. And then there is man, who kills for many reasons, not all of which make sense. You have found no blood. Whatever took your boy did not take him to feed. This was the work of man. I would wager my life on it."

"But for what purpose?" Madoc demanded.

"I don't know." Dodinal felt burning anger rise up inside him, and forced it down. This was not the time to release it, not when there was nowhere to direct it. His wrath was aimed at whatever had taken Wyn and the other children. None of them was known to him, but he would not tolerate innocents being preyed upon. "But I will find out, I swear. Now, where are these other villages?"

Madoc etched a map in the snow with his spear point. "We are here. The villages are here, here and here." He made three marks, one to the northwest, the other two to the northeast. "There are others, but too far away to travel there and back again inside a day."

"And each of the three has had children taken?"

Madoc nodded. "Two of them lost one child apiece. The other had two taken. Once their people realised what had happened, they kept their children inside and posted guards. No more were taken."

"And were any of the missing children found, dead or alive?"

A long sigh. "No."

Dodinal walked to the forest edge. He needed a moment alone so he could think without interruption. With no tracks to follow, a search seemed a hopeless cause, yet he was certain where they needed to go. Even when he tentatively cast his senses out and found nothing, he remained in no doubt.

It could not be mere coincidence.

He returned to the waiting men. They watched him approach with curiosity and apprehension. "We head north," he said.

"North?" Madoc was doubtful. "We could set out in any direction and be no more certain we are on the right path."

"Do you not heed your instincts when you hunt?" Dodinal asked. He waited for an answer, but none was forthcoming.

Finally it was Idris who spoke. "If Dodinal says north, then north it is. I trust his instincts as I would trust my own."

"Very well," Madoc said. "It is decided." He called out orders to his men. Three of them stayed with him. The remainder returned to the hut, to protect their people. "A smaller group travels faster. Between us, we will find anything that is there to be found."

Dodinal glanced up at the cobalt circle of sky above the clearing. They had four hours of daylight left, five at best.

The men were pensive as they prepared to move out. Dodinal was not of the Christian faith, he did not concern himself with Heaven and Hell. He had often escaped to the Church of St. Stephen during his time in Camelot, but only because it was the one place where he could find peace. Here, though, so far from civilisation, it would be easy to believe in gods and devils. Some still followed the old religion. He might not share their beliefs, but he understood their fears. Even Gerwyn looked anxious. The air of arrogance had gone. If anything, his expression was that of a man with much on his mind.

They set off, fanning out as they advanced to sweep a wider area of ground, looking for anything untoward. Afternoon sunlight had burned away the worst of the cold; before long, Dodinal was sweating beneath his cloak. He took it off and slung it over his shoulder. The snow still lay thick on the ground, but if this weather lasted it would not be there for long. He would not be sorry to see the back of winter, even if the onset of spring brought him closer to a decision he would not relish having to make.

His stomach rumbled. Dodinal cast his senses outwards, hoping in vain that the milder conditions might have enticed game to return. He could still taste the venison they had feasted on. The thought of fresh meat made his belly ache, so he turned his thoughts elsewhere.

An image of Rhiannon came to mind. He smiled, despite the grim nature of their task. That she might not feel the same about him as he had come to feel about her was something he did not want to dwell on. It was not only possible, but likely; while she had been kind, even affectionate, there had been no hint of anything deeper.

"Over here!" a voice cried out, tearing Dodinal away from his thoughts. Looking across, he saw Hywel away to his left, crouching and examining the ground. The other men hurried over, then waited for Dodinal, who was the last to arrive.

"What have you found?" the knight demanded.

Without waiting for an answer, he crouched alongside Hywel, tugging thoughtfully at his beard as he tried to make sense of what he saw; tracks that, to inexperienced eyes, would have appeared as little more than a confusion of churned-up snow. Dodinal, however, saw with eyes that pierced the secrets of the wildwood.

What strange tracks they were. He reached down and ran his fingers slowly around the edge of the imprint closest to him. Such was its size and shape it could have been made by a man, but a man whose feet were deformed. The print was curved, as though the foot was badly twisted, and it possessed only three toes.

"You have seen this?" he said quietly to Hywel.

The tracker nodded. "It could have been someone who had lost two toes in battle, or to frostbite."

"It could," Dodinal conceded. "But that does not explain *this*." He indicated another print. It too was curved; the only difference between it and the first was this one had six toes.

Dodinal straightened, so he could follow the course of the tracks leading away from them, northwards into the depths of the forest. He counted eight pairs, all displaying similar deformities. One set was noticeably deeper and better defined than the rest. He nodded. One of the eight had been carrying something heavy enough to have driven its weight further into the snow. "Neither does it explain why they would be running around barefoot in this weather."

"There's something else," Hywel said, looking back nervously. "There are no tracks behind us. They start right here."

Dodinal grunted, struggling to accept a truth that defied logic. The evidence was plain to see. The tracks started in the middle of nowhere. For all his scorn of the men's talk of devilry, the knight nevertheless found himself gazing at the cloudless vault overhead. It was indeed as if something had come down from the sky. Something that walked like a man but on feet that were not quite human.

"Well?" Madoc demanded.

Dodinal chose his words carefully, not wanting to spread alarm. "We have their tracks now."

"Men?"

Dodinal nodded, far from convinced. "Eight of them. One was carrying something. I suspect it was your missing boy."

Madoc brightened. With no blood trail, it was possible the child might still be alive, making it all the more vital to find him. Dodinal looked up again, not out of anxiety but to study the light.

"We have perhaps three hours left to us. If we have not overtaken them by nightfall we will have to give up the search. We cannot track if we cannot see."

"What? But we cannot give up!" Madoc sounded aghast.

Dodinal frowned. They had given their word they would help, and he would not halt the search until the very last moment, but they could not stay overnight. Idris had left armed men behind and given instructions for the young to be kept indoors at all times. While there was nothing to suggest their village was at risk – no sign of any tracks, strange or otherwise – the chieftain had taken no chances while he was away.

It had disturbed Dodinal greatly to hear of children elsewhere being stolen. The raiders were on the move. There was no way of predicting how far they would travel. He would not rest easy until he was back with Rhiannon and Owain. "I am not suggesting you give up the search," he told Madoc, with quiet authority. "We will help you for as long as we can. But no longer than that. We have our own people to consider. Surely you would no more expect us to abandon them than we would expect you to abandon yours to help us."

"Of course not." Madoc slumped. "Believe me, we are truly grateful for any help you can give us. So let us make haste while we can."

They set off again, moving swiftly now they had a trail to follow. Dodinal kept a tight grip on the spear, although at the first sign of trouble he would want his sword in his hand.

An hour passed, then two. The sun eased down the sky, and a sound like rain filled the air. Water dripped from branches as the ice began to thaw. Where it drummed on the ground, the snow started to melt, a sure sign that spring was at last upon them.

Then the trail suddenly ended, the tracks vanishing as abruptly as they had appeared. Dodinal raised his hand and the men came to a halt alongside him.

"What is it?" Idris asked. Dodinal pointed. "Ah. I see."

Madoc went to push past them. "What kind of man can appear out of nowhere and vanish just as easily, eh? You say there is an explanation for everything, Dodinal. Explain *that*."

Dodinal put a hand on his chest to hold him back. "I cannot."

"Then let me pass. I will find the answers you cannot give."

"No," Dodinal said softly. "If there are answers to be found, I will find them. Stay here. The less we disturb the snow, the better."

"Do as he says," Idris advised. "He knows what he is about."

Madoc's lips tightened into an angry line but he gave way.

Dodinal drove the point of his spear into the hard ground and unsheathed his sword. He made his way slowly to the point where the trail abruptly ended, next to a small, snow-covered rock.

His eyes scanned the forest for movement, but the woodland was populated only by the long swaying shadows of the trees. Sweat broke out on his forehead and he impatiently wiped it away. He did not believe in devils. Even so, there was something unarguably wrong here, something out of kilter with the natural order. He could try to deny it for as long as he drew breath, but he had learned years ago never to deny his instincts.

He drew close to the rock. The tracks did not peter out. They simply stopped. Beyond the last print, the snow, while thinner on the ground than it had been, was unbroken. The forest stretched away before him. Nothing had passed beyond here. If Dodinal had been religious he might have fallen to his knees and prayed for guidance. But he was not, and so could rely only on intuition and his senses.

While he contemplated the tracks, his eyes were drawn to the rock, streaked dark beneath its melting white coat. For a moment he had no idea why it captured his attention. Then it was as though his eyes had suddenly opened. His heart drummed and his breathing turned ragged. He put the sword away and reached out until he could place his hand on the rock. It was soft to the touch.

There was a sick feeling in his stomach, for he already knew what he would find. Sure enough, when he gently pushed, the rock shifted and tumbled over, sending up a cloud of snow as it collapsed. An arm unfurled to show a child's hand, clenched into a fist. More snow skittered away to reveal an unruly mop of dark hair.

Footsteps hurried towards him and he waved them back, wanting to spare Madoc and his men. The boy was a stranger to Dodinal, yet even so the sight of his frozen body, curled up as though he had fallen asleep, was almost unbearably sad.

His eyes burned and his vision blurred. Dodinal reached down and lifted Wyn in his arms. The boy felt as light as the snow covering him, as if his departed soul had taken with it the weight of all he had been.

Madoc, face distraught, took the child from him. The chieftain set off, taking great striding steps back towards his village, his men falling in around him. Dodinal followed at a respectful distance, Idris and the others behind him. Not a word was spoken.

When they reached the village, Madoc was immediately surrounded by people, the women keening their grief and men surrounding him, wanting to take the boy. He refused their help and disappeared inside his hut, his people hurrying in after him.

"We'd best wait here," Idris said. "This is a private moment."

They loitered outside the hut for an age, while the shadows thickened around them. Dodinal, still shaken from the shock of finding the child's body, wandered from the clearing to the edge of the forest, where he prowled restlessly. Through the trees he could see fires being lit in pits dotted here and there around the village. A sentry stood guard outside the main hut, but otherwise the place appeared deserted. No defences other than the fence, one man and a few desultory fires. Little good they would do against something that could appear and vanish at will, that could take a child, snuff out its life and discard it like a broken plaything.

Nothing could bring the boy back. But there were questions Dodinal would have answered before they left this place, which they must do, despite the tragedy in which they had become unwitting players. Soon, though, there would come a time of reckoning. If that meant his quest for peace had to wait, then wait it must. Whether he liked it or not, Dodinal was a knight. He had sworn to protect the innocent. He would not allow such cruel deeds to go unpunished.

TEN

MADOC'S HUT WAS so crowded that there was barely enough room for Dodinal. But when people saw him enter with a look as dark as the encroaching night on his already fearsome face, they moved aside to let him pass. He made his way to the table in the centre of the hut on which the child's body had been placed, wearing the clothes he had been found in, arms folded across his chest.

He looked to be asleep, at peace.

A woman sat on a chair beside him, elbows on the table and hands clasped together, lips moving as she whispered a prayer. Her eyes were closed. Tears had left trails like glistening scars down both cheeks. A man stood trembling behind her, a hand on each of her shoulders, either to comfort her or to prevent himself from collapsing. He looked up at Dodinal with swollen red eyes.

"It was you who found him?"

Dodinal nodded.

"Then my wife and I thank you." The man's voice quivered with barely suppressed emotion. "To have lost him forever ..."

He broke off, unable to continue.

Dodinal said nothing. There were no words in the world that had meaning at a time like this. He could not begin to imagine the torment Wyn's parents had suffered when their boy had gone missing. Even then, they could have at least held out hope that he would be found alive, however unlikely that was. Now, that hope had been dashed; there was nothing left to shield them from the unbearable burden of grief. When Dodinal had lost his parents, and for many years after, he had been certain there could be no worse feeling. How wrong he had been. A child's pain at the death of a parent was nothing compared to a parent's suffering at the death of a child.

He looked around. The villagers were standing two and three deep around the table, Madoc prominent at the front. Idris, Gerwyn and the three hunters were at the back, looking uncomfortable. All were there to honour the dead, as was Dodinal, but he had other reasons for intruding. "May I look at him?" he said softly.

The woman ceased praying and raised her head, seeing Dodinal for the first time. In the hut's shadowy interior, her eyes were black pits. "Who did this?" she hissed. "Who did this to my boy?"

"I don't know," Dodinal answered. "I'm sorry."

Without asking her consent a second time, the knight leaned over to take a closer look at the boy. He was around the same age as Owain, maybe a year or so older. Dark brown hair framed a pale, thin face. The child's eyes were closed, his mouth partly open. There were no rips or tears in his clothes and no visible wounds on his body. No trace of blood either.

Dodinal turned away. He had seen all he needed and had no desire to see any more. "I'm sorry," he repeated, feeling the emptiness of the words even as he uttered them. Then he gestured towards Madoc and made his way to the door. Idris and his men quickly fell in behind. looking glad to escape.

Once outside, Dodinal breathed in deeply. The last time he had seen a dead child was after the Saxons had destroyed his village, and there had been many dead children then. In life they had shunned him for being different, but in death they were just victims. They had not deserved their fate, no matter how cruel they had been to him, just as Wyn had not deserved his. "Whoever took the boy was careful not to harm him," he said, as much to himself as the others. "There were no signs of violence. Not so much as a scratch that I could see."

Madoc nodded tersely. He looked on the verge of tears. In a community this small, any death would be hard felt, let alone the death of one so young. "They wanted him alive. They could not have known the child was sick. He has... had... always been frail. His chest was weak. Sometimes he struggled for breath. The shock..."

"The shock of it would have stopped his heart." Dodinal spoke the words that Madoc could not. "And then, once they realised he had died, they abandoned him and left him where he lay."

"Whoever *they* were," Idris said. "We still have no idea."

"Neither does it explain the tracks," Hywel added.

Dodinal stared into the forest. They were in there. Far away by now, no doubt, but those who had taken Wyn and the others before him were in there somewhere. And who was to say they were done?

"I have been thinking about that," he said. "Ellis told us it was like they had come down from the sky. He was not far wrong, though he did not know it. They used the trees."

Madoc pulled a face. "Used the trees? How?"

"Consider it. They came into your village as if out of nowhere. They took the boy. The tracks vanished again." Dodinal gestured towards the darkening wood. "They moved from tree to tree while they carried him, keeping off the forest floor to leave no trail. Once they were far enough from the village to leave you with no means of following them, they returned to the ground to move faster."

"That is nonsense," Madoc argued. "No man can move through the trees that swiftly, let alone eight of them."

Dodinal rubbed his eyes, feeling suddenly weary. It had been a long hard day and its outcome had drained him of strength. "There is no other possible explanation, aside from your devils. And I have no time for them."

He made no mention of the strange twisted footprints he and Hywel had found, and for which he had no ready explanation.

To do so would only deepen the atmosphere of dread and despair that already blighted this place.

Madoc paced for a moment, mulling over the knight's words. "Very well, then," he said at last. "I am not entirely convinced, but I would sleep easier believing men are behind this and not something from the spirit world. We can defend ourselves against men."

"Then make sure you do," Dodinal told him. "Your village is far too open. Enclose it as best you can. There is timber all around you and you have enough strong men. You don't need me to tell you to make sure your children are never left alone."

"The children are fine. As for the defences, I'll see to that as soon as it's light. But what of you? Do you still intend to leave?"

"We do, and we will leave now," Dodinal said. "Our village is fortified, but its stockade has been left to rot for too long. We will strengthen it so that nothing, man or beast, can get through. Once we are done, we'll return here with as many people as we can spare to make sure your defences are as strong as they can be."

"Then travel safely." Madoc held out his hand. Dodinal shook it, as did Idris and the others. Farewells made, they turned and set off through the forest, Dodinal taking the lead.

They made good progress even after the sun had set and the forest was shrouded in darkness. After a while, however, it became clear Idris was not up to the arduous pace Dodinal had set, so the knight gathered the others to him and told them to push on ahead.

"Idris and I will follow," he said. "We have much to discuss, but we cannot talk if we're gasping for breath."

Gerwyn nodded. He looked shaken by what he had seen.

"Make sure everyone stays indoors," Idris told him. "No one goes outside alone. I want a watch kept overnight."

"You really believe they're in danger?" Gerwyn asked, eyes darting around anxiously. "Our village is far from here."

"The other villages are even further," Dodinal pointed out. "Yet they have been attacked. We cannot take anything for granted."

Within moments the four men had vanished into the darkness, leaving Idris and Dodinal alone. They walked at a brisk pace to keep warm, for while the day had been mild, the night air was as cold as winter. The moon was full; the constellations shimmered. The wind had dropped to a whisper.

They talked of inconsequential things to while away the time: the onset of the spring, plans to hunt together once the palisade was repaired. Imaginary feasts were prepared and they laughed when their stomachs rumbled in unison.

It was only after their conversation had reached a natural break and the two men were travelling in companionable silence that Dodinal realised he had made the decision not to leave, without being aware of it. Perhaps the boy's death had been enough to convince him that, having found people he cared for, he should not risk losing them.

Neither man spoke of what had happened that day. There was no need. Each was painfully aware of the events he had witnessed, and each preferred to come to terms with it in his own way.

It was past midnight when they reached the village. Dodinal yearned for nothing more than a hot drink and a bed to sleep in. Anything else could wait until morning.

When they staggered into the Great Hall, blinking against the heat and smoke from the fire, it was to find Rhiannon sitting at the table waiting for them. Of Gerwyn and Owain there was no sign; presumably they slept at the back of the hut, beyond the hanging skins. He thought he could hear snoring.

"Sit down," Rhiannon ordered, getting to her feet and bustling across to the fire. "You must be exhausted, both of you. The others got back hours ago."

The knight groaned as he lowered himself to the bench. Idris almost collapsed into his chair. "Next time, go without me."

Dodinal managed a laugh that quickly turned into a yawn.

Rhiannon returned with two steaming bowls of cawl, and the men fell on them. This time the meal was rich with meat.

Rhiannon must have decided that, with spring here, the game would return and so there was no need to ration their supplies quite so rigorously.

Although he had doubts, and his senses had found no signs of life to contradict his suspicions, Dodinal was too ravenous to care.

A second bowlful, and a beaker of ale, disappeared in short order, and finally he was sated. Wiping his mouth with the back of his hand, he thanked her for her kindness and then made to leave. "Get yourself to bed," he told Idris, who appeared to be having difficulty keeping his eyes open. "We have work to do tomorrow. Everyone will need to be well rested."

"And that includes you," Rhiannon said. "I have tended to the fire in my hut. You will not be cold tonight. But if you would prefer to stay here, you are more than welcome."

Dodinal politely declined and was disappointed to see a look of relief on her face. He took his leave. Once inside the warmth of Rhiannon's hut, he hung up his cloak, rested the spear against the wall and tugged off his boots, leaving them where they dropped. Finally he removed his sword belt and dropped it on the floor beside the mattress before sinking gratefully onto the bed.

Yawning, he closed his eyes. But even though he was light-headed with fatigue, sleep proved frustratingly elusive. He kept seeing that poor boy's lifeless face. Madoc had been right; what kind of man could leap from tree to tree while burdened with a struggling child? And what kind of man left footprints in the snow that were twisted and had too few or too many toes?

He was just drifting off when the door swung quietly open.

Dodinal reached out and slid his sword silently from its sheath. There was only one man arrogant or foolish enough to dare skulk into the hut at this hour and, chieftain's son or not, he was about to learn the hard way that Dodinal was not to be fooled with.

But then came a soft rustle as a cloak was undone and dropped to the floor. The furs on his bed were pulled back, and a warm body slid in beside him. Dodinal immediately recognised her scent. "What are you..?" he started, then her mouth closed over his, silencing him. He resisted for a moment, then reached down to pull her closer, and was startled when his hands touched bare flesh. She had not just removed her cloak.

Rhiannon broke off the kiss and started undoing his shirt buttons, then gave up and pulled it impatiently over his head. Dodinal did not protest. She was in control and he was content to allow her to take the lead. Her hair brushed against his chest and stomach as she lowered her head, then he moaned deeply in his throat as she took him in her mouth.

When it seemed he could bear it no longer, she clambered up onto him and guided him inside her; she was already wet. Now it was her turn to moan as he wrapped his arms around her and began to move. He became lost in the moment, feeling nothing but the heat of her around him, hearing nothing but their hitching breath, seeing nothing but her face above his, radiant in the firelight, contorted by her rapture.

When they were done she collapsed on him, her mouth finding his. "Thank you."

"You're welcome." He almost cringed when he said it. If only he possessed Arthur's gift for eloquence.

They made love again, slower this time but no less intensely, then lay entwined for a while before she disentangled herself from him and got up from the bed.

"Stay," he said, one hand reaching out for her. Warm fingers briefly grasped his, then released him as she stepped into the shadows beyond the fitful glow of the fire. He caught glimpses of her as she moved about the hut, picking up her clothes and dressing.

"I dare not," she said. "Idris and Gerwyn were exhausted; I knew I would not rouse them when I left. But it will be dawn before long, and they might wake before I return if I do not hurry. Fear not, though, sir knight" – and despite the darkness he could tell she was smiling, teasing him – "there will be other times. Assuming, that is, you are not about to desert us now winter has finally passed."

Dodinal, still basking in the warmth of their lovemaking, said lightly: "Not much chance of that. Not after tonight."

"Oh, I see." Rhiannon bent over him. "You're happy to stay, now you've had your evil way with me."

"It seems to me it was you who had your evil way with me." He grunted then laughed as she poked a finger into his ribs.

"The time is not yet right for us to be together openly," she said, her manner serious. "I have been widowed long enough as far as I am concerned, but perhaps not long enough in the eyes of others."

"By others, you mean Gerwyn?"

"You're very perceptive."

"Hmm. You'd have to blind not to see it."

"He'll come around, don't you worry. Now I must return, and you must rest. If you weren't tired before, I'm sure you are now."

When she had gone, Dodinal put his hands behind his head and lay staring into the darkness. So much for avoiding complications. Still, as complications went, this was one he could happily live with. During the short time Rhiannon had been with him, the horrors of the day were driven from his mind. This had been a celebration of life in defiance of the death he had witnessed.

Of course he would stay. He had a life here, friends, a family almost. He had been so obsessed with searching for peace that he had almost failed to see that peace had found him. Still thinking those thoughts he eventually fell asleep, a smile on his face.

ELEVEN

He slept later than he had intended. By the time he rose it was past nine, and the men of the village were already up and about, emerging from their huts like hibernating animals roused by the spring sun. Some tended to the livestock, others inspected roofs for damage after the months of harsh weather. Dogs raced around, relishing the freedom of the outside world after being kept inside the huts for so long. They paid no heed to Dodinal.

Thuds reverberated from the forest, followed by a loud tearing sound and a crash as a tree fell.

Idris was inspecting the rotten palisade. The moment he saw Dodinal emerging from the hut, blinking and rubbing his eyes to clear them, he called out a greeting and marched over. "I was just about to send Rhiannon to wake you!"

A blush coloured Dodinal's face at the memory of last night's encounter; he hoped it passed for the lingering effects of sleep. "You should have roused me earlier."

The chieftain made a dismissive gesture. "Plenty of time. Get yourself to the Great Hall, there is food waiting. A man cannot work on an empty belly, especially after yesterday's exertions."

Dodinal narrowed his eyes and looked for some sign that Idris knew what had happened last night. If he did, the old man was giving nothing away. He looked preoccupied. "I've already sent men into the forest to start cutting down trees to replace the missing or rotting timbers. But the damage is extensive and I do not have enough men. We will not get it all done today, even if they work until sunset."

"Then we will do what we can." Dodinal clapped Idris on the back. "There are other defences. We can talk about it later."

The Great Hall door was open, and the window shutters had been removed, letting in light and venting the smoke from the fires. Even so, the atmosphere was sombre. The hut was filled with women, using brooms to sweep the floor and to brush the worst of the soot off the walls. While they greeted him warmly enough when he ducked inside, he could see they were anxious too. They would have heard of the tragedy. They knew that, but for the grace of their god, it could have been one of them sat at the table, crying and whispering prayers.

They kept their children close. The little ones sat on the floor in groups or ran around playing noisy games. Rhiannon was there; apart from a fleeting smile and a wave of greeting, she paid him no attention. Instead she tended to a pot suspended over the fire, shooing children away if they ventured too close to the flames. Dodinal was disappointed they would not have a chance to talk.

Platters on the table were heaped with nuts, dried meat, fish and bread. There were jugs of ale too. It was a banquet, compared with the meagre fare of the past few weeks. Dodinal thought that the villagers must be confident finding fresh food would be easier now that spring had arrived. He hoped their confidence was not misplaced.

Keen to get working, he grabbed handfuls of nuts and berries and stuffed them into his mouth, chewing them greedily while he took as much meat and fish as he dared without feeling guilty and put them in his pockets, to eat while he worked.

Once he had swallowed, he gulped down some ale and hurried outside, partly to make the most of the daylight and partly in the hope that Rhiannon would follow him the moment she could. He wanted to find a quiet place to talk to her about last night and the nights ahead, now he had decided to stay.

His eyes sought out the old chieftain, who was deep in conversation with Gerwyn. They were too far away and there was too much noise around for Dodinal to hear what was being said, until he got closer. The younger man gesticulated vigorously, clearly making a point with some force. "Father, please, you have to let us go."

"I have to do no such thing," Idris said coolly.

"If we don't hunt, then we don't eat. You'd prefer to build a fence than plough and sow the fields. What is the point of barricading ourselves away if it means us starving to death?"

"Good morning," Dodinal said pleasantly to Gerwyn, as if there were no bad feelings between them.

"Let me hunt," Gerwyn persisted, addressing his father as if Dodinal had not spoken. "The men you have put to work will need fresh meat to keep up their strength. You know my words make sense."

Idris caught Dodinal's eye. "He wants to go hunting. Reckons he'll be more use to us that way than if he stays here, chopping down trees. I don't know, though. I think we need every man available to rebuild the defences. What do you think, my friend?"

Gerwyn made an angry gesture with his hand. "Who cares what he thinks? He has far too much say around here. He's not *brehyrion* and not my father. I don't have to listen to him and neither should you."

"I did not ask you," Idris said. "And I value his opinion far more than I would ever value yours."

Gerwyn simmered, but for once he held his tongue.

"Where will you hunt?" Dodinal asked.

"South," Gerwyn answered testily, as if the answer was blindingly obvious. "Best chance of finding anything."

Dodinal cast out his senses. There should be prey around by now, awoken from its winter slumber and foraging for food. Yet there was nothing. He almost told Gerwyn he would be wasting his time, then bit back the words. How could he explain how he knew there was no fresh meat to be found within a day's march or more?

He suspected Gerwyn was less interested in hunting than in avoiding having to work. He also suspected the chieftain's son would be more hindrance than help if he were made to stay.

"Let him hunt," said Dodinal. "We have enough men to manage here with the two of us helping out. I'm certain we will all appreciate any meat he can put on the table."

Gerwyn gave him a suspicious look, as if sensing he was being mocked. Then, apparently satisfied this was not so, he nodded with almost childish eagerness. "I will take a few friends with me, the better to track with and to help carry back whatever we find."

"You appear to have all this worked out," Idris grumbled, but without malice, and with a sly look at Dodinal. He, too, thought they would be better off without Gerwyn under their feet. "Go on, then. Get your friends and be off with you. And you'd better not return without meat for our bellies or there will be trouble."

"Don't worry. I won't let you down." Gerwyn grinned at his father and nodded in an almost friendly fashion at Dodinal before scurrying off. The two men watched him go.

"You weren't planning to stop him," Dodinal murmured.

Idris's eyes gleamed. "No, but if he wants to run around while the rest of us toil, then I wasn't going to make it easy for him. Now he's out of the way, his idle friends too, we can really get to work. You said something about other defences. What did you mean?"

Dodinal set off for the gates, Idris beside him. "We cannot secure the palisade today. So we do what we can for now and then fill in the gaps. There is blackthorn in the forest. Get your strongest women, give them blades and whatever cloth can be spared..."

Between them Dodinal and Idris quickly got the villagers organised. Ten men had already taken axes and saws to the forest, so Dodinal allocated another ten to haul them to the village. The timber was left on the ground alongside the gaps in the fences, ready to be hoisted into place later. Those women young enough and strong enough to work were sent into the woods to find blackthorn. They wrapped their hands in cloth and furs and took scythes to hack at the shrubs and drag back bundles of branches. Bristling with vicious thorns, they would serve as a makeshift but effective barricade.

Even the children were set to work, those that were old enough, carrying tools and nails and rope wherever they were needed, though always within the village. They went about the chores with feverish excitement, after months trapped inside their smoky huts.

Dodinal busied himself digging out the stumps of the posts that had rotted beyond repair. It was hard going under the hot sun. Sweat pooled at the base of his spine and he found himself having to stretch with increasing regularity to ease the stiffness in his back.

He lost track of time. When a shadow fell over him and a hand reached down to offer a beaker of ale, he took it and drank it greedily without looking up. "Thank you," he said.

"You're welcome," Rhiannon answered. "But didn't we have this same conversation last night?"

Dodinal almost coughed up the ale. He looked around quickly to make sure there was no one within earshot. They were alone, though Idris was ambling towards them, casting an eye over the defences as he walked. "I was hoping for a chance to talk to you earlier. But not now. We're about to have company."

"Then it will have to wait until tonight." She grinned down at him. "Assuming Gerwyn is successful and I can get the two of them drunk enough not to hear me leaving while they sleep."

She took the beaker from him and her fingers lingered on his. "And if not tonight, well, no matter. There will be other nights."

"Yes," Dodinal answered. "Yes, there will be."

They worked throughout the afternoon, stopping once to eat and drink before returning to their labours. Fifteen posts were needed. Fifteen trees were felled, their trunks stripped of branches before being dragged to the palisade.

Once the posts were ready, the men lifted the first of them into place. They drove them deep into the holes Dodinal had helped to clear, then packed earth and stone around them before lashing and nailing each post to its neighbours.

As conscious as they were of the slowly fading light, they could not work any faster. They pushed their tired bodies until they were close to collapse. Even then they were not done by the time it had become almost too dark to see.

At least the gates had been repaired and stood true on their hinges. An iron bracket had been fixed to each gate to take the sturdy wooden bar that would hold them shut. But four of the posts in the palisade had not been reinstated. Dodinal was glad he had got the women to drag back the bundles of blackthorn. They were needed.

He sent the women to the Great Hall but gave neither the men nor himself any respite. They had more to do. It was slow going. They had to keep their hands away from the thorns as they lashed the bundles into stacks, then hauled them to the palisade and nailed them into place to close the gaps. Despite their caution, their palms were scratched and bleeding by the time they were done.

"We are finished for tonight," Dodinal said, and the words were met with mutters of relief. He eyed Idris with concern. The chieftain had worked as hard as men half his age, ignoring Dodinal's pleas for him to rest. Now he swayed on his feet as if drunk.

Cooking smells drifted across from the Great Hall, and aches and pains were immediately forgotten. Dodinal salivated. Even Idris shrugged off his exhaustion, standing up straighter and licking his lips. "Let's get inside," he said, his voice stronger than his body appeared. "And then get some food inside us!"

The men needed no further prompting and hurried away. Dodinal watched them go. Idris went straight to the Great Hall as his men called the dogs and tethered them outside their huts. It would be the first night the hounds had slept in the open for months.

Dodinal assessed the palisade, pushing hard on the new posts and feeling a sense of relief when they stood firmly in place. He had no concerns about the temporary defences. Nothing could get through those blackthorn stacks without ripping itself to bloody shreds.

He rubbed his hands briskly together, suddenly cold. As he hurried towards the warmth of the Great Hall, he saw the gates were closed and secured. Idris had left a man standing guard, a spear in his hand. The knight nodded his approval; they could not be too careful.

Inside, the mood was subdued. Even the children sat still. Only the mastiff, stretched out by the fire, its eyes flickering orange pools, was at ease. People ate without enthusiasm. The encroaching night had subdued appetites, for everyone knew now of the terrors the darkness held. They may have strengthened the defences, but there was no fortification strong enough to hold back fear.

Owain sat next to his mother, the boy's eyes following Dodinal as he entered the hut and took Gerwyn's chair. The knight smiled at him, to try to reassure him that all was well. The child smiled back, then turned his attention to his food. Rhiannon and Idris both nodded a greeting but neither said a word.

A bowl of cawl had been set out for him, along with some bread and a beaker of ale. He chewed listlessly, for once affected by the tension around him. A young woman, suckling her baby, left with her husband to put the child down for the night. The silence seemed to deepen once they were gone.

"Gerwyn is not yet back, I see," Dodinal said, the air of despondency making him edgy.

"He will stay out until he kills something, or the cold sends him back," Idris said. "He would hate to return with nothing after you brought us meat."

"And if he does not find anything to kill?"

Idris shrugged listlessly, as if he did not care either way.

Rhiannon said: "There is a river a day's travelling from here. If the game does not return we will send men to catch fish."

Dodinal nodded. It would not have been possible to reach the river during the worst of the winter. Now with the onset of milder weather the journey was well within reach. Little wonder they no longer concerned themselves with hoarding the last of their food.

"Then we have no fear of going hungry," he said.

Idris pulled a face. "Fish is for the old and for babies, those without teeth. No, we will not go hungry, but that is about the best that can be said. Why the forest is so barren this year is beyond me."

Dodinal kept his suspicions to himself. It did not matter what dwelled in the north. It did not matter what had taken the children, not at that moment. They were warm and safe. That was what mattered.

It was, he knew, a selfish attitude, given what had happened the previous day. But what had happened could not be undone. The only sensible course of action was to make the best of what they had.

He finished his meal and washed it down with the last of the beer. As he wiped his hand across his mouth, he noticed Owain sitting up straighter. The boy had cocked his head as though listening to something beyond anyone else's hearing.

Again, Dodinal thought, wondering what was approaching this time. Owain looked at him, then shifted his gaze towards the door.

His message could not have been clearer.

The mastiff was immediately on its feet. It growled and ran to the door, where it leapt up and began scratching at the wood.

Villagers edged away, deeper into the hall.

Idris pushed his chair back and stood.

"No," Dodinal said. "Stay here. I will look outside."

"You cannot go alone," the chieftain argued.

"Don't worry, I'll be fine." He kept his tone light, but he was glad he had not left his sword inside Rhiannon's hut this time. "It's probably no more than your hound having a bad dream. Nothing can get in. Even if it had, the guard would have raised the alarm."

"Then take me with you." It was Hywel. "We can check the ground outside the palisade together. For tracks."

Dodinal considered this. "Let me see if there's anything to track first. Just make sure you keep the hound inside. If there are any prints I don't want it churning them up."

He didn't want the mastiff turning on him in the darkness either, not when it had already gouged chunks out of the door.

Idris held the dog by its collar. It growled and tried to break free when Dodinal opened the door, but Idris was stronger. Once outside and with the door shut firmly behind him, Dodinal drew his blade and surveyed the village. It appeared deserted in the moon's cold light. Nothing moved, save for the ghostly plumes of his breath that appeared and vanished before him.

Dodinal sheathed the sword as he approached the gates, so as not to startle the man standing sentry. He need not have bothered. The guard, no doubt exhausted from his labours, had succumbed to fatigue and sat on the ground, back against the gates, legs stretched out. Not even the sound of the knight's boots thumping across the hard earth was enough to rouse him from his slumber.

Dodinal was unimpressed. Words would be had. There was no purpose in having guards if they were going to sleep on duty, no matter how tired they were. It was inexcusable.

"You," he said gruffly. There was no response. Dodinal's mouth tightened. He reached down to shake the guard by the shoulder. The man toppled slowly onto his side, head flopping loosely to reveal a deep, ragged wound across his throat.

TWELVE

INSTINCT TOOK OVER, and the knight wheeled around and drew his sword. He had considered the village unassailable. He had been wrong. Something had got inside. Something that had opened up the guard's throat so fast he hadn't had time to cry out.

Dodinal searched the ground for tracks, but there were none to be seen. Branches creaked in the wildwood beyond the palisade. Whatever had taken the children had used the trees to move through the forest. Even so, climbing trees was hardly the same as scaling a wall three times as tall as a man.

Dodinal squinted up at the top of the palisade rising high above his head. He could not imagine anything that could scale it with no branches to haul itself up by. Yet something *had* got in.

The tethered hounds barked. A baby started crying shrilly. Dodinal winced. Between the barking and the infant's wailings, he would not be able to hear any sound the intruders might make that could lead him to them.

He set off for the Great Hall, body tensed to strike at anything that came out of the shadows. The intruders had come for the children, no question of it. Dodinal was certain they were still inside the village; why kill the guard if they were prepared to leave empty-handed? He moved silently. If they had not seen him already he wanted them to remain unaware of his presence.

From the barn he could hear oxen shuffling nervously. A sheep bleated, low and mournful, and fell silent. As Dodinal neared the hall, a furtive rustling made him look up. Moonlight etched a shadowy figure, the size of a child, crouched on the roof. It was such an incongruous sight that for a moment he took it to be one of the village youngsters, up to mischief. The figure straightened, stepped forward and launched itself off the roof at him, leaping higher and farther than any child ever could.

It moved too fast for Dodinal to react, crashing into him and sending him sprawling to the ground, his sword flying from his hand. He scrambled to his feet and raised his fists, looking around wildly for the intruder, catching a glimpse of it darting into the shadows. Dodinal stood still, watching, listening, but he could hear nothing other than the barking of dogs and sounds of livestock roused to panic by the presence of a predator close by.

His face stung. He raised a hand and felt a thin cut down one cheek. His fingers came away bloody. Another scar to join the others, he thought darkly, but it could have been worse. Far worse. No wonder the guard had not had time to raise the alarm. Dodinal had been sliced so fast he had not felt it. A few inches lower and his life would have been draining out of him.

He bent to retrieve his sword. The Great Hall door crashed open and Idris and a handful of men spilled out, all unarmed.

"What's going on?" the chieftain called, stepping towards Dodinal. His eyes widened in surprise as he took in the knight's face. "And what happened to you?"

"No time to explain. Something got in."

The chieftain's eyes were drawn to the palisade, which stood as solid and impenetrable as a rock. "Impossible."

"Do as I say and be quick about it. Your man is dead. I would prefer it if no one else was killed while we stand around talking. Keep the woman and children inside, and the hound to guard them."

Idris hurried the men back inside, returning with swords and spears and shields. Idris held a second shield, which he gave to Dodinal. The knight nodded his gratitude and slipped his arm through its strap. It was unadorned. Nothing like as fancy as the shield Arthur had presented him with, rimmed with gold and bearing the King's motif of a red lion set against a crucifix. This was made of old wood and cracked leather, with a battered metal rim. It looked older than Dodinal, yet could not have been more valuable to him if it had been fashioned from gold.

Dodinal ordered the men into pairs. "Two remain in the Great Hall. Nothing gets inside, understand? The rest of you, scour the village. Be careful. Whatever it is, it's fast and it's dangerous."

"There's only one of them?" Idris looked surprised, as if he felt Dodinal had overreacted.

"I hope so, for all our sakes. You haven't seen it move."

The dogs continued their ceaseless barking. The baby's crying suddenly got louder. Its parents must have carried it outside. Almost immediately a scream rang out around the village, bouncing off the high walls so that it was impossible to tell where it came from.

"*Move*," Dodinal hollered. "Search the huts. You find anything, you kill it. It might have got in, but there's no way it's getting out."

Another scream came, from Dodinal's left. "Move," he shouted, breaking into a sprint. Idris and his men followed close behind him.

As he rounded the nearest hut a dog lunged at him, growling and straining its leash. Distracted, he almost ran straight into the couple who had left the Great Hall with their baby. They were now racing headlong back to it, the woman holding the infant to her chest. She gave a startled cry, and her husband gasped at the sight of the towering shape looming out of the darkness towards them. Both slumped with relief when they saw it was Dodinal.

"What happened?" he asked, voice low and urgent.

"Rebecca wouldn't stop crying." The woman's face was pale with shock. "I took her outside, hoping the air might help get her to sleep." Her voice broke. She shook her head and clutched the baby tighter to her chest. Whatever she had seen, she could not bring herself to speak of it. Dodinal looked at the child's father.

"I ran out when she screamed," the young man explained. "I saw her looking up and..." He raised his hands helplessly, as if suspecting Dodinal would not believe him if he said what he wanted to say.

"And you saw something on the roof."

The man gaped. "How did you know?"

"No time for that. Which hut is yours?"

The man pointed it out. There was nothing on the roof. They had neither seen nor heard it flee, so Dodinal assumed it was hiding somewhere nearby. "Get your wife and child into the Great Hall. Stay with them, a third man will not be unwelcome. Make sure the door is bolted. Don't open it unless you know for sure who is outside."

The husband nodded. He took his wife by the elbow and led her away. The baby cried relentlessly. Dodinal heard its lusty bawling even after they had carried it indoors. The parents were lucky they had not been killed, the child snatched from them.

"This way," he said. Idris and the men followed him without hesitation. When they reached the couple's hut he raised a hand for silence. The door was ajar; from inside came the flickering glow of a fire. Dodinal listened hard, but heard nothing. He edged forward.

The door exploded outwards, slamming against the wall with a resounding crash. A squat figure bounded out on all fours, straight at the startled men. They swung their swords, but the figure was faster than anything Dodinal had ever seen, weaving sharply left and right without losing pace. They may as well have been trying to strike the moonlight.

The creature suddenly reared up on its hind legs and lashed out at a villager as it loped past him. The man clutched at his throat and went down, a gurgling scream torn from his lips. There was no time to tend to him. The quicksilver figure was making directly for the Great Hall, and by the looks of things the man was already beyond saving.

Dodinal gave chase, determined to run it down, his heart thumping so he was only just able to hear the thud of footsteps behind him as the men struggled to keep pace.

Anger spurred him on. Two dead. How many more would die before they cornered this thing? They would have to kill it; it was too dangerous to be allowed to live. It had already reached the hall, where it sprung up to the roof with a freakishly powerful leap. Dodinal was thunderstruck. What manner of creature was this?

He slowed and stopped. The men clattered to a halt alongside him, gulping air into their lungs. They had the creature where they could see it, and as long as they could see it, it could not harm their children. The only way it could get inside from where it crouched was through the smoke hole. Dodinal quickly discounted that as a possibility. Every living thing feared fire.

They had it trapped. Dodinal was determined it would not get away from them. Eyes fixed on the hunched figure, he pointed left, then right. Idris nodded understanding. The chieftain whispered hurried orders to his men. Moving slowly, not wanting to provoke it into attempting to escape, they spread out until they had taken up positions on all four sides of the hall. There was nowhere for it to go. If it tried to break through the cordon they would be ready. They would not again be caught unawares by its speed and lethal claws.

It must have realised they had it surrounded, for it stood on its back legs and paced the roof, yelping in an oddly high-pitched fashion. Dodinal peered into the darkness, wanting a clear sight of it, but there was too much distance and too little light between them.

Idris edged closer. "What now?" He had to raise his voice to be heard above the dogs. It was fortunate they were tethered. If they had been allowed to run loose they would either be in the way or dead.

"We wait."

"And if that... whatever it is... stays up there all night?"

"Then we wait all night. Until it starves to death, if needs be."

The baby would not cease its interminable crying. Dodinal wished they could do something, anything, to muffle it. Then, as if in mocking imitation, the creature threw back its head and howled. It was too big a sound to have come from such a small body, loud and piercing enough to hurt Dodinal's ears. When it stopped he swore he could hear it echoing around in his head.

For a moment there was silence, and then there came a howling chorus from the forest beyond the walls. The men exchanged nervous glances. Dodinal tightened his grip on his sword.

He knew what was coming.

During one of Arthur's sorties against the Saxons a volunteer had been needed to infiltrate an enemy camp while they slept, in order to determine their strength. Dodinal had stepped forward, aware he would be killed if caught. He slipped past the guards and out again with ease. The victory the next day was a resounding one, with every Saxon slaughtered but few casualties on Arthur's side.

The creature on the roof had also been sent in under cover of darkness to scout the enemy terrain. Unlike Dodinal, it had been caught. Now it had summoned its kind to rescue it.

But what was its kind? Dodinal had never heard of a man who ran on four legs. For now it did not matter. He need only concern himself with staying alive so he could prevent any harm coming to those he had sworn to protect.

The ululating calls abruptly ceased, and there was a charged silence. Even the baby stopped wailing. Then they heard the sound of claws on wood, drumming rapidly. A man-like shape appeared above the palisade, a dark silhouette against the moon. It leapt up and balanced effortlessly on top of a post before flowing headfirst down the inside of the wall, its movements swift and sinuous.

A second figure appeared, then a third. No sooner had they set off, scuttling down the wooden posts, than more followed in their wake. Dodinal counted eight in all, including the scout. He nodded grimly, recalling the tracks at Madoc's village.

Even from a distance he could see the creatures were as big as the chieftain's mastiff, maybe bigger. They were certainly larger and bulkier than the scout on the roof, and it had already killed twice. Dodinal could not imagine the devastation they would cause if they were allowed to run loose. He had to take the battle to them, and strike the first blow before they could wreak havoc.

With a roar he hoisted his sword and ran at them, reaching the palisade as the first creature dropped the last few yards to the ground. It landed on all fours and immediately went for Dodinal.

The knight did not break his stride; to hesitate would be fatal. When the creature reared up and lashed out, Dodinal met its forelimb with his sword. There was a sudden jarring in his wrist as the blade scraped along bone. Blood splattered his face and filled his mouth with a hot coppery taste.

The thing shuddered and howled. Dodinal tore the sword loose and drew it back, ready to strike again. The creature was too fast, despite the wound, spinning lithely around and loping away into the darkness. More of them bounded towards him; Dodinal began to fall back. Voices were raised in battle cry behind him, and he grinned wide as Idris and his men, swords and spears aloft, stampeded towards him, boots rumbling like thunder as they charged across the ground.

A dark form sprang forward. Dodinal felt the air rush across his face as its claws swept past him. Hell, but those things could move. If he had not instinctively jerked his head back, the creature would have taken his face off.

Its momentum threw it off-balance. It was too close for the sword to be of any use, so Dodinal slammed the shield against the back of its head, knocking it to the ground. The blow should have caved its skull in but it leapt to its feet and scrambled back before rounding on Dodinal, growling but staying just beyond the blade's reach.

The smaller creature leapt down from the roof and joined the others. They attacked as one, scarcely making a sound as they tore across the ground towards the waiting men.

Dodinal stood firm, as did the villagers who had spread out to either side of him. As soon as the creatures were within reach, he thrust and slashed with the sword, lashing out wildly, using the shield to deflect the swiping blows aimed at him, some striking it with enough force to splinter the wood.

The beasts had no fear. They darted around at dizzying speed, fighting with jaws and claws. A man to Dodinal's right screamed as one of the creatures snapped its teeth shut on his groin, and shook its head like a terrier worrying a rat. When the man lost his balance and fell, it let go of his groin, twisted and buried its head in his throat. With a wet ripping sound, the man's screams were abruptly cut off.

Idris wielded his blade with reckless abandon, exhaustion forgotten. His voice rose above the din as he bellowed taunts and insults at the foes that scurried around him. When one of the creatures barrelled into the man at his side, upending him, Idris deftly spun the sword and rammed it deep into the thing's flank. His roar was louder than its squeal of pain. They were fighting for their lives, and the chieftain relished every minute of it.

Dogs were unleashed to join the fray. They fell upon the creatures but were torn apart. Dodinal saw men go down. More wives widowed, more children doomed to grow up without fathers. Rage flared inside him, and he struggled to contain it. He could hurt people, kill them even, if he gave in to his anger, which did not distinguish friend from foe. Yet not giving in would get them all killed.

By now the creatures were cut and bleeding. Their movements were slowing down, but none had fallen. A sick feeling came over Dodinal. This was a battle they could not win. The villagers were brave but unskilled fighters. The creatures were fewer in number, but had strength and ferocity to compensate. Unless he could tilt the odds in their favour the men would not live to see daylight.

Slowly but surely they were forced to give ground. He realised the creatures were driving them deeper into the village, herding them like cattle. They must have sniffed out what was inside the Great Hall and were forcing the men away from it to leave the women and children vulnerable. Even as the thought occurred to him, the largest creature peeled away from the pack and leapt onto the roof.

Its weight was too much for the supports to bear. Splintering and cracking, the roof gave way beneath it. The creature tried to scramble clear, claws scrambling for purchase on the wooden struts beneath the thatch, and Dodinal watched in horror as it plunged out of sight, howling as it vanished inside the hut.

THIRTEEN

FOR A MOMENT both sides froze, as if time itself stood still. Then the sounds of terrified women and children, helpless wails and disbelieving cries of despair, erupted inside the hall.

The seven creatures turned and raced towards the sounds, aware their prey was within reach. Dodinal reacted quickly. With no thought for his own safety, he took off in desperate pursuit.

The door was flung open and a handful of women ran out, screaming wildly, heading for the gates. Dodinal yelled at them to get back inside, but they were scared out of their wits. They did not know what they were doing or where they were going.

They never had a chance. The creatures swarmed over them like a dark tide, and their screams gave way to the tearing and crunching of flesh and bone.

Dodinal was sickened, but while there was nothing he could have done to save those poor women, there were others, children too, trapped inside, one of the beasts loose in there with them.

He ran to the Great Hall, past the frenzied slaughter. As he reached the door, he heard a clamour go up from behind him. He turned to see the village's men seeking retribution for the slaughter. They rampaged across the ground and set about the creatures, bloodlust pushing conscious thought from their minds. They were so intent on revenge they were too slow to defend themselves when the creatures turned away from the mangled corpses and fought back.

One of the things threw itself up on two legs and lashed out at Elfed, the big tracker they said was strong enough to have wrestled a bear. Maybe that was true and maybe it was not. Either way, the blond giant was no match for the creature. He cried out and grabbed at his belly, dropping to his knees as steaming viscera tumbled out over his desperately grasping hands. The creature struck out a second time, snapping Elfed's head around and breaking his neck. The big man hit the ground. Dodinal turned away and ducked through the doorway. Elfed was beyond his or anyone's help.

Inside, he was confronted by a maelstrom of sights and sounds. He took them in within the space of a heartbeat. Broken wood and thatching lay strewn around the floor. Some of the debris had landed directly on the main fire and was burning. More debris smouldered around it. The air was hazy with dust and smoke. Sparks gusted up towards the gaping hole in the roof.

Women and children cowered in a corner beyond the table, directly across from where he stood. They cried and whimpered, mothers clutching infants to their chests and standing in front of the older children to shield them. Rhiannon had her arms wrapped tightly around Owain, holding her son with his face to her midriff. The look of sheer terror on her face was one Dodinal hoped never to see again.

Two men lay in crumpled heaps on the floor, blood spreading out around them. The mastiff was dead too, its head ripped from its neck. The dog's eyes stared glassily at Dodinal from across the hall.

The father of the screaming baby had survived the onslaught, although he was bleeding from several wounds. He held out a spear, all that stood between the women and children and the great beast that prowled the hall. Fortunately for them, it was hurt and unsteady on its feet. Blood bubbled up from a deep gash in its head.

By the fire's light, Dodinal saw it clearly for the first time.

It was an abomination. No other word would suffice. Its body was that of a man, but hideously deformed, and so emaciated that every rib stood out. Yet its arms and legs rippled with muscles, and where a man would have toenails it had claws, four on each hand and foot, long curved nails that tapped and scratched against the wooden floor as it paced from wall to wall, seeking a chance to strike.

The creature sensed or heard Dodinal enter, and swung its head to regard him. He found himself gazing into human eyes that gleamed with malevolent intelligence, set deep into a face that resembled one of the gargoyles that leered down from high on the walls of the Church of St. Stephen.

Its chin was long and protruding, its snarling mouth wide and bristling with sharp teeth, too many even for a mouth that big. Its skull was lumpish, as though it had been squeezed in infancy before its bones had properly hardened. A low forehead was set above heavy, ridged brows. The nose was flattened, the nostrils flared. Its body was devoid of hair, its skin leathery and ash grey in colour, pale enough for the firelight to clearly define every cut and scratch it had sustained in the fall.

Devils, the men had said. Maybe they had been right.

Dodinal threw the shield aside. A large piece of it had broken off; it would disintegrate if it took another blow. Better to be done with it now and have both arms free to wield the sword.

He stepped forward. "Leave this to me," he told the injured man, voice low, eyes not once moving from the growling, pacing creature. "Take the women and children outside. Keep away from the fighting. Run from here as quickly as you can."

The man's face was tight with pain and fear. "And you?"

"Forget about me. Just go."

The man nodded gratefully and hurried away. Dodinal had his back to the women and children. He did not see them leave, but he heard them, the rapid clatter of shoes on wood, the swish and rustle of cloth, the nervous whispering of children, older voices hushing them. Heard them, but paid them no heed, for he dared not turn away from the beast even for a second. He knew how fast it could move.

Even now it was coiling to leap at them as they rushed outside. Before it could pounce Dodinal yelled and struck out with the sword. The beast shrieked in agony when the cold iron slashed its flank; it spun and darted away from him, claws splintering the floorboards as it scrambled further into the hall, out of the reach of the firelight.

Dodinal had a feeling it would not be content with skulking in the shadows for long. He skirted the fire, intending to drive the thing further back and buy the women and children more time while they made good their escape. His foot kicked against wood, and he glanced down. A piece of timber as long as his sword had fallen from the roof and lay partly ablaze in the flames. He stooped and grabbed the unlit end, holding it out before him as he straightened.

The creature barked and growled, its movements increasingly agitated as Dodinal advanced step by cautious step. He waved the makeshift torch from side to side in one hand. In the other he held the sword aloft and poised to strike.

It reared up and arched its back to display its genitals, taunting him. Dodinal responded by ramming the torch into its exposed belly, and the acrid stench of burning meat filled the air. Its gargoyle face made even more hideous with pain, the creature screeched and dropped down on all fours, then twisted round and clattered to the back of the hall where it disappeared behind the hanging hides, leaving them swinging and flapping in its wake.

Dodinal's mouth tightened. It was time to end this. He lifted the torch to the hides. They were as dry as parchment after countless years hanging in the heat of the Great Hall's ever-burning fires. They singed smokily, and then burst into flames. Fire clawed at the roof timbers until they too began to smoulder.

Cold air gusted between the open doorway and the hole in the roof, creating a draft that intensified the heat still further. Then came a *whoosh* and a shower of sparks as the thatch ignited. A searing wave swept over Dodinal, so fierce it was all he could do not to fall to his knees. He felt his hair burning, and he brushed at it violently to put it out.

Suddenly the hut was filling with choking black smoke. Dodinal spun on his heels and dashed for the door. He had to get out before the entire structure collapsed and burned him alive.

He lost his way in the dense smoke, and could not find the door. Sheathing the sword and keeping hold of the torch, he reached out, pressing his hand against the wall, and followed it blindly, trusting to luck he was moving in the right direction. His fingers found the empty space of the doorway and he stumbled out into the blessedly cold night air, retching and coughing up the oily soot that filled his mouth and lungs.

He slammed the door and used the torch to wedge it shut, shoving the burning end against the wood. It would not hold for long if the creature tried to break down the door, but with any luck the fire would have reduced the godless thing to bone and ash before it had time to get out.

Chaos reigned around him. Some of the creatures were mauling bodies on the ground while others harried the surviving men, darting in to cut and then scampering away, giving the villagers no chance to strike back. Women and children who had fled the hut ran screaming into the village, but the flames from the blazing roof reached high into the sky, driving back the darkness and leaving them nowhere to hide.

The beasts suddenly broke away from the men and went after the women and children, bounding across the open ground, moving as one like a pack of wolves hunting game. Dodinal struggled to head them off, but his chest felt as though a band of steel had tightened across it, and he could not find the breath for speed.

A woman screamed and went down, arms flailing wildly as the creatures tore into her. A child's piercing cry rose above the sound of slaughter. Immediately the creatures turned aside from the savaged body and took off, heading straight for the palisade.

Dodinal could not fathom why they had abandoned the attack. Then the light from the rising flames intensified, and he saw that one of the creatures was running on two legs, holding a young girl aloft like a trophy. It barked and howled and gibbered. The rest of its hellish brood howled and barked in return.

He heard a woman's despairing voice ring out.

"*Annwen.*"

Then they were scrambling up the stockade. Shadows cast by moonlight striped their hairless bodies as they clambered and leapt from post to post. The girl wailed as claws scraped and splintered the wood. The beast that had taken her held her pressed to its chest with one muscular arm. It was using its free hand and both clawed feet to propel itself up the wall. They were gone within seconds. The child's cries faded as the creatures carried her into the forest.

Dodinal's boots kicked up earth as he came to a shuddering halt. His chest heaved with exertion and the lingering effects of the smoke. Without waiting to catch his breath, he turned and pounded across the ground. He rushed past the Great Hall, the flames clawing at the sky, running towards the gates.

The guard lay where he had left him, forgotten in the carnage. Blood formed a dark aura around his body. Dodinal charged past the corpse without a second glance. He hoisted the wooden bar free of the brackets and hurled it aside, shouldering the gate open.

The barking and yelping had ceased. Nevertheless, he could hear the creatures as they escaped through the forest, the distant crashing and groaning of branches as they hurled themselves from tree to tree.

He stood just outside the gate, torn by indecision. Part of him wanted to give chase, to find the girl and save her if he could. The other part, the part not driven by anger, recognised he lacked the pace and strength to catch them. That aside, he knew they would change direction at random before coming down to ground. Finding their tracks in the moonlight would be impossible. They would make their way north, of that much he was certain. But there was a lot of country to the north and he was not familiar with the land hereabouts.

They could be anywhere.

Dejected and livid, he stowed the blade and went back inside the village, telling himself he would go after the girl as soon as possible. His first concern was Rhiannon and the boy. He had lost track of them in the confusion, after they had fled the Great Hall.

It was with relief that he caught sight of Rhiannon, moving slowly among the dead and wounded, stumbling as she walked even though she did not appear injured. He hurried towards her, feeling heat on his face as he passed the Great Hall, its roof ablaze. Sparks and smoke boiled into the night sky. Flames bathed the village with their fitful orange light. The walls were charred, but their oak frames were slow to burn. Before long, even they would ignite, and that would be the end of it. Idris would have to build another home.

Rhiannon gasped and fell to her knees. Dodinal turned suddenly cold. Please, he thought, let it not be Owain.

He quickened his pace, guts tightening with dread.

When he reached her, he saw it was not her son that lay still on the ground, but Idris. Rhiannon was kneeling alongside his body. She had lifted his head to place it on her lap and was bent over it, fingers running through the long white hair that spilled across her waist.

One side of his skull had been crushed and was seeping blood and grey matter. No man could have survived such a blow, not even a man as full of life as Idris had been.

The old *brehyrion*, and this time Dodinal had no trouble remembering the word, was dead. His eyes stared at the stars. Crouching wordlessly beside Rhiannon, Dodinal reached out and passed his fingers over the man's eyelids to close them.

He was dimly aware of people moving and talking in hushed tones around him, but he paid them no notice. His mind struggled to comprehend the enormity of the man's passing. He got down on one knee and put his arms around Rhiannon, saying nothing, just holding her, feeling her body stiffen and then relax at his touch. Moments later she shuddered as she began to weep, and he held her tighter still.

They stayed like that for a minute or two, and then Dodinal leant across to lift the old man's head from Rhiannon's lap and lower it gently to the ground. "There will be time to grieve for the dead," he told her as he helped her to her feet. "But that time will come later. For now we must concern ourselves with the living."

People had gathered round and were standing there helplessly as they looked down at Idris, traumatised both by the sudden ferocity of the attack on the village and by the death of their leader. They seemed to be at a loss to know what to do or what to say.

Then all heads turned as one towards the Great Hall as its door was hurled open with a mighty crash. Dodinal had given the creature no further thought, assuming it had perished in the flames, but it had not. It leapt out of the burning building, alive if not unscathed. Its body was blackened and blistered. It rolled on the ground, yelping in pain.

Rhiannon went rigid and screamed her son's name.

"Oh no," Dodinal groaned when he saw why she had cried out. Owain was running past the Great Hall, towards the gates. The boy, oblivious as always of his own safety, was perhaps trying to rescue the stolen girl. He gave no sign of having seen the creature, but the creature immediately saw him. It twisted around on the ground, jumped up and reached out to snatch Owain off his feet. Dodinal had left the gates open. There was no need for it to scale the palisade. It vanished into the darkness in the blink of an eye. Dodinal heard it howl in triumph.

He saw red and went after it.

The smoke in his throat and his lungs was forgotten as he tore between the trees. Their life lights, though dim, were bright enough for him to avoid them even with his eyes closed. Behind him he was aware of the sound of villagers hurrying after him, but he did not slow; he didn't want them anywhere near him.

The moon bathed the forest in its unforgiving light. Ahead of him, a shadow flitted and leapt high up in the trees. Dodinal's fury coalesced as he realised it was pulling away from him. The distance between them was growing even though he was running so hard his heart felt like it was about to burst through his chest.

Consumed by the fire of his seething rage, he had no sense of time. So when the mist cleared and he was finally forced to break off the pursuit, throat ragged, legs burning, pulse thudding, lungs puffing like bellows, he had no idea how long he had given chase.

He doubled over, hands on his knees, head bowed, gasping for breath, hearing nothing above his heart's relentless pounding. When at last it calmed, he realised with dismay that the forest around him was silent.

The creature was gone. He had lost it.

Baying his frustration and anger, he drew his sword and hit out at the tree closest to him, striking it repeatedly, roaring with each blow. The force of the impacts was like a hammer against his wrists, until it seemed the blade must surely break. He hated himself for failing, for letting down the people he had sworn to protect. He hated Arthur, too, for making him take the oath to begin with. Dodinal had not sought knighthood. But neither had he refused it.

Now he would give anything to turn his back on it.

He hurled the sword away and wiped his eyes. Blood and ash and sweat smeared the back of his hand. Then he slid to the ground and sat with his back against the tree, elbows resting on his knees, and held his head in his hands. Men called out to him. Dodinal did not call back. He was too troubled to want anyone near him. It was the first time in his life he had failed. He hated the feel of it. Anger, despair and inadequacy battled for supremacy inside him. He raised his head to stare into the inky darkness of the forest. There was a good chance Owain and the girl were alive; whatever those things were, the children were no good to them dead.

Perhaps there was time to save them, and redeem himself.

Even if there was not, he would go after them regardless. He would not suffer the creatures to live. Not after what they had done and would doubtless continue to do. They would continue probing south, attacking village after village, unless they were stopped.

So he would stop them. They did not deserve to live.

Dodinal nodded solemnly. His mind was made up.

He got to his feet and retrieved his sword from where he had thrown it. Then he set off for the village to say his last farewells.

FOURTEEN

THE MEN DID not find him; he found them. He could have passed them unseen had he wanted to – certainly he was in no mood for conversation – but his fight was not with them, and he had no reason to treat them discourteously. Even so, when they asked him what had happened, he gruffly informed them the creatures had gone. With that, he fell silent and did not speak again until they reached the village.

Rhiannon paced anxiously at the gates. Her shoulders slumped when she saw Dodinal had returned alone.

"Owain is gone. I'm sorry," he told her. The words sounded woefully inadequate. "It was too fast for me."

"What do you mean, gone?" Rhiannon's voice had risen in pitch. She was close to hysteria. Dodinal did not blame her.

He reached out and held her by the shoulders. When he pulled her towards him, she resisted briefly and then collapsed into his arms as his words hit home. "I know it's hard," he murmured into her ear. "But don't despair. Owain is alive. He is strong, not like the child they took from Madoc's village. You have to be as strong as he is."

She pulled away from him, beating both fists hard against his chest, her voice rising to a shout. "And what good is it to me to know he is alive after those... *devils* have taken him? How is that supposed to make me feel any better?"

Her voice broke and she hit him again and again, putting all her strength into each blow, screaming in denial. Dodinal said nothing, did nothing to stop her, waiting for the storm to pass, until she lacked the strength to strike him and the screams had dwindled into sobs.

Then he held her tight and pressed his face to her hair and whispered: "Owain is alive. I will get him back, I swear."

She did not resist when he led her through the gates. The guard's body was gone. The ground was stained black.

He steered her past the Great Hall, now completely alight. The firelight painted a picture of hell.

Bodies, battered and bleeding and not all of them intact, lay where they had died. Wives and husbands knelt alongside them, crying and wailing their grief, whispering prayers, holding the fallen even while torn flesh cooled and broken limbs stiffened, as though they could hold on to the life that had been extinguished.

Someone must have taken the children to a place of refuge to spare them further trauma, for there were none to be seen. Many of them were now orphans. Not all of them would yet know it.

Idris had been moved, his body placed before the smouldering remains of his home, with his arms crossed over his chest. His head rested on a folded cloak, his hair arranged to conceal his shattered skull. His sword and shield had been placed next to him. Two men with spears stood, one each side of his body, a guard of honour. Dodinal held back his grief at the loss of a man he had come to regard as a friend. There was too much to do.

Villagers flitted through the smoke, comforting the bereaved and gently separating them from the bodies. Now the initial shock had worn off, the living were taking care of the dead, carrying the fallen to a place out of sight where they could be readied for burial.

Ordinarily the dead would need to be buried soon so as not to attract predators and vermin. Now there was no need to hurry. It was too soon after winter for flies, and in this abandoned wilderness the corpses would not attract so much as a single carrion bird.

Now Dodinal understood why this was. It had nothing to do with the weather, as they had assumed. The wild beasts had not gone south to survive the winter, but had fled there, scared away by the gargoyle creatures that swept through the forest like a plague.

Dodinal hailed a passing woman and asked her to accompany Rhiannon to her hut, not wanting her left alone. But Rhiannon would have none of it and insisted on seeing to the wounded, since she was the village healer. Dodinal did not try to stand in her way. Far from it; he felt that with her work to distract her, she was less likely to spend the night fretting over her missing son, even if there was no distraction great enough to keep him far from her thoughts.

So he left her to it and wandered through the village, giving out words of condolence or reassurance to the survivors, who wandered around helplessly, unsure of what to do in the absence of any clear leadership. He had no desire to interfere in their affairs, but with Idris dead and Gerwyn yet to return, he felt he should guide them, for their sake and not his own.

As he walked, he searched for familiar faces. Eventually he found one, gratified to see Hywel, the quietly-spoken tracker, among those who had embarked on the grisly task of carrying the dead to the hut where their mortal remains would be stored overnight. Its original inhabitants were presumably among the lost.

There was no preamble. Each man understood what had happened. Neither felt the need to speak of it, only of what should be done. "They will start digging at first light," Hywel told him, taking a break from his grim duties to walk the perimeter with Dodinal so they would not be overheard. "What happened here tonight... people have yet to come to terms with it, let alone consider what will become of us after the burials. Idris is dead. His son is his heir, but no man here will accept Gerwyn as their *brehyrion*. I fear for us."

"Until tonight they only took children by stealth," Dodinal said. "Then word spread, and villages started keeping their children indoors. The creatures will not give up. Direct confrontation was inevitable.

"We were unlucky. We were the first. But we hurt them. They will be in no hurry to return. You have nothing to fear."

"That's not what I meant," Hywel said. He stopped and looked up at the moon. Another two days and it would be full. "Idris did not know you for long, but he held you in great respect. As do we all. We would do well with you to guide us through the hard days ahead."

"You honour me." Dodinal remembered how he had laughed off Rhiannon's suggestion that he might one day take over from Idris. So amusing then, so tragically prescient now. "But I will be leaving come dawn. The children are alive. I will find them and bring them home. I made a promise to Rhiannon and I intend to keep my word."

"Then I will leave with you, if you will take me."

Dodinal shook his head.

Hywel scowled. "Those things were like nothing I have seen before. You know what they did. They tore our people limb from limb, yet we failed to kill even one of them. You are a great warrior, but you would not stand a chance alone."

Dodinal shrugged. "Perhaps, perhaps not. If I have to give my life to save others, then so be it. I am not afraid. But too many people have died tonight, Hywel. The village needs good men like you if it is to survive. Besides, a man travels faster when he travels alone."

"And a man dies faster when he fights alone," Hywel snapped back. Dodinal could not help but laugh, despite the night's shattering events. Even so, he would not be swayed and when the two men parted he shook Hywel's hand solemnly. Whatever happened, he was certain he would not see the tracker again.

He intended to return directly to Rhiannon, to offer whatever comfort he could. But on his way he heard a familiar voice raised in anger, and he knew that Gerwyn had returned.

FIFTEEN

As THE KNIGHT cast eyes on Gerwyn, the late *brehyrion*'s son saw him and came storming across the ground towards him, hands curled into fists. His eyes shone a deep amber in the firelight, lending him a feral, almost demonic look. "What happened here?" he demanded, his voice loud and strident. "My father is dead and I want to know why."

Dodinal looked beyond him to the two men guarding the old man's body. Standing close to them, awkward and fidgety with nerves, were the brothers Gerwyn had taken on his hunting trip. It came as no surprise to him that they had returned empty-handed. One of the brothers shrugged helplessly as Dodinal held him in his gaze. The knight ignored him and returned his attention to Gerwyn.

"We were attacked."

"Really?" Gerwyn spat. "You think I have not worked that out for myself? I am no simpleton, no matter what you think."

One of his hands now clasped his sword hilt, but as yet he had made no effort to draw it. Dodinal tensed. He was willing to forgive the man his hostility in the light of his father's death, but if he spilled over into outright violence, the knight would put an end to it. "I did not intend to suggest that you were," he said. "If you let me speak, I will explain what happened."

Gerwyn dismissed the words with an angry gesture. "You are alive. My father lies cold on the ground. Even a simpleton can see you were more interested in saving your own hide than protecting his."

"He had no duty to protect your father, you gutless bastard."

Dodinal turned his head at the unexpected interruption.

Rhiannon marched towards them, wearing a furious expression. "He had no duty to protect anyone, but he did because he chose to." The words tumbled out of her in a torrent. "He led the fight against the creatures that attacked us. Yes, your father is dead, but know that he died valiantly. If it were not for Idris and Dodinal, and the other brave men of the village, we would all be dead and our children would all have been taken."

Gerwyn assumed a condescending air. "'Creatures'? You must have taken a knock to the head, woman."

"That's enough," Dodinal growled, but the words were lost as Rhiannon drew level with Gerwyn and, without breaking stride, slapped his face with the palm of her hand, hard enough to rock him on his feet. She thrust her face into his, spraying him with spittle. "Where were you when all this was happening? Far from here, shying away from hard work, just as you have always done."

Gerwyn was frozen in place.

"It's a pity you weren't around to help defend us when we were attacked. My son might still be here if you had been, and your father might still be alive." Rhiannon jabbed a finger hard into his chest. "If you want to blame anyone for his death, then blame yourself."

With that she spun on her heel and stormed off, leaving Gerwyn thunderstruck, with a livid welt on his face. The fight had gone out of him. When he turned to Dodinal, he appeared to have just surfaced from a sleep filled with confusing dreams. "What did she mean about Owain? And what is all this talk of creatures? Has the world gone mad?"

Dodinal was too weary to care whether Gerwyn understood what had happened or not. "Believe me, I am deeply sorry about your father, but my place is with Rhiannon. Find someone else to tell you what occurred here tonight. You will find it hard to believe, but believe it you must. And, yes, the world *has* gone mad."

He had no more to say and so he left, to find Rhiannon and do whatever he could to help her through the long night ahead. She had commandeered another of the huts whose occupants had been killed. One by one the injured were carried in for her to assess their wounds, and stitch them or bind them as necessary. Candles had been lit all around to boost the light from the fire.

It was ceaseless, demanding work. Dodinal watched her with increasing concern, she seemed to age years as the night passed. There were dark circles under her eyes, and her skin was wan and taut. He could have wept at the sight of her.

Midnight came and went and still she was not done. Her hands were painted red with blood, her clothes were spotted with dark patches. She was so tired her body swayed, and she had to pause from her work while she rubbed her eyes into wakefulness, smearing blood across her face. Her fingers trembled as she stitched torn flesh with needle and sinew until the only way she could hold them steady was by gripping one hand with the other.

Finally Dodinal could bear it no longer and insisted she rested. "You have seen to the most badly injured," he told her, ignoring her protests and guiding her away from the healing hut towards her own. "The others have but minor wounds. They can wait until morning."

Once inside, he ordered her to lay on the pallet. He found a cloth and used hot water from the pot to wash the blood from her hands and face despite her weak protestations. Then he pulled the furs up over her. "I will not sleep," she insisted in a drowsy voice. Her eyelids drooped. Only her anger and fear were keeping her awake.

"No matter, as long as you rest. You have been through a terrible ordeal. You need to take time to regain your strength."

At that, she cried out and sat bolt upright. "What about Owain? How can I sleep when he is all I can think of?"

Dodinal gently pushed her down. "Rest, I said. Think of your son, by all means. Only, think of the joy you will feel in your heart when I bring him safely back to you."

She looked deep into his eyes, seeking the truth of his words and finding it. Satisfied, she nodded and settled down, turning onto her side and pulling the furs up to her chin.

Dodinal busied himself with tending to the fire, then sat at the table and stared into the flames while he slowly sharpened his sword. He went over his memories of the attack and asked himself if there was anything he could have done to have altered the outcome.

After a while he noticed Rhiannon's breathing had slowed and was deep and steady. The anxiety had fallen from her face, and she looked once more like the kind and beautiful woman who had tended to his wounds. He would do anything for her, and for her son. It vexed him greatly to be sitting in the warmth of the fire while Owain was in the forest at the mercy of the gargoyle creatures. Every fibre of his being demanded he should be out searching for him, and for the girl. Now he knew what to look for, he would be mindful of signs of the creatures' passage. Yet for all his gifts, he could not see tracks in the dark. Blundering off blindly in the wrong direction could set him back hours, or even days.

It was frustrating, but he had to wait.

He rested the sword against the wall and sat in silence.

Finally he drifted into sleep too.

He woke with his head at an awkward angle, his neck stiff and sore. Weak grey light seeped like watery gruel through the gap between door and floor. He had slept straight through until dawn. He stood and stretched, twisting his head from side to side until he could move it freely. It was cold. The fire had burned low. He fed it wood and banked it until it flared into life.

He warmed his hands above the flames, then crouched by the bed where Rhiannon slept, her chest gently moving, her lips slightly parted.

He let her remain undisturbed, holding on to that image of her while he pulled on his cloak and fastened it at his shoulder. There was every chance he would not survive to see her again. This was how he wanted to remember her. Restful, without the weight of the world on her shoulders. He gathered his sword and the spear Idris had given him before slipping silently from the hut.

To his surprise, Gerwyn was waiting outside, leaning against the wall close to the door, bow held loosely in one hand. Judging from the dew that glistened on his cloak, he had been there for some time, since before sunrise, waiting for Dodinal to emerge. He had a pack over one shoulder and a quiver bristling with arrows over the other. When the knight stepped out, he straightened and cleared his throat nervously. "How is Rhiannon?"

"Asleep," Dodinal said shortly, setting off for the gates, not only because he was anxious to make a start but also to draw the other man away from the hut so their voices would not disturb her.

"Good." Gerwyn hurried after him. "I... I wanted to apologise."

"You should be apologising to Rhiannon, not me."

"I will, the next time I see her. But I didn't just mean about last night, though I admit I spoke out of turn. If you want to know, I am ashamed of myself. I've been less than courteous to you since you arrived. My behaviour has been unforgivable. Even so, I hope you will forgive me." He shrugged helplessly. "Give me a second chance."

Dodinal pondered this as he passed the remains of the Great Hall. It was a charred wreck: the roof gone, the walls reduced to the blackened bones of their frames. The air around was still rank with the acrid stink of burning. Would anyone have the heart to rebuild it now that Idris was dead?

He had no reason to trust Gerwyn, but the man sounded sincere enough. Of course, he was now aware of what had transpired while he was away hunting. Perhaps the shock of losing his father had rattled him sufficiently to bring him to his senses. If so, it was encouraging. There could yet be hope that Gerwyn had it within him to one day follow his father as *brehyrion*. One day. He still had a long way to go.

"I forgive you," Dodinal answered flatly, hoping that was the end of it and he could be on his way. He had a long journey ahead.

"Really?" Gerwyn sounded almost pathetically grateful.

"I said so, didn't I?"

"You really don't mind if we travel together?"

Dodinal halted and glared down at the younger man, who defiantly stood his ground. "I said I forgave you, nothing more. Anyway, what makes you think I am going anywhere?"

Gerwyn raised an eyebrow. "You creep out of here at dawn with sword and spear, and expect me to believe you're not leaving?"

"I could be going hunting, for all you know."

"But you're not. You're going after them, aren't you? Owain and the girl, and those... whatever they were, that took them."

There was no point pretending otherwise. "Yes, I'm going after them. Thank you for your offer, but I prefer to travel alone."

"If you will not let me walk with you, I will follow." Gerwyn had a determined set to his jaw. His voice was hoarse with emotion. "My father is dead because of those things. Rhiannon was right. I should have been here. That's something I will have to live with for the rest of my life. I cannot change what has happened, but I can at least try to make amends by revenging his death."

"A man who thirsts for vengeance grows to despise himself." Dodinal could not disguise his bitterness. "Believe me. I know that all too well."

"It's not just about vengeance," Gerwyn insisted, his hands becoming as animated as they had been when he talked his father into letting him go hunting. "Owain is my brother's son. He is blood kin. I may not show it as openly as my father did, but I care for him a great deal. Go ahead, leave alone, if that is what you want. I will not be far behind you and you cannot stop me."

Dodinal raised his eyes to the brightening sky and sighed long and hard. He could stop him if he wanted to. But even if he knocked Gerwyn down, he would just get back up again. He was a man on a quest of his own now. There would be no standing in his way.

"Why don't you wait until after your father's funeral?"

"My reasons are similar to yours. You want to be gone before Rhiannon wakes, because of your feelings for her."

"I have no feelings for her," Dodinal interrupted testily, the words sounding false even to his own ears. He turned and walked away. Again Gerwyn pursued him.

"Yes, you do. She has feelings for you, too. It's clear to see. That is why you leave while she sleeps: if she were to walk out here now, you would have second thoughts."

"No, I would not," Dodinal said, although he wondered if, despite having sworn to find her son, his resolve would falter if she did come hurrying after him. "Besides, you still have not answered my question. Why won't you wait until after your father's funeral?"

"Because I would be shamed to stand among the villagers while they paid their last respects." Gerwyn dropped his head. "I do not deserve to be here, not until I have redeemed myself by bringing Owain home. I could not bring myself to look Rhiannon in the eye."

Dodinal studied him for a moment, searching for any hint of insincerity or duplicity and finding none. Short of killing him, there was no shaking him off for now. Gerwyn may be an ass, but he did not deserve Dodinal's sword run through him. Fine, then. Let them walk together, if that was how it had to be. Dodinal could always lose him in the wildwood if he began to get on his nerves. "All right."

Gerwyn smiled. He went to speak, but Dodinal forestalled him. "As long as you keep your mouth shut. If you annoy me any more than you have done, I will not be responsible for my actions."

He lifted the sword half out of his sheath, then let it drop back.

The smile faltered. When they passed through the gates, Dodinal understood why.

Waiting for them were Gerwyn's two friends, the brothers whose names he still did not know. They carried spears and had swords in their belts. Like Gerwyn they had packs as well as bows, and quivers, bristling with arrows. There, too, was Hywel the tracker, and with him was Emlyn, who had the surest aim of all the village's hunters. Both men were armed and carrying packs of their own.

"What is the meaning of this?" he demanded, although the meaning was all too apparent. They had planned it well in advance.

"You were prepared to travel in company," Gerwyn answered, flashing his teeth in a nervous grin. "So what difference does it make if one man travels with you or several? You have nothing but the clothes you stand in and the weapons you hold. You could not even start a fire. Between us, we have everything an expedition needs. Well, except food. But we will hunt. We will not go hungry."

Dodinal doubted that, but otherwise Gerwyn's words rang true. Having lost his pack, he was woefully equipped for the journey.

"Besides," Hywel said, looking somewhat sheepish, "Idris was our *brehyrion*. We all respected and loved him. We have come to respect you, too. We will not let you fight this battle alone."

"Then it's decided," Gerwyn said. "There is safety in numbers. We will be safer as a group than we would be going it alone."

Dodinal's grumbles were half-hearted. He really had intended travelling alone, but had not rated his chances of success very highly. He was just one man. The creatures had torn through the village. Twenty dead, almost a third of them women, many more badly injured.

The odds were still against him, but not, now, quite as heavily as they might otherwise have been.

"Well, seeing as you're all here, we might as well set off," he growled. Giving Gerwyn a last baleful look, he also saw a way of turning the situation to his advantage. If the young man did make it back with the children, the villagers would doubtless be less reluctant for Gerwyn to take over from Idris. So he leant forward to whisper to Gerwyn. "I'll track, you lead. Show these men you have the courage to become *brehyrion*."

Gerwyn jerked his head back in surprise. Then he nodded.

As they set off towards the forest, Dodinal paused to look back at the sleeping village. He was struck by a sudden premonition he would never pass this way again.

SIXTEEN

They moved at a steady pace, driven by a sense of urgency but wary of tiring themselves out too quickly. Tendrils of mist rose from the ground as if the land itself were sending guardians to walk with them. Gerwyn led, with constant glances over his shoulder towards Dodinal to make sure he was heading north. The knight either nodded or subtly gestured left or right if they had drifted off course. If Gerwyn possessed any tracking skills at all he would only have had to look up to see what direction they needed to travel.

The creatures could move at will through the trees and so must know which branches would take their weight. But their instincts were not infallible; branches that looked strong may have been weakened by disease or age. Some of them had been left hanging loose or had snapped off and fallen to the ground.

Of course, Gerwyn saw nothing of this. He was a hunter, but his prey was only ever to be found on the ground, not above it.

Soon after they left the village, the trail of damaged branches petered out and vanished. Dodinal was not unduly concerned. He kept his eyes on the forest floor. Sure enough, it was not long before he found a single set of tracks; the burned creature's spoor.

He said nothing. The others only had to know which path to follow. When he looked around, his companions were oblivious to the trail. All save Hywel. He nodded briefly to show he had not missed it. Dodinal smiled; he would have expected nothing less of such an accomplished woodsman.

Time passed. Shadows fled the forest as dawn gave way to early morning sunlight. The travellers spoke little, aware of the need to conserve their strength, and breath, for the long journey ahead. Along the way, however, Dodinal learned that Gerwyn's two friends were named Tomos and Rhydian. They were brothers, as he'd assumed; indeed, so similar were they in looks that he found it difficult to tell them apart. Not that it mattered. They were so jittery around him that they walked a good distance away, speaking only between themselves and to Gerwyn, and even then in lowered tones.

As the sun climbed the sky, the day became pleasantly warm. The air carried more than a promise of spring. Dodinal walked with his cloak carried over his shoulder. He wondered if Rhiannon was awake, and whether she had forgiven him for leaving while she slept.

He wondered, too, what she would make of Gerwyn's absence, and what words might be said at the *brehyrion*'s funeral. But there was no gain in thinking about that. At least the villagers were in good hands. If anyone could get them fed and sheltered, it was Rhiannon.

Around them were the first true signs of the new season: green buds speckled the branches, and daffodils, snowdrops and bluebells pushed up through the ground, filling the air with their scent.

Memories of the hard winter just past were already fading. All that was missing was the birdsong that usually greeted the season. Its absence was jarring and wrong, as if Dodinal had looked down to find he had no shadow.

"I expect you're in a bad mood with us." It was Hywel. He had fallen in beside Dodinal, as had Emlyn. The knight had been too lost in his reverie to notice their approach.

"What? Why?"

"For not letting you travel alone."

Dodinal shrugged. "Say nothing of this to Gerwyn or his friends, but I'm glad to have company, even though it is not the company I might have expected. I suspected you might impose your presence upon me, whether it was wanted or not."

Hywell and Elwyn grinned at him.

"But I did not expect you to conspire behind my back, not with Gerwyn, of all people."

Hywel pulled a face. "I did not conspire with him. I overheard him tell his friends he was going with you, and they said they were going too. I wasn't going to let them go without me, and I said as much to Emlyn here. Of course he then insisted on coming along."

"Aye," Emlyn confirmed. "So we confronted Gerwyn and, well, that was that."

"Sounds more complicated than any conspiracy," Dodinal said, with a low chuckle.

They continued in companionable silence.

After a while they heard sounds in the distance, and Dodinal realised they were close to Madoc's village. He said as much to Gerwyn, who was keen to call on the chieftain, to tell him what had happened. "He knew my father. He would want to know of his death."

Dodinal would rather have continued uninterrupted, so they could cover as much ground as possible before having to make camp for the night. They had no idea how far north the creatures had travelled but it was reasonable to assume they were many miles ahead of them. Any delay could mean the difference between finding Owain alive and finding him dead.

At the same time, he understood why Gerwyn would want to talk to one chieftain about the passing of another. So he agreed with good grace. There would be no need for them to stay long. Let Gerwyn tell his story. Then they would be away.

Sawing and hammering and the thump of axes on wood rang out through the forest well before Madoc's village came into sight. Dodinal nodded his approval. His warning about strengthening their meagre defences had obviously been heeded.

The cropped-haired chieftain seemed surprised but pleased to see them. The work continued around him when he walked out to greet them at the edge of the forest, calling out to announce their presence. A trench was being dug around the village perimeter. Stakes had been piled on the ground nearby, ready to form a palisade, while two men were nailing lengths of timber together to fashion a gate. Dodinal could not bring himself to tell them their efforts would have all been for nothing should the creatures come in search of fresh prey.

Madoc summoned his men and they put down their tools and gathered around, while Gerwyn told the tale as it had been recounted to him. Their faces darkened when he spoke of the creatures that had attacked the village. Several men made quick gestures to ward off evil. Then Gerwyn described how his father had died, and several of them cried out in dismay. He told the tale so well, for one who had not been there, that Dodinal was impressed despite himself.

"I am sorry," Madoc said, reaching out to clasp Gerwyn's shoulder. "Your father was a good man. We shared many a drink and plenty of laughter at the gatherings over the years. For him to meet his end in such a manner is an insult. He deserved better."

"That is not the end of it." Gerwyn explained how Owain had been taken, and the girl Annwen too. When he was done, there was a heavy silence. Men bowed their heads, or stared with renewed anxiety into the forest, as though fearful the creatures were lurking just out of sight within the trees, waiting to pounce.

"So you are hunting them down?" Madoc asked eventually, looking not at Gerwyn but at Dodinal.

Dodinal nodded.

"Then I will hunt them with you."

Dodinal inwardly groaned, having heard the same too often already. Before he had the chance to respond and decline the chieftain's offer with as much grace as he could muster, another voice called out, "As will I."

It was the man he had last seen trying to comfort his wife as she prayed over her son's dead body, laid out on the table in Madoc's hut. The father of the boy Wyn. His eyes had been red with grief then; now, they were bright with anger.

"Gwythyr, no," Madoc said. "I forbid it. This is no time to forsake your woman. She needs you at her side."

The man Gwythyr barked a short, bitter laugh. "She does not know I am here, does not even know who I am. She just sits at the grave we dug for our boy, whispering her prayers over and over. You cannot leave and expect me to stay, Madoc. It was my child those inhuman bastards took, not yours."

Gerwyn followed this exchange silently. Then he spoke. "Any man who wishes to join us is welcome."

Dodinal's shoulders slumped. The way this was going. their small group would soon grow into a small army. More people meant more noise, for no man could travel as stealthily as he. They would have to move quietly if they were to avoid alerting the creatures to their presence, when they eventually tracked them down.

Yet, for all his reluctance, he did not object. Gwythyr's point had been well made. Who was Dodinal to refuse him when it was not his child who had been taken; nor any of his kin, come to that?

Again Madoc gazed around at his assembled men, then glanced at Dodinal. Dodinal gave an almost imperceptible shake of his head. "I hear what you say," Madoc told the grieving father. "You have the right to avenge your son, and so you will come with us. As for the rest of you, you will remain here, to work on the fortifications and defend the village if there is need of it."

Once he had finished speaking, the men wandered off and returned to their tasks without a word of protest. None of them had volunteered to join their quest. If anything, they had looked relieved when they were told they must stay. Dodinal bore them no grudge. He could understand their fear.

Madoc and Gwythyr went briefly inside the chieftain's hut. When they emerged, they were burdened with shields, weapons and packs. Wyn's father made no effort to bid farewell to his wife, shaking his head firmly when Madoc suggested it. Dodinal was no stranger to the hatred that smouldered inside the man. It did not allow for sentiment. Gwythyr would want to be away without delay or hindrance.

They departed without fuss or goodbyes, Dodinal picking up the trail almost as soon as they had crossed the village boundary. The forest echoed with the sounds of labour. It would not be long before the defences were complete. He hoped they were not put to the test before Madoc returned. He suspected the village would stand or fall depending on whether the chieftain was there to help defend it.

The afternoon passed uneventfully. They stopped to rest only briefly for, by unspoken agreement, all seven men were keen to push on and take advantage of the daylight hours. Once night fell, they would have to pitch camp.

After a time they began to hear a rumbling in the distance.

"We'll not go hungry tonight." Madoc gestured vaguely ahead of them. "The river's half an hour away, maybe less. Good fishing."

Dodinal smiled sadly as a memory came to him, of Idris dismissing fish as food for babies and the very old, for the toothless. Like the effusive chieftain, he, too, preferred the taste of meat. But even fish was better than nothing, and they had to eat. Men did not fight well, or march well, on empty stomachs.

The roaring grew louder the closer they got to the river, until it was like the roar of a gale through the trees and they had to raise their voices to make themselves heard. Finally they emerged from the forest onto the wide bank of a raging torrent, the clear water swollen with snow-melt, foaming and turbulent, alive with eddies and swirls as it swept past them. The spray quickly soaked them through.

The far side of the bank was an unbroken wall of forest, mirroring their own. Dodinal sensed the land there was bereft of game too, yet even had it teemed with wildlife, it would have been cruelly out of reach. They had no way of crossing the river. They dared not even attempt it. Dodinal was consoled by the realisation that the creatures could not have crossed it either.

The constant rumble and rush was deafening, but their ears soon became accustomed to it as they proceeded upriver along the bank. The ground was rocky, the going firm underfoot, but even so, they made sure not to wander too close to the edge. After the melting snows, the water was almost level with the top of the bank, where the earth had turned to slippery mud. A man who lost his footing would be swept away to certain death.

Dodinal remained within the forest to follow the trail, catching glimpses of his companions beyond the tree line. The creatures had followed the straight path of the river until its course ahead of them veered eastwards, when they had moved away from it, relentlessly heading north. Dodinal called out to the men and hurried to catch up with them. "They left the river behind them. We must do the same."

Hywel squinted up at the sky. By now the sun had lowered until it appeared to touch the treetops, lengthening the shadows around them and turning the air so cold that their breath plumed misty white. "Better to wait until morning, maybe? We won't be able to follow their trail much longer and at least there's fresh water to be had here."

"Where there's fresh water there's fresh fish," Madoc added, rubbing his stomach in a slow, circular motion.

There were indeed fish. Dodinal could sense them. He pulled a face but said nothing.

It was agreed they would establish a camp while there was some daylight left. Given the stiff, damp breeze that blew off the river they decided to return to the forest.

Once they had chosen the site of their camp they split up, with Dodinal, Gerwyn, Emlyn and Hywel gathering firewood and the other four taking their spears to the river's edge. Madoc and Gwythr knew this territory well while Tomos and

Rhydian professed to be as adept at catching fish as they were hunting game. Dodinal had his doubts but let them go; they only needed so much firewood.

"How are you two going to catch anything with those?" Gerwyn taunted them as they carried their spears towards the river, a friendly grin on his face.

"It takes a lot of skill," Madoc answered mock-indignantly. "What you have to do is stand perfectly still until the very last moment... then shove your spear in and hope for the best."

They left, laughing, and went about their chores. Soon there was a fire blazing within a circle of stones, a stack of gathered branches heaped alongside it to ensure they would not get cold.

Dodinal had even more reason to be thankful these men were with him. He had been left so poorly equipped after his encounter with the wolves that he lacked the means to start a fire.

The wood they had gathered was green, unseasoned, spitting and smoking in the flames. But that was all for the best: to Dodinal's mind, fish came closest to being palatable when flavoured with smoke.

At dusk, Madoc and Gwythyr returned to the clearing. Between them they clutched enough fat trout, strung together on a cord, for the men to have one apiece. Too hungry to wait for the brothers to come back, they scaled and gutted the catch and threaded the fish onto sharpened sticks over the fire.

Oil dripped from the fish as they cooked, sizzling and flaring as it struck the flames. The aroma of cooking trout made them salivate. They ate once the skin was blackened and peeling, blowing and sucking on their fingers as they burned them in their haste.

Although he usually disdained fish, and it was far from enough to satisfy his hunger, it was Dodinal's finest meal in a long time. He devoured it quickly, picking over the last of the flesh carefully until there was nothing left but head, tail and bones.

He tossed the remains away and stretched his arms over his head, stifling a yawn. Dusk had given way to dark; the moon was rising and the sky was ablaze with stars. The air began to cool rapidly. He pulled his cloak tight around his shoulders. It had been a long, tiring day. He suspected they would all want to sleep early so they could rise and leave early come the morning. For all their levity, they had not once lost sight of their purpose.

Then Rhydian stepped into the camp, holding a brace of trout in one hand and his spear in the other, water dripping from the blade like rain. He looked around the fire. A frown creased his forehead.

"Where's Tomos?"

"We thought he was with you," Hywel answered.

Rhydian looked anxious. "I haven't seen him. He complained all the best spots had been taken, said he would find a good place a little way downriver. I was watching the water, but I looked up now and then to see how he was getting on. When I left there was no sign of him. I thought he had returned here."

Dodinal got to his feet, suddenly uneasy. There could be any number of reasons why Tomas had not returned. He could have gone into the woods for a piss or to empty his bowels. Perhaps he, too, hated the taste of fish, and had taken his spear into the forest, hoping to outdo the rest of them by returning with game. Or he could have fallen in. That was as likely as an explanation as any, though not one Dodinal wanted to entertain after witnessing so much bloodshed.

"We have not seen him," he said. "But we'll find him. Probably squatting behind a bush with his trousers around his ankles."

The men laughed at that, even Rhydian, but the laughter sounded empty and forced, as though they all feared the worst.

They gathered their weapons and followed Rhydian as he led them downriver to the place where he last saw his brother. The earth was soft, and it was plain to see where Tomas had stood, spear in hand, waiting to skewer the fish. A trail of boot prints led further along the bank. Perhaps he had decided to try his luck elsewhere, having failed at the first attempt. They looked around and called out, but their efforts to find him were in vain.

Finally Dodinal sighed deeply. "Rhydian, I'm sorry to have to tell you this, but it looks like your brother must have fallen in."

"What makes you think that?" Rhydian answered sharply.

Dodinal gestured at the ground close to the bank. "There are no footprints beyond this point."

"That's impossible." Rhydian stepped back unconsciously, as though fearing the river could pull him into its lethal embrace. "We have fished wilder rivers than this. He knew what he was doing. He would never be stupid enough to fall in."

Gerwyn reached out and grasped Rhydian by the shoulders, pulling him close in an awkward embrace. "Your brother was not stupid. But anyone can make mistakes." He looked up bleakly at Dodinal. "Anyone."

Rhydian shrugged free of him. "Believe whatever you want. Tomos would not have fallen in, he's here somewhere. Go back to the fire, all of you. I will search until I have found him."

"As you wish," Dodinal said softly. Let the man search, if that was what he wanted. He would find no trace of his brother. Tomos was dead. His body would be far from here already, carried away by the implacable torrent until it either snagged on some obstruction or was washed out into the faraway sea. But it would be better to let Rhydian reach that conclusion for himself than try to convince him he was wasting his time.

They watched him go, picking his way along the path, calling out his brother's name, until he was far enough away for the roar of the river to drown out his voice. When they made their way slowly back to the camp, the fire did little to warm them. Even Dodinal, for all that he had barely known the missing man.

He suspected Gerwyn would have remained with Rhydian if he had held so much as a glimmer of hope that Tomos may yet be alive. Perhaps, like Dodinal, he felt his friend should be allowed to make his own decision as to when to abandon the search, rather than have others make it for him. That might have caused resentment.

Dodinal observed Gerwyn guardedly. If that had been his reasoning, it was another encouraging sign he was not as selfish and shallow as everyone, Rhiannon especially, considered him to be. Then again, he thought ruefully, it could have been that he was simply too lazy to want to bother helping with the search.

The brace of trout Rhydian had caught lay untouched on the ground. The men had been ravenous, but now not one of them was hungry. It did not matter whether they had liked Tomos – indeed, Madoc and Gwythyr had barely known him – but they were all in this together, and he was one of theirs.

The men sat and brooded, each aware it could have been he who had fallen in, whose lungs had filled with water as he struggled, terrified, trying desperately to swim to the bank only for the current to sweep him away, consigning his body to the river's crushing embrace forever.

Each of them had lost someone, whether it be a father, kinsman or child, *brehyrion* or, in the case of the absent Rhydian, brother. The mood around the fire was as dark as the woodland around them.

Other than the crackle and spit of the fire, the woods were eerily silent. In forests elsewhere there would be the hooting of owls, the howling of the wolves, the furtive rustling of small creatures in the undergrowth. Here, the stillness put Dodinal on edge.

After an hour or so spent in mainly silent introspection, they heard something move swiftly across the woodland towards them. At once the men leapt to their feet, reaching for their weapons, relaxing only when a forlorn-looking Rhydian stepped into the circle of firelight.

"Well?" Gerwyn hurried across to him.

Rhydian shook his head. "Nothing. I walked until I reached a turn in the river, where the forest closed in and the bank narrowed until there was not enough room to walk safely. Then I searched through the trees while I made my way back here. You were right, Dodinal. He must have fallen in, though for the life of me I cannot understand how." He hurled his spear to the ground and sat down wearily. "Why him?" he asked no one in particular. "Why not me?"

"You should eat," Gerwyn said tentatively. "You'll feel better with a full belly."

Rhydian waved the idea away. "I'm not hungry."

"Then rest," said Dodinal. "Conserve your strength. The same goes for all of us. It has been a hard day. We should sleep now so we can be away again with the dawn. I will stand first watch."

Hywel looked at him sharply. "Why is that necessary? Are you worried those things may still be out there?"

Dodinal did not immediately reply. He had assumed the creatures were long gone, but had no way of being certain. At least he knew they had nothing to do with Tomos's death; they would have left tracks if they had. He realised the men were afraid of what might be prowling the deep forest beyond the camp. Frightened men made mistakes, and in their situation errors could easily prove fatal, as Tomos had discovered to his cost.

"Better safe than sorry," he said to reassure them. "We have cooked fish and their remains are scattered around us. Too late and too dark to gather it all up now but it could attract bears or wolves."

There were no predators within range of his senses, but his companions could not know that. "I would rather miss a few hours of sleep than be woken by something taking a bite out of me."

"Good point," Hywel conceded. "Wake me in two hours. The rest of you can take turns after me."

They seemed satisfied with that and, one by one, wrapped their cloaks around their shoulders and settled down to sleep, resting their heads on their packs. Dodinal undid his sword belt and placed it on the ground to his right, with the spear within easy reach to his left. The fire blinded him to anything outside the reach of its light so he closed his eyes and listened, wary for sounds that might betray the presence of anything that did not belong in the forest.

There was nothing, save for the ceaseless roar of the river and a night breeze that whispered its secrets to the trees.

Snores and coughs soon sounded around the camp. Bodies shifted and turned on the hard ground. Someone quietly farted.

When his legs started cramping, Dodinal got to his feet and, fastening the sword belt and picking up the spear, crept away from the fire to avoid disturbing the men. He walked slow circuits of the camp, treading carefully so he would not be heard above the endless din of the river.

He thought of Camelot and the life he had left behind in the hope of finding the life he longed for, a life of peace, free of war and of bloodshed. A mirthless smile played across his lips. How much blood had been spilled since then, despite his best endeavours to prevent it? How much more would have to be spilled before there could finally be an end to all of this?

Without intending to, he found himself thinking about Rhiannon. He was glad he had taken with him the image of her asleep in her bed, the cares of the world lifted from her shoulders, for a short while at least. It gave him something to hope for. Something to *live* for. That was the woman he wanted to return to, her son safely with him, not the dead-eyed husk she had been the night before he left.

A twig snapped with a whiplash crack and he froze, holding the spear ready before him, his breathing silent and shallow. It had come from somewhere close to the camp. He strained to listen.

"Dodinal?" someone whispered. The knight relaxed.

Rhydian picked through the undergrowth towards him.

"Didn't I say to get some rest?" Dodinal said.

"I couldn't sleep. Too much to think about." Creeping about the forest at night was perhaps not the most sensible idea, at times like this, but Dodinal was gratified to see Rhydian at least had the presence of mind to carry a sword. "I still can't believe Tomos is gone."

"I did not know him, but I share your pain."

"You have lost a brother too?"

"Not a brother, but others close to me. You may be hurting now, but it will pass, in time." That was a lie. The hurt did not pass. It dulled, yes, but it was always there, a silent, haunting presence that would never go away. Neither would he want it to. His past was more than the sum of his memories; it had made him the man that he was.

"Thank you," Rhydian said quietly. He scratched the back of his head. "You might as well rest. No point in us both being awake."

"Are you sure?" Dodinal was bone-tired and appreciated the offer, but it felt wrong to leave the man alone with his grief. "If you want to talk about your brother, I will listen."

"Another time, perhaps. Right now it just doesn't feel like he's gone. I keep expecting to look up and see him walking towards me, dripping wet, a big embarrassed grin on his face." Rhydian stared into space. Pain had etched lines around his eyes and mouth. "Go ahead, sleep while you can. I will keep watch until I start to tire. Then I'll wake Hywel."

"Very well." Dodinal hesitated, thinking he should say more, but realising there were no words in the world to make Rhydian feel any better, or any less alone. "Goodnight, then."

Rhydian responded in kind, and Dodinal went back to the fireside, where he returned his spear and sword to the ground. As Rhydian had no immediate need of his pack, Dodinal took it to rest his head on. Wrapping his cloak tightly around him, he settled down close to the fire and closed his eyes. With his thoughts as turbulent as the river's harsh lullaby, sleep was a long time coming. When at last it did come, it was filled with dark and twisted dreams.

He was back in the village, in the chaotic aftermath of the attack. With a groan of horror he saw it was not Idris who lay dead on the ground but Rhiannon, her dark hair matted with blood where her skull had been staved in. Owain sat cross-legged next to her, rocking back and forth, holding his mother's limp hands in his. He looked up accusingly at Dodinal and opened his mouth as if to say something.

No words emerged from his lips, only a long drawn-out scream, a shrieking so ghastly the battle-hardened knight clapped his hands to his ears to try to drown it out. There was no stopping it. The scream went on and on. It drilled into his skull until he felt it would burst.

He woke with a start. His eyes snapped open and he bolted upright, looking wildly around in confusion. It was only when he felt the heat of the fire and heard the scream again, cutting through the air like a knife, that he realised he was no longer dreaming.

SEVENTEEN

IT CAME AGAIN, weaker this time, ending with a kind of choking sound that was more dreadful than the scream had been. There was no need for Dodinal to rouse the men, who were climbing to their feet and arming themselves. Hywel pulled a strip of cloth from his pack, bound it around the end of a branch and thrust the torch into the fire to light it.

There was a name on every man's lips, but they did not say it. There was no need. They could see Rhydian was missing from the camp. Tomos was surely dead, so there was no one else it could be. Even those who had not known him well were shaken by what they had heard; they grasped spears and shields with sweating hands as they hurried from the camp after Dodinal, who had not waited the short time it took Hywel to light the torch.

Instinctively they followed his lead, not once questioning how he knew which way to go or how he could move so assuredly in the darkness. Such was their trust in him it did not cross their minds. For their part they could only see the stately trunks the torch's guttering light revealed as they ran, struggling to keep up with the knight. There were no more screams, for which they were thankful.

Gerwyn forged ahead of them, almost losing his footing in the tangled undergrowth in his haste to draw level with Dodinal. "It's those devil creatures, isn't it?" he gasped. "They have Rhydian."

For a moment Dodinal did not respond. Then he nodded, too distracted to realise that Gerwyn could not see him. "Yes, they have him." His voice was barely louder than a whisper. "No more talk. Forget about what they might have done to Rhydian. Start worrying about what they might do to you if they are still around."

They rushed through the forest, Dodinal at the van with Gerwyn at his shoulder and Hywel immediately behind. The remaining three followed, grouped close together so that no man was left alone. They knew all too well how silently and swiftly the creatures could strike. None of them had heard Rhydian being taken.

They reached a small clearing, and Dodinal raised a hand to halt them. This was the source of the screams. It was nothing more than a feeling in his bones, but he trusted his feelings enough to know that from here on they had to continue with the utmost care.

He hung his shield over his shoulder so he could hold the torch in one hand and the spear in the other, mouthed *wait here* to his companions and stepped cautiously into the clearing.

It was deserted, as far as he could tell. He turned slowly, eyes straining to catch sight of anything out of place. There were no tracks to be seen. The ground was undisturbed.

Dodinal turned to face the men, shaking his head. He was on the verge of returning to them when he heard a soft tapping like rainwater dripping from the trees after a storm. Except it had not rained that day; the sky had been a cloudless blue from dawn until dusk. Almost afraid of what he might see, Dodinal held the torch aloft and looked up.

Lightning had struck one of the huge, ancient trees that edged the clearing. It had sheared off high above Dodinal's head, ending in a ragged stump and a thick bough, no longer than a man's arm.

Rhydian had been impaled on it, the branch's broken end protruding from his chest. The corpse stared at Dodinal with empty eye sockets. The skin around them was pierced and bleeding where the creature had dug in its claws to grip him before gouging out his eyes.

But that was not the worst of it.

Dodinal backed away, a groan of revulsion building in his throat.

Rhydian's groin was a gore-soaked mess where his manhood had been torn away. It had been rammed into his mouth so that his cheeks bulged and his genitals protruded from his lips like a swollen tongue, resting against his red-smeared chin.

Dodinal was vaguely aware of someone violently retching.

Then his own stomach rebelled and he had to turn away before he too emptied his guts on the ground. In his time, he had witnessed the most barbaric deaths on the battlefield. Truth be told, he had been responsible for a great many of them. But that had been in the heat of battle. He had committed violence only against men who would have ended his life had he not ended theirs first.

This was different. If Rhydian's death had been intended to scare them away, the creatures could have just killed him and left his body for them to find. Instead they had tortured him, broken him with acts of the most obscene cruelty. They had not merely wanted to frighten the men. They had wanted to drive them mad with terror.

He staggered away from the clearing.

It was Gerwyn he had heard retching. The *brehyrion*'s son was bent over at the waist, dry-heaving. The other men gathered around him, stunned, faces ashen as they stared with appalled expressions at the body, mercifully returned to the shadows now that Dodinal had lowered the torch. Gwythyr was visibly shaking, his eyes wide, his hands pressed to his mouth. Perhaps it had occurred to him that his son had been lucky to die how he did.

"We have to get him down," Gerwyn said weakly. He straightened and wiped a hand across his mouth, then spat on the ground. "We can't leave him up there. It isn't right."

"Have you taken leave of your senses?" Madoc snapped. "We have to get away from here now. Those things could still be around."

This was met with a general murmur of agreement.

Anger flashed across Gerwyn's face. "Would you be as hasty to leave a friend of yours like that? He deserves a decent burial."

Dodinal held up a hand for silence. "I understand. He was your friend. But Madoc is right. It's not safe to stay here. We assumed those creatures were long gone, and Rhydian paid for our mistake."

"But –" Gerwyn started.

Dodinal spoke across him forcefully. "Someone would have to climb the tree and cut him down. Will you? And even if you do, then what? We have nothing to dig a grave with. We would have to leave him on the ground for wolves and carrion birds to finish what those creatures started."

Gerwyn tried to interrupt, but Dodinal would not be silenced.

"We have to go, now. Only a fool would believe they would have gone after slaughtering Rhydian. They are out there, waiting. Waiting for one of us to wander off, and then..." He did not finish the sentence. There was no need to. " But we will not give them that chance. We stay close at all times, understand? If any of you needs to piss, we all stop and you piss where you stand."

Gerwyn fumed for a moment, but relented. The men had given him no choice. If he had insisted on getting the body down they would have left him behind and carried on. They could not wait to get away from the clearing. It was in their faces and in the way they shifted nervously on their feet, waiting for Dodinal to take the lead.

The knight shouldered his shield and set off away from the clearing, going around rather than through it. He listened for the sound of pursuit, but soon gave it up as hopeless; he could hear nothing over the noise of the men following behind him.

Dodinal became increasingly anxious. He might not hear the creatures, but the racket the men were making would carry a long way. Glancing over his shoulder he realised

Hywel was still carrying the burning torch. While there was nothing he could do about silencing them, he could at least make it harder for the men to be seen.

He quietly called out the tracker's name and beckoned him closer. "Put that out. They'll see us from miles away."

They stopped while Hywel did as Dodinal had told him. He rammed the torch into the ground and twisted and scraped until it was blackened and dead. Tiny flames began to dance across the undergrowth and he stamped on them until they too were out. Starting a forest fire would do none of them any favours.

"I should have thought of that," Hywel said apologetically.

Dodinal did not answer. His eyes flicked forward as a sharp crack like a branch breaking came from ahead of them.

His searching eyes picked out something smaller than a bird arcing down from the trees, hurtling towards them.

Before Dodinal had the chance to bellow a warning, Hywel's head suddenly snapped back. The tracker gave a soft grunt, sounding more surprised than hurt. Then his hands flew to his face and he staggered backwards, twisting in a slow half-turn, and collapsing heavily to the ground.

Acting without thinking, Dodinal dropped his shoulder and let the shield slide down his arm, then lifted it to protect his head. No sooner had he done so than the shield was struck a thundering blow.

Dodinal crouched over Hywel's unmoving form, holding the shield up at an angle to protect them both as best he could. There was a small rock on the ground close to where the tracker lay. Now Dodinal wondered if Tomos had fallen into the river after all.

The sudden assault had left the men frozen. Now they shook off their inertia and erupted into action. Following Dodinal's lead, they held their shields at the ready and crouched around him, covering him while he reached out with his free hand to feel Hywel's neck for a pulse. Though fearing the worst, he was relieved to feel a faint tremor beneath his fingers. In the moonlight he could not see the tracker's head but it seemed Hywel had only been caught a glancing blow.

They crouched and waited until their cramping muscles began to complain. Even then, they dared not move, dared not speak, hardly dared to draw breath. Dodinal braced himself as his keen ears detected a faint whistling racing towards them. A moment later he heard stone strike hard against wood, followed a moment after that by a grunt of pain. Whoever had been hit had not been badly hurt, though; the barrier of shields remained unbroken and steady.

Minutes dragged by. All Dodinal could hear was the fast and ragged breathing of men in fear of their lives. He listened for the creaking of branches.

A moment later, a stone hit the barricade, followed rapidly by another and then another, booming out like thunderclaps as they clattered against the shields. Wood began to splinter and leather began to tear with the ferocity of the onslaught.

"I've had just about enough of this," a disgruntled voice suddenly muttered in the darkness. Emlyn. "Time to make those filthy bastards regret starting a fight with us."

Dodinal glanced at the shadowy figures beside him, he could just about make out Emlyn putting down his shield. Madoc adjusted his arm so that his own shield covered them both, lowering it just far enough for them to see where the next stone came from.

Emlyn reached over his shoulder for his bow, notched an arrow and pulled it back, waiting. He did not have to wait long. "*There,*" he called. Madoc's reflexes were sound for a man of his age. He hoisted the shield a second before a stone slammed into it. Emlyn was instantly on his feet, loosing the arrow. As it flew away into the darkness he reached over his shoulder for another, notching it and firing it with a speed born of many years of practice, then immediately ducked back under cover.

They did not hear either arrow strike, but the wildwood was suddenly filled with an agonised screeching and a frenzied clatter of branches. Dodinal got to his feet, ignoring the screaming protests of his legs, leaving the other men where they were to protect Hywel.

The knight held his shield and spear at the ready, trying to gauge whether the creature was heading towards them or away, deeper into the forest. Soon enough, the screeching and crashing faded out of hearing.

Even then he waited. Those gargoyle monstrosities may be savage, but they were cunning too; a fearful combination. He dared not let his guard down, not when there could be more of them out there, hiding in the trees, biding their time, patiently waiting for the men to lower their defences so they could launch another ambush.

They had to move quickly. At least one of the creatures knew their location. It would be safer for them to get away than stay where they were, especially as they no longer had the torch to give away their position. Unless, that was, the creatures could see in the dark.

Dodinal shuddered at the prospect.

Undecided, he stood for several long moments, eyes closed and listening. There was nothing save the soft breathing of men and the shifting of cloth and creak of boot leather as they moved.

Finally, Dodinal abandoned his vigil. If there were any more devils were out there, they were in no hurry to attack.

He crouched and whispered, "We have to get away from here."

"Have they gone?" Gerwyn whispered back.

"Yes. But I think there was only one of them, holding back to make sure they were not being followed. It's impossible to be certain; those things are devious. So we'll have to keep our guard up."

"What are we going to do about Hywel?" Emlyn asked.

Dodinal had already asked the same question of himself.

While it was never wise to move a wounded man, especially a man with a head wound, they had no other choice. Leaving Hywel in the forest alone would be as good as condemning him to death.

"We either take him with us or someone will have to stay here with him until he comes around," he said.

"I'm not staying." Gerwyn responded immediately and with fierce determination. "Don't get me wrong. Hywel is a good man. But I owe it to my father. Besides, they still have the boy. Rhiannon would kill me if I returned without even trying to bring him home."

Then Madoc spoke. "There is not a man among us who would be prepared to abandon the search, Dodinal. We all have reasons for wanting to track down those godless bastards. But neither would we leave Hywel here. I say we take him with us, carrying him if needs be. If he recovers soon, all well and good. If not... we'll worry about that when the time comes."

"That's what I was hoping to hear." Dodinal grinned, his heart lifted by this spirit of brotherhood. It took him back to his days of fighting alongside Arthur, when they had been outnumbered more often than not. Now, like then, they needed to stand together and fight as one if they were to stand any chance of victory.

"We will bind his wound and be gone from here before that devil has chance to return with more of its kind," he said.

Hywel groaned but did not wake when Dodinal turned him to see his head in the moonlight. Fortunately for Hywel, the stone had whipped across his forehead, where the bone was thickest. A flap of skin hung loose, bleeding copiously. Gerwyn handed Dodinal a strip of cloth, and he bound the wound to keep it clean.

It could have been worse, he supposed. What worried him was that it may yet prove to be. Sometimes a hard blow to the head left a man damaged in ways that would only become apparent later.[9]

"How bad is he?" Emlyn's concern for his friend was heartfelt.

"Too early to say. The wound should heal quickly enough."

[9] Medieval medicine commonly attributed dementia and brain damage to imbalanced humours or spiritual influences, but there is evidence that soldiers – including knights like Malory – and military surgeons were at least broadly aware of the effects of brain trauma.

"Aye, but will he still be the Hywel I have known since we were babes in arms? I have seen such injuries before, Dodinal. I have seen good men turned into dribbling wrecks."

"There is nothing we can do about it for now. As long as he breathes, there is a chance he will fully recover. I will carry him for as long as I can. Then we will rest. I want two men before me and two behind, shields at the ready."

Madoc took hold of Dodinal's shield and sword while the other three men shared out Hywel's belongings between them to lighten the load. That done, Dodinal placed both hands beneath Hywel and lifted him, placing him gently over one shoulder, giving silent thanks that the tracker was such a small man.

They set off, chancing to luck that they were heading north, for they had lost all sense of direction. The river grew quieter as they moved away from it, until it was no more than a distant rumble.

Gerwyn and Madoc walked a few paces ahead of Dodinal, with Emlyn and Gwythyr following closely behind. The knight kept one hand resting on Hywel's back to try to hold him still.

After a couple of hours of uneventful travelling, he called a halt, although he could have carried on with no discomfort for several hours more. He lowered Hywel to the ground, using a pack to cushion his head, and they sat in a rough circle around him, shields raised while they debated with lowered voices whether it would be wiser to wait for the dawn or push on once they had rested.

In the end, it was agreed they would move on. They were tired and craved sleep, but recognised they would only lose time they could not afford to lose, if they sat around until daylight. Dodinal lifted Hywel again and they gathered up their belongings and continued on their way at a steady pace.

Occasionally the tracker would let out a low moan or would shift on the knight's broad shoulders as though coming around, only to remain dead to the world. Dodinal hoped he would make it. Putting aside their friendship, they had lost two men already and could not afford to lose a third. Before long, they would have to decide what to do with him if he did not regain consciousness. Their options would be limited. Dodinal pushed such thoughts from his mind. He was already dizzy from too little sleep and too little food.

Night headed towards dawn; the forest brightened almost imperceptibly around them. Soon it became apparent the woodland was no longer as dense and oppressive as it had been. It would not be long before they left the forest behind. Dodinal yearned for the feel of the sun on his face.

They had lost the trail in their haste to get away, after the attacks on Rhydian and Hywel. For now that did not seem important. They could return to the woods later, if needs be, and search around until they picked up the tracks. Once they had rested, that was. Their eyes drooped and they stumbled as they walked. They had travelled a long way, and were still reeling from the night's horrors. They would be in no fit state to resume the search until they had slept.

They reached the tree line, grinning and laughing as they emerged from the forest. After so many days in the wildwood, the world suddenly opened up into an endless expanse. They stopped and looked about them as though they had forgotten what the land looked like, drawing fresh, clean air deep into their lungs.

The sky was cold purple, streaked with pale salmon to the east. Ahead of them were piled banks of clouds, high and dark, looming ominously like great castles on the horizon. While there was not enough light for them to see clearly by, the men could hear the soft swish of a breeze skimming the grassland.

Finally Dodinal spoke up. "We have to keep moving."

"Oh, what?" Gerwyn groaned. "I'm dead on my feet."

"You will be if any of those creatures are still in the forest. If you feel too tired to walk, just remember what they did to Rhydian. There is open ground ahead. We can make camp once we're far enough away from the trees that we can see them coming if they attack."

He led the way, shuffling through the knee-high grass away from the forest until they reached a small stand of trees. Dodinal turned to look back the way they had come.

The forest was a great sleeping beast, a shadowy monster stretching across the land from east to west for as far as the eye could see. For a man who was most at home in the wild, he was surprised at how relieved he felt to be leaving it behind.

Packs and weapons thumped and clattered as they were dropped to the ground with groans of relief.

"Here, let me help you." It was Madoc. Dodinal crouched until Hywel's feet were touching the ground, the chieftain holding him so he did not fall. Between them they carried him over to the nearest tree and gently lowered him until he was resting beneath its branches. Dodinal lifted his head and placed a pack beneath it, then took off his cloak and draped it over the tracker's supine body. He pressed his fingers to Hywel's neck; the pulse was stronger than it had been.

"Get some sleep," Madoc told him. "That goes for the rest of you. I'll rouse the next man in two hours."

"Are you sure?" Dodinal asked. The chieftain was the oldest of them all by many years. The journey would have been hardest on him.

"Yes, yes, I'm sure. Don't worry about me. I can rest later. I'll stay close to Hywel and keep an eye on him in case he comes round."

Dodinal nodded. He trusted Madoc to stay awake. He settled down under the trees, the other men close by, and reached for a pack, pulling it over to rest his head on, and was asleep almost immediately.

When he felt hands on his shoulders, shaking him awake, it felt like only moments had passed. He opened his eyes and saw the sun was high in a clear blue sky. "What time is it?" he asked in a thick voice.

"Noon, or thereabouts," Gerwyn answered.

"You should have woken me sooner."

"We decided to let you sleep on. You carried Hywel for hours."

Dodinal's eyes flicked towards the stricken hunter, who lay where they had left him. "Has he come around yet?"

Gerwyn shook his head. "He opened his eyes once when Emlyn was checking the wound, but only for a few moments. Even then, he did not seem to be aware of anything. I'm worried about him."

Dodinal said nothing. He was worried too. He got up, brushing dirt and dry leaves from his clothes. Stretching his arms and back, he wandered out from beneath the stand of trees and stood in the long grass, absorbing the view. It was enough to take his breath away.

Behind him, the forest was as dark and forbidding by daylight as it had been by moonlight, and to the east and west was open land, gently undulating as it stretched away for as far as the eye could see. But ahead of him, rising into the sky like a mighty fortification, was the range of mountains he had mistaken for clouds in the deep darkness that preceded dawn. Beyond the green, gentle foothills towered peaks higher and more formidable than any he had ever cast eyes on. They possessed a strange and desolate beauty. That was where they would find the gargoyle creatures. They could only have been spawned in so wild and dangerous a place.

He returned to the men. "We have to find the trail. It should not be difficult, but we have a lot of ground to cover. Gerwyn, you come with me. We'll head west and search for tracks. Madoc, you and Gwythyr head east. Emlyn, stay here and watch over Hywel. All of you keep sharp. We can't assume those things are only out at night."

They set off, leaving their cloaks behind in the warm spring sunshine. Seeing the long grass they left broken and flattened in their wake, Dodinal had no concerns about picking up the creatures' trail. Sure enough, he and Gerwyn had not gone far when they heard Madoc call out. They turned to see him in the distance, waving his arms above his head, and made their way over to him. Dodinal was not in the least surprised to find the trail led straight for the mountains.

When they returned to the stand of trees, Dodinal was relieved to see Hywel awake and sitting with his back against an oak. Emlyn crouched by him, talking quietly. The tracker looked up as they approached; a good sign. But as they drew closer they saw the anxiety on Emlyn's face.

"How are you feeling?" Dodinal called out.

"Not good." Hywel's voice was strained.

"A headache?" Gerwyn asked. "If so, it should pass."

"I wish it was just a headache. I could live with that."

"Then what?" Madoc demanded. "What is it?"

Hywel passed a hand in front of his eyes. "I'm blind."

EIGHTEEN

THEY DID NOT know what to say. Men like Hywel were set apart from the rest by their skills. Sharp eyes had defined him, made him a great tracker. Now he had lost his life's calling along with his sight. It was as cruel a fate as losing his sword arm would be for Dodinal.

"Don't despair. I have seen this before. The loss may not be lasting." He hoped he sounded more convincing to Hywel's ears than to his own. "I'm sure you'll be fine."

"Maybe, maybe not. Either way, you'll go on without me."

"I carried you from the forest. I'm not leaving you now."

Hywel blinked slowly. "You carried me here?"

"What did you think? You flew?" Emlyn jabbed a finger into his friend's shoulder. He was trying hard to sound cheerful.

"Then you have my thanks, Dodinal. Even so, surely you can see there is nothing to be gained by taking me with you." He raised his hands in a gesture of helplessness. "I will only slow you down. And what if those things attack again? I couldn't see them coming, let alone fight them off. I'd rather take my chances. Just turn me towards the west. If I can walk in a straight line I'll find the river eventually."

"And then what?" Emlyn demanded bitterly. "You'll jump in?"

"I'll have a spear to fish with. What was it you said last night, Madoc? You just shove the spear in and hope for the best? Doesn't sound that difficult to me." His sightless eyes creased as he grinned. "I can light a fire by touch and I'll have plenty of water. I'll be fine."

"You'll be fine until you get too close to the edge or some hungry beast comes looking for food," Emlyn snapped back.

Dodinal looked around at the men, his expression clear. They nodded without a flicker of hesitation and began to gather up their belongings as, saying nothing, the knight stooped and lifted Hywel to his feet, ignoring his protests.

"You'll walk in a straight line, my friend. Except you'll be heading north, not west, and you will not be walking alone."

"But this is insane. Leave me. Find me on your way home."

"Shut up," Dodinal said pleasantly. "And start walking before you feel the point of my sword in your arse."

Muttering curses, Hywel did as he was told, but he had no sooner taken a few steps than he stumbled and almost fell over some hidden tummock. Before Dodinal had a chance to react, Emlyn brushed past him and took hold of Hywel by the elbow. Dodinal was glad to see the tracker made no effort to push his friend away. He might not like it, but he must have come around to the fact that they were not going to leave him behind. Instead, the two continued on their way together, heads close, talking quietly as they walked.

They followed the trail of broken grass, cloaks tossed over their shoulders, weapons stowed. There was no danger of being caught in an ambush, not with open land all around them. As they walked, the mountains, stern grey and featureless with distance, seemed to grow steadily higher. Their peaks would have been lost in the clouds, had there been any.

Dodinal felt rested after his long sleep, but his empty stomach gurgled and rumbled. He wished they were close to the river. He would willingly break off the pursuit for a while if that meant they could find something to fill their bellies with.

The afternoon wore on, and the sun began its slow descent. They began to feel the strain as the ground rose, the gradient so gentle at first that they had scarcely noticed it. They had left the lush grassland behind and now followed an ancient path leading up towards the hills. The earth was firm and rocky, with hardly a tree to break the monotony of the landscape; with the dying of the light, it had become hard to make out the creatures' trail.

Even with Hywel to slow them down, they moved at a brisk pace that would take them well into the foothills before dusk, where they would have to find a place to pitch camp. Somewhere defendable. Dodinal's fingers stole to his sword hilt. By now he had come to expect trouble. It was more a question of *when* than *if*.

They pressed on until the sun dipped low enough to ignite the horizon and suffuse the air with a soft golden light, and Dodinal called a halt. It would be dark in less than an hour. Turning back, they could see the great forest spread out like a slumbering serpent below them. Ahead, the land rose steadily upwards, the great mountains already lost to shadows, harbingers of the encroaching night.

Dodinal gathered the men around. "I don't like the idea of sleeping out in the open, but there's no shelter that I can see. I say we continue on uphill for as long as the light lasts. If we're lucky, we'll find a cave. If not, we'll have to get to higher ground. We'll have a better chance if they come after us."

"I don't think we need worry too much about that," Madoc said. He was gazing uphill, towards the shadow-clad mountains, and sounded distracted.

"Why not?" Dodinal said, a little irritably. He was tired and hungry, in no mood for games.

Madoc stretched out an arm and pointed. "Look."

Dodinal saw a flickering glow, carrying a pillar of smoke out of a hidden fold in the hills.

They were not alone. Someone had started a fire.

"That's settled, then," Emlyn said. "Those creatures seem to be afraid of fire. If there are people up there, we'll be safer with them than making camp out in the open. You never know, they might even have food going spare."

"There's no guarantee they'll be friendly," Madoc observed.

Dodinal nodded. "Quite so. We know the creatures passed this way. There's every chance these people, whoever they are, will have been attacked. They may not welcome strangers in their midst."

"I wasn't suggesting we should just go charging in." Emlyn looked offended. "I'm not an idiot. But we should at least go and check out the lie of the land."

Dodinal considered this. They would have to skirt the fire in any event. It would do them no harm to find out who had started it, and they would be foolish to turn their backs on what could prove to be a safe haven for the night. Tiredness and hunger had left them snapping tetchily at each other. The chance of a decent night's sleep was too good to pass up.

"Sound thinking," he said, speaking directly to Emlyn. "We'll get as close as we can without being seen. If it looks dangerous, we keep going and find someplace else to make camp. And listen out. It's nearly dark. Those things could have killed us all, last night. They might try to do so again."

The gradient became steeper, and he slowed the pace for Hywel's sake. Before long, they were all puffing like a smithy's bellows.

They halted briefly to catch their breath and to rest their aching legs, then continued upwards. The air turned chilly as the sun dropped out of sight and dusk turned to full dark, but their exertions screened them from the cold. Each man walked with his cloak draped over one shoulder. The fire, though still unseen, drew them in like moths. Dodinal sniffed at the air. Wood smoke. Encouraging. A lot more encouraging than the acrid stench of burning flesh.

Then he felt the ground levelling off, and sensed they were close to cresting the hill. He drew his sword; he did not need to turn around to know that each man save Hywel would have his own sword and spear at the ready. His stomach knotted, as it did in the final moments before battle. A warrior who felt no fear did not last long. The skill was not in disregarding the fear but in learning how to control it.

He pushed on until he reached the summit, where he waited while the men fell in beside him. They stood in silence and stared down at the village nestled in the narrow coomb below them, lit up by the fires that had been set around its perimeter. The fires aside, the place appeared deserted. Nothing moved. Even from a distance they could see most of the buildings were in disrepair, gaping holes in their roofs, walls half collapsed, fallen timber scattered haphazardly across the ground.

"What can you see?" Hywel hissed.

"A village," Dodinal answered with quiet urgency. "Looks abandoned, but obviously someone's about."

"You think they've been attacked?"

"Hard to say. Stay here. I'm going down to find out."

"You're not going alone," Madoc said. "Too dangerous."

"That's why I'm going alone. No sense putting all of us at risk. Besides, if they have been attacked, they're less likely to be hostile if they only see one of us." Dodinal raised his sword. It flashed amber with reflected firelight. "And if they're still hostile, well, I can look after myself. Be patient. I'll signal as soon as I'm sure it's safe."

He left his spear and shield with them, not wanting to look any more threatening than his bulk already made him appear. Then he began to descend, treading carefully for there was no path now, the valley wall falling steeply towards the village. Slender trees somehow managed to cling to the thin rocky ground, and Dodinal in turn clung on to them as he slipped and slid down the slope.

By the time he made it to the valley floor, he was breathing hard; he was not getting any younger. It was just as well Arthur had brought peace to the land when he did.

He remained concealed in the trees while he considered his options. There was nothing except open ground ahead of him, and fires lit up the entire area. Other than edge his way around the valley to approach the village from behind, there was no way for him to avoid being seen. With that in mind, he judged it would be better to make no attempt at stealth and instead to walk openly into the village, sword sheathed and hands in sight to show he had nothing to hide. He could have the blade drawn in seconds if he came under attack.

He felt a familiar churning in his guts as he stepped out from under the trees. He counted half a dozen fires around the village's edge. Close up, the bonfire stacks were smaller than they had appeared from above. These fires would not keep the creatures out. They might serve some other purpose. A beacon, perhaps. Or a warning.

Dodinal could feel the heat from the nearest fire as he approached. The skin on the back of his neck prickled and the hair on his arms stood on end. He sensed he was being watched by someone or something unseen. It took a conscious effort to resist reaching for his sword.

He stopped when he reached the first building, an indistinct structure twice his height. A barn, he supposed. Most of the wall boards had fallen from the frames and lay like broken bones on the ground. He peered inside and saw only shadows dancing in the firelight. Moving on to the next building he found it had fared no better. He stepped inside, his boots kicking up dust and clumps of dried thatch. Even with the roof and walls mostly gone, the air was musty and stale; it must have been abandoned a long time ago. Suddenly uneasy, he hurried outside and looked around for some sign of life, anything to suggest he was not the only soul around. Surely whoever had started the fires had not lit them and then left the village? What purpose would that have served?

Fighting the urge to give up and return to his friends, he drew his sword – to Hell with appearances – and forced himself to head further into the village. He passed between huts that were all in such a ruinous state he was certain they would collapse if he so much as brushed up against them. Little fear that the creatures had attacked the place. There was nothing left to attack, and certainly no children to steal. Dodinal had a distinct feeling there had been no children here since before he was born.

That was when he stumbled across the graveyard.

At first he did not recognise it for what it was. In the glimmering light it resembled nothing more than an uneven common, that had perhaps been worked for crops in the past, but had since been left to grow over until brambles and weeds had choked the life out of it. Yet as he closed in on it he saw otherwise. The grassy mounds of the graves, four dozen or so at a rough count, were laid so close together they almost touched. A stone had been placed at the head of each grave; they were inscribed, but Dodinal had no intention of lingering to read them. They were weathered, some more than others, but even the most recent must have been put there a generation or two ago.

It was a dead village in more ways than one.

Almost dead, he thought, eyes flicking towards the fires.

Blowing air from between his lips, he turned away and resumed the search, relieved to be putting the graveyard behind him.

Only a few huts remained. He hurried past two that were obviously dilapidated, before he came to a third that was more or less intact. His stride became measured and cautious and he held his sword at the ready as he approached in absolute silence.

He was close enough now to see a soft amber glow spill out from under the door. Amidst the flames that burned around the village he had not noticed it before. For the same reason, he had neither seen nor smelled the smoke rising from the hole in the thatched roof. Questions jostled in his mind, but he silenced them at a stroke. It would not be long before he had all the answers he needed.

Dodinal crept up to the door and stood with one ear pressed to the wood, but heard nothing from within save the muted crackle of a fire, like hundreds of tiny bones snapping. He waited, but still nothing. He sighed. There was nothing else for it. Reaching down with his free hand, he took hold of the latch and eased it up, then pulled the door open hard enough that it smacked against the outside wall. Even before the thudding crash had done reverberating around the dead village, he was inside, sword clasped two-handed.

There was a man sitting on the floor by the fire, or rather, there had been right up until the moment that Dodinal flung the door open. As the knight filled the open doorway, the man let out a piercing shriek and leapt to his feet, only to get tangled in the moth-eaten cloak he had draped around his shoulders. The fire danced hectically and the man, arms flailing, let out another yell as he lost his balance and landed heavily on his arse, recovering quickly to scurry backwards away from Dodinal, his eyes bulging with fear.

The knight sheathed his sword and stood by the door with his palms raised, showing he intended no harm. The man cowered against the far wall, shaking like a beaten dog. He was older than any man Dodinal had ever seen. His body, clearly visible through the tattered rags that passed for clothing, was thin to the point of skeletal, and the hair on his head was sparse and a lacklustre grey. His mouth was parted in a grimace of fear, revealing blood-red and largely toothless gums.

"It's all right," Dodinal assured. "I'm not going to hurt you."

The man said nothing. His chest was heaving and his breath came in gasps.

"I swear, you have nothing to be afraid of. I am a traveller. I saw the fires and came here in the hope of finding shelter for the night."

The man licked his lips and swallowed loudly. "Traveller?" He frowned, as if unused to hearing his own voice, which was dry with age and fear. "No travellers ever come this way. So what could bring you here, eh? Tell me that, damn your heathen hide."

And with that he let out a high-pitched cackle.

Dodinal's shoulders slumped. Whatever answers he had hoped for, he doubted he would find them here.

"It's a long story," he said tiredly, wondering why he was bothering to answer at all. "I am travelling with friends. Some of their kin have been taken. We are going to get them back."

The man's jaw dropped. "You're going up into the mountains? After those black-hearted bastards?"

Dodinal nodded. He was not in the least surprised the man knew about the creatures. Of course he would, living here in these hills. Who was to say what misery he had endured over the years? Perhaps the reason there were so many dead and only one living was because the creatures had wiped the village out long ago. It would explain the man's strange manner. To be the only survivor...

"Why didn't you say so!" The old man suddenly clapped his hands together and hurried to his feet, beaming a gap-toothed grin. "Do you have any idea how long I have waited for you?"

"Waiting for me?" Dodinal found himself backing away as the man stumbled barefoot towards him. "But you couldn't have known I was coming this way."

The man waved impatiently. "Not *you*, oaf. Not you in particular. All these years I've waited for someone with the balls to go after those things. I was starting to think I would not live to see it. And yet here you are. At long last."

Dodinal flinched as the old man held out both arms as if to embrace him. This close, he smelled as though he had recently risen from one of the grass-covered graves. The stink was enough to bring tears to anyone's eyes. "Well, then, that's good," he said helplessly.

The man's eyes suddenly widened and he flung up his hands as though suddenly remembering something. "Travelling with friends, you said? Quickly, go fetch them. Bring them to me. You will be safe here. I have food. We'll eat, and talk. Oh, I have such a story to tell."

Dodinal suspected the man's story would amount to little more than deranged raving, but was persuaded to stay by the prospect of food. None of them had eaten anything since the fish from the river, and they had walked a long way since then. Now his stomach was so used to being empty it no longer gurgled in protest.

That aside, the man could possess information that might help them. He knew about the creatures. Perhaps he knew where to find them. The mountain range was huge, and they could be anywhere.

"I'll be back as soon as I can," he said, turning on his heel and setting off into the darkness, breathing deeply to clear the graveyard stench from his nostrils. He retraced his steps to the steep slope of the coomb and called out to the men waiting above. Having assured them the village was safe, since the old man, as crazed as he was, could not present a threat, he waited patiently while they negotiated their way down through the trees. With Hywel hampering them, it took them twice as long as it had taken him.

While Dodinal waited, the aroma of cooking meat began to drift across the valley floor towards him. At once his mouth was awash with saliva. The old man had not lied about having food. Dodinal suspected it would be better for their peace of mind that they did not question him too closely as to its provenance.

Finally the men had made their way down, and crowded around him, wanting to know what he had found. "A crazy old man who might just be able to help us," was all he would tell them before he started back towards the hut. They wanted to hear more, but then they, too, caught the waft of roasting meat. They would have devoured any food set before them, but fresh meat was like a gift from the gods.

Before they reached the hut, Dodinal stopped and gathered them around him. "Don't do anything that might frighten him."

"We'll be on our best behaviour," Madoc promised. "Any man who can get his hands on fresh meat deserves our respect."

"I don't know about respect, but we need to be careful. I think he knows where we will find those creatures. It could save us days of searching. We need him to trust us; if he gets scared or takes a dislike to anyone, for whatever reason, he might refuse to talk."

"There are other ways," Madoc growled.

"He is a helpless old man who has done nothing to harm us," Dodinal answered levelly. "Anyone who lays a finger on him will answer to me. Besides, he has been through so much, I doubt we could do anything to break him if he did turn against us. But it won't come to that. He seemed eager to help."

He went into the hut first so as not to startle the old man. The others followed hesitantly behind.

"Come in, come in," the old man urged them. He was crouched by the fire where a half-leg of meat was spit-roasting over the flames. His eyes widened when he saw Hywel, who was almost dead on his feet and would have collapsed had Emlyn not taken him by the elbow to support him. "What happened to your friend?"

"We were attacked," Dodinal said. "It's a long story, which I will tell you later. For now, though, we would be grateful for the chance to rest. It has been a long and tiring day."

"Of course! Make yourself at home. Not that it's much of a home, but you're welcome to it."

Gerwyn rolled his eyes at Dodinal, but he knew enough to say nothing. They sank to the ground, groaning with relief to be off their feet at last. Hywel sat with his back resting against the wall. The swelling on his forehead was going down, but the bruise was even more livid than it had been. It would get worse before it got better.

"What meat is that?" Gerwyn asked. Dodinal wished he hadn't. They might not be so eager to eat on hearing the answer.

"Goat."

Dodinal blinked. "Goat?"

"Yes, goat. Haven't you ever heard of goat before?"

"Yes," Dodinal said, not wanting to offend. "Of course. But... well, there hasn't been any fresh game around for many months, with the winter we've had. I was surprised you had managed to get your hands on any."

"It has nothing to do with the winter." The man turned the meat with one hand and waved vaguely in the direction of the mountains with the other. "It's those black-hearted devils up there. They've been on the move. I've heard them, going down to the forest, screeching and yelping like mad things. Heard them come back, too. Wherever they go they frighten everything away. They scared off the goats for a while. But that was a long time ago, and the goats came back. They learned it was safer up here than down there, even with the creatures on the prowl. Bears and wolves eat goat. *They* don't."

He nodded towards a small stash of swords and spears, all of them faded with age, piled against the wall in one corner. There was a bow and a quiver of arrows too. "The goats know all about me. I still have good eyes, even if the rest of the me is slowly falling apart. But I only ever take what I need, so they're wary of me and no more than that."

Dodinal cast his senses out. He had become so used to the empty world he had not thought to do so until now. Sure enough, there were life-lights in the hills around and above him. Whatever else happened, they would not go hungry. Goats were nimble and fast on rough terrain, but if a frail old man could bring them down, seasoned hunters like them should have no trouble doing so.

"Do you know what the creatures are?" Emlyn asked. Dodinal winced. So much for the subtle approach.

"All in good time," the old man said dismissively, and devoted his attention to the meat. "Eat first, then talk. We have all night."

They sat in silence, eyes closed, only the tantalising smell of the goat keeping them from falling asleep. Finally the old man judged the meat to be cooked, and he let it cool for a few moments before taking an ancient knife to it, slicing thick chunks away from the bone and handing them around. The men were too hungry to worry about his grubby fingers and snatched the meat off him, scarcely managing to utter their thanks before cramming their mouths full. They chewed like ravenous hounds, swallowed and held out their hands for more.

Once the last scraps had been prised from the bone they sat back with hands resting on bellies, picking their teeth.

"I'd offer you more, but that's the last for now." The man's voice was muffled. It took him longer to chew because he had so few teeth. "I'll be out with the bow come morning. Don't suppose there's any point asking you along. You'll be wanting to be on your way."

"That we will," said Dodinal. "Perhaps you'd be good enough to tell us where we can find what we seek. And the quickest way to get there."

The man nodded. Something about him had changed. The manic intensity had vanished from his eyes. Perhaps that had only been an act to scare away strangers. He looked almost sad. "You can leave your injured friend here if you like." He nodded at Hywel, who had fallen asleep sitting up, head tilted to one side. "He is no use to you blind. Oh, don't look so surprised. I'd have to be blind myself to miss it. Don't worry, I'll look after him until you return."

He did not say *if you return,* but he might just as well have.

Dodinal looked at Emlyn, Hywel's closest friend, and was more than a little relieved to see the bowman nod his approval.

It made sense. As much as they liked him, there was no denying Hywel was a dead weight. He would hold them back when they needed to hurry. He would be no use in a fight, and could not defend himself from attack.

No, it would be better this way. At least they knew one of them would survive the journey. Maybe one day, if his sight recovered, he would make his way home and tell the villagers what had happened.

"We accept your kind offer," Dodinal said. "Seeing as we will be away with the dawn, perhaps you will tell us now where to find the creatures, to save us having to disturb you before we leave."

"You first," the old man said. "Tell me what brought you here. Not just you, Dodinal, though I sense you're different from the rest. All of you. What happened to bring you to this cursed place?"

Dodinal saw no reason to complicate matters by telling of his own past. So he began at the point where Ellis had arrived in their village and recounted the tale from there on as quickly as he could. The old man listened intently. His eyes clouded with pain when he heard how they had found the missing boy's body in the snow. His face twisted with anger as Dodinal described the attack on the village and the ensuing slaughter, followed by the taking of the two children.

When the story was told, the old man sat in silence. Then he slowly shook his head. "Dear God, it's worse than I thought." His words were thick with emotion. "And it's all my fault. All *our* fault."

"Don't blame yourself." Dodinal failed to see how one frail and elderly man could have been responsible for any of it. "Please, just tell us what you know so we can sleep. They are so far ahead of us we will have to leave as soon as it is light. Even then, I fear we might be too late."

"I'll stand first watch," Madoc volunteered.

"And I'll stand second," said Emlyn.

"No need," the old man answered wearily. "The creatures will not trouble us. They have not bothered me for so long now, I suspect they have forgotten I even exist. No, they will be long gone now."

"Then why light all those fires?" Gerwyn asked.

"Because I don't want to be alone in the dark, that's why, not with the restless spirits of the dead haunting these hills." He looked deep into Dodinal's eyes. "You saw the graves, didn't you? Have you not asked yourself why one man is alive when so many are dead?"

Dodinal nodded, feeling an icy trickle down his backbone. "The creatures did this to you?"

The man's laugh was brief and harsh. "No, we brought it upon ourselves. This village died of shame. You want to know what those things are and where to find them? I will tell you. Then you will understand why I am the last man alive, here in this place of ghosts."

NINETEEN

My MOTHER GAVE birth to three daughters before I was born. Two of the daughters died of fever. The eldest also fell ill, but she was strong and survived. Her name was Megan, and we were as close as any brother and sister could be. If anything, we were closer than most. I was small, the runt of the litter, but if any child threatened me or pushed me around, Megan had a way of finding out, and she would make them sorry for whatever it was they had done to me.

In those days, the village was thriving. There were fish from the lake and the river. We kept cattle and sheep and feasted on meat from the goats, hares and deer that were plentiful then, and crops that were grown in the fertile land around us. We wanted for nothing.

Each autumn and spring, we would load up our carts and set out for the forest, where villagers from across the region would gather to trade. And more besides; my mother said that when a son or daughter was old enough, it was where they were taken to meet a wife or a husband. Otherwise they would end up marrying their cousins and their children would be soft in the head. It was God's judgement.

All my young life I had thought of Megan as nothing more than my sister. Until a certain age you do not see *boys* or *girls*, only other children like yourself. Megan was Megan, and that was that. But then, one summer, that terrible summer when the barking of the dogs brought madness and death, I saw her for what she was; a beautiful girl on the cusp of womanhood. I was fourteen, Megan two years older. For the first time I began to notice the soft golden sheen of her hair, the gentle swelling of her breasts, her clear grey eyes and high brow.[10]

Don't misunderstand me. I did not desire her, at least not then. Rather, I was sad, for I knew that, come the autumn and the next gathering, my parents would take her with them in the hope of finding her a husband. I also knew there would be no shortage of suitors. She had a sweet nature and her voice fell as happily on the ear as her form did on the eye. Any young man fortunate enough to talk to her would be smitten in an instant. That day was fast approaching.

Every morning we would do the chores assigned to us, and then we had the day to ourselves. It had been a hard winter, if not as hard as the winter just gone. We relished our freedom, and loved being able to run as far as we wanted after the long months in the snowbound valley, trapped in our huts while the roaring wind shook the timbers.

On that hot August day we decided to climb out of the valley, higher into the hills, to the lake and the woods that surrounded it. We often went there to fish or hunt for hares. Not because we needed the food; more because it gave us something to do, away from the others.

Away from *him*, I thought, although I did not say so aloud.

Megan led the way, as usual. As I followed I found my eyes drawn to her buttocks, swaying as she walked. As young as I was, I understood that was not how brothers were supposed to look at their sisters. I walked with my head lowered so I was watching the ground rather than her.

Eventually we reached the woods. It was cool in the shade of the trees after the sun's fierce onslaught. We were both dripping with sweat and stopped for a while to catch our breath.

[10]Grey eyes and a high forehead were much-prized in medieval women. Wealthy women would even pluck or shave their heads to raise their hairlines, in some cases as high as the crown of the head.

Megan was wearing a thin white dress in the heat, a gold braid tied around her waist. When she reached round for her pack, the dress stretched across her chest so that her nipples were clearly visible through the fabric. Embarrassed, I hurried on ahead of her, as if impatient to get to the lake. My face felt hotter than the sun blazing overhead. I had not experienced feelings like that before; they left me bewildered and more than a little ashamed.

I reached the lake, a great burnished shield in the sunlight. It was hot beyond the shadow of the trees but the breeze that came off the water caressed and cooled my skin. I removed my pack and began setting lines, using slivers of meat as bait. I did not turn around when I heard Megan approach.

"Why didn't you wait?" She sounded hurt.

"Sorry," I said. "I thought you were right behind me."

It was the first time I had lied to her, and I felt certain she would see through it. But she smiled and tousled my hair. The touch of her fingers sent a thrill down my spine. "Daydreaming again. I'm surprised you didn't keep going until you walked into the lake."

With that she put down her pack and rummaged around in it until she found her own lines. We worked together in silence for a while. Then, once all the hooks were baited and cast, we retreated to the trees and sprawled out in the shade while we waited for the fish to bite. All the while the sun beat down on us mercilessly until we started to feel our skin burn, and we knew that before long we would have to give up and return home.

Then, without warning, Megan got to her feet. "I can't stand this heat for a moment longer. I'm going for a swim."

I thought about trying to persuade her otherwise. The lake was shallow at the edge but fell away sharply just a few yards out. From experience, though, I knew there would be no talking her out of the idea now her mind was made up.

"Good idea," I said, the exact opposite of what I was feeling. I insisted on going with her. Megan was a strong swimmer but anything could happen, and I wanted to be close by if she got into trouble.

Giggling like small children, we ran back to the lake. Megan got there first; she had always been quicker on her feet than me. "Turn around," she ordered. "Don't look at me until I say you can."

I did as I was told and stared at the woods. My stomach lurched and tightened, and I felt a tingling between my legs. Then I heard her feet splashing through water. When she gasped with the sudden shock of cold it was all I could do to stop myself crying out.

"You can turn around now," she called, and I did so gladly.

She had gone far enough out that the water had risen to the top of her chest. Her long blonde hair drifted out like a golden fan behind her. Squinting against the dazzling reflection of the sunlight I caught a glimpse of her body beneath the surface, the twin pink mounds of her breasts and, dimly, the mysterious dark triangle below her flat belly. It was wrong – oh, so wrong – but I made no effort to avert my eyes.

"Aren't you coming in?"

I shook my head, not trusting myself to speak.

"Don't be such a baby. The water's not cold."

"It's not that, I'm just hungry," I lied. "Let's go home and eat."

"Once I've cooled down. Come on, you might as well get in. We're not going back just yet."

I knew how stubborn she could be once she got a notion inside her head. Uncomfortable with the thought of swimming naked like she was, I settled for slipping my shirt over my head and kicking my shoes off, and stepped gingerly into the lake. It was cold enough to take my breath away. Knowing she would only mock me if I scurried back out, I made myself wade out, squealing with each advance, until the water was over my waist, when I paused to get used to the cold.

Without warning, Megan put her hands on my shoulders and pushed. I stumbled, fell, went under. Suddenly my ears were filled with a booming rumble. All I could see was a cloudy blur as my feet kicked against the steeply sloping bank. I panicked and swallowed great mouthfuls, flailing uselessly.

Then I felt a burst of pain in my scalp as Megan grabbed my hair and pulled me up.

I stood on unsteady legs, coughing and retching up water, snot running from my nose, my eyes streaming. I was scared and angry at the same time. Megan was an indistinct shape the other side of my tears. I almost yelled at her in fury. But then her arms reached out and she hugged me, crying that she was sorry, so sorry, over and over. The anger drained out of me. I pressed my face into her shoulder and whispered that it was all right and that I forgave her.

Then I had to hurriedly break free from her and turn away before she felt the painful hardness that had sprung up between my legs. I rubbed at my eyes and spat the last of the water from my mouth until it had subsided. Then I grinned at her and she smiled back. I could not stay angry with her for long; she teased me at times, but she looked after me too. She would never deliberately hurt me.

We swam around for a while, scaring away any fish that might otherwise have taken the bait. Eventually the cold started to get to us, and we decided that we'd had enough.

"Y-you get out f-first," she said. "Keep your b-back turned."

I nodded and splashed out of the water, hurrying past Megan's clothes, which she had left just far enough away from the lakeside to keep them dry. I had dropped my shirt and shoes closer to the woods. The afternoon sun was still strong but the breeze was cold against my wet skin. I pulled the shirt on to keep off the chill while the rest of me dried and was just reaching for my shoes when I heard an echoing voice in the woods, calling out for Megan.

"Oh no," she groaned. "It's only bloody Arwel."

Let me tell you about Arwel. He was our *brehyrion*'s son. It was said he had been born with the cord around his neck, stopping him from breathing. The midwife had shaken him hard enough to get his lungs working again, but it seemed as though it had broken something in his head.

Although the same age as Megan, he had the mind of a child and was apt to lose his temper if he did not get his own way. He was big for his age, too, tall and wide and ungainly with it. He had a habit of tripping over his own feet. Unfortunately for my sister, this bovine oaf was obsessed with her. He followed her around, trying to join in with whatever she was doing. I was convinced she escaped to the hills whenever she could simply to get away from him.

I couldn't see him, but I could hear him, crashing through the undergrowth, calling her name. Having him find Megan would be bad enough; having him find her when she was as naked as a newborn babe would be mortifying.

I heard running feet from behind and turned to see Megan sprinting towards me, naked and dripping water, arms crossed over her chest, holding her clothes in an untidy bundle. "Don't look," she snapped. "Just get into the woods before he sees us."

I ran for the cover of the trees and slowed my pace once I had reached them, lest Arwel hear me. We hurried away from him, moving as quickly as we could. I could hear the soft slap of my sister's feet on the dry earth and her hitching, nervous breathing.

"Megan!"

I started. He sounded close but the woods made his voice echo; he could have been anywhere. Megan was not willing to risk being seen. I felt her hand grasp my forearm and she dragged me off the path. I kept my eyes on the ground, as though anxious not to lose my footing in the tangle of undergrowth. Megan put her hand in the small of my back, pushing me forward, guiding me between the trees.

"There," she whispered into my ear, and I looked up to see we had reached a place where the ferns grew dense and tall.

We heard him call again. He sounded like he was almost on top of us. By chance, he must have taken the same path as us. We wasted no time, hurrying over to the tall ferns and hurling ourselves to the ground where we lay as still as we could, our faces pressed against the cool mossy grass of the forest floor, barely daring to breath. Heavy footsteps crashed towards us. I risked raising my head from the ground to peer through the greenery.

"Megan!"

Arwel was on the path directly ahead of me, walking slowly, looking into the ferns as though he could somehow sense us hiding there. He was big and ungainly, and ugly with it, piggy eyes squinting through the trees. His thin hair was parted down the middle and hung like damp fur on either side of his face. His heavy forehead glistened with sweat and his fat cheeks were flushed.

I ducked out of sight, afraid he would see me. I could neither see nor feel Megan, but I sensed her at my side. Despite our predicament I felt myself becoming aroused again, doubly so when her hand found mine and squeezed it. Lake water had cooled and softened her skin.

Then, from somewhere far away, came the barking of dogs.

I frowned. There were hounds in the village, of course, but these sounded as if they were coming from high in the mountains overlooking the lake and woods. But there were no villages to be found there; the land was too rugged and desolate for anything other than wild goats and sheep to survive. And there were so many of them, more than we kept in the village. The noise was cacophonous. I could not be certain exactly how many; at a guess I would have said two or three dozen. Not wolves, either. There was no howling, only the belling of hounds. I recalled the tales we had been told as children, stories of Cwm Annwn, the hell hounds of Gwynn ap Nudd's wild hunt. Arwel must have heard it too. I heard him cry out with fear and he ran headlong back along the path as though in mortal danger.

The barking did not stop. It grew louder. I was certain the dogs were running towards us, that they would find us and tear us apart. I reached out and pulled Megan towards me, to protect her with my body if I had to. Her eyes met mine, wide and bright, her mouth twisted with fear. I could not help myself. I pressed my lips against hers and kissed her.

For a moment she struggled in my arms. Then, as the sound of the dogs worked deep into my head, I felt her relax and she returned the kiss, her probing tongue sliding between my teeth until it found mine.

The sound of the dogs faded away and took the fear with it. I was lost in the moment, completely surrendering myself to the taste and the smell and the touch of her. One of my hands strayed to her breast.

Megan pressed her hand to my belly and then slid it down into my trousers. I moaned as she took me in her hand. It was all I could do not to cry out.

I squeezed my eyes shut and pressed my mouth harder against hers as a delicious pressure built inside me. Her hand moved, and I moved in time with it, the pressure building and building until something exploded within me. I was overwhelmed by a thrill so intense it was nearly painful.

Suddenly she let go of me and groaned with disgust, whipping her hand from beneath my trousers and shoving me away.

Whatever foul spell had been cast over us was now broken.

I felt like a man waking from a troubled sleep. I lay on the ground, blinking in confusion at the sky, filled with revulsion at the thought of what we had done. We were brother and sister. What madness had possessed me? Possessed *us*, for it was fair to say I had not sinned alone. Megan had been as desperate for me as I had been for her. All that day I had felt strange yearnings for her. Now I began to wonder if she had harboured the same shameful desire for me.

I could not bring myself to talk, and neither could she. I sat facing away from her while she dressed in silence, and did not move when she strode past me, without a word or a backwards glance. When she had walked far enough away that I could not see her, I got to my feet and set off back towards the village. Then I changed my mind and, stepping from the path, made my way to the lake. The lines were where we had left them, one swinging back and forth. I was not interested in taking the fish from the hook, so I left it to its struggle for freedom. I felt dirty, tainted. I needed to wash myself clean.

I waded into the water. Once it had reached past my waist I held my arms out straight before me and dived in...

The sun was close to setting by the time I reached home, but it was still uncomfortably warm and my clothes scratched my damp skin. I heard voices from the hall and could smell roasting lamb. Lacking the stomach for food or company, I continued straight on to our hut, hoping Megan and my parents would have joined the others for the evening meal. I ducked inside. It was deserted.

I lay on my pallet and stared miserably at the smoke hole; the sky was turning dark. I still struggled to accept what Megan and I had done. I thought perhaps I should leave home, gather up what few possessions I had and make my way down to the lowlands, lose myself in the forest, search for a village where I could start a new life where no one would ever know of my disgrace. I would have done, too, except that I would be dead in a day, food for a bear or a pack of wolves. I was small and weedy.

Eventually my mother returned with my sister. I feigned sickness to explain my absence at the hall. Megan did not so much as glance my way. She had reached the age where they felt they needed to shield her from my eyes – and what a success that had been – so they had suspended a blanket from the ceiling above one end of the hut where she could dress and sleep without being seen.

Muttering that she was tired, she pushed past the blanket and disappeared.

That was a long night. My mother and I talked quietly for a while, then she yawned and said she, too, was going to bed. I lay on my back, staring up at the ceiling, as laughter and raised voices drifted across from the hall. It was always that way. Once the women and children had left for the night, out would come the ale and the men would drink themselves stupid, and then my father would stagger home and pass out. That night he collapsed on his bed, with a grunt that wafted beery fumes over me, and was snoring in seconds.

Minutes felt like hours, hours passed like days. I could not sleep. The heat did not help. I pulled the shirt over my head and dropped it to the floor beside the pallet. Still too hot, I took off my trousers and dropped them next to the shirt, leaving on my braies to preserve my dignity. An owl hooted. A sheep bawled. I closed my eyes and willed sleep to come.

It must have, for I was aware of nothing until I felt a weight on my mattress. Someone was climbing quietly into the pallet next to me, and warm, moist flesh brushed against mine. *Megan*, I thought, with a sick feeling in my belly. I sat up and tried to push her away but the hands that gripped my wrists were too strong, forcing me back to the mattress. A heavy body, much heavier than Megan's, slid over mine, pressing me down so I could not move.

"Mother?" I gasped. There was no mistaking the smell of her. I tried to protest but her mouth smothered mine and my words were muffled and lost. Away in the hills above the village, I heard the barking of those hellish hounds, insinuating itself into my head like worms boring into the flesh of the dead. At once I was filled with a lust so strong it eclipsed all other thoughts. I was helpless to resist, it was as if it were happening to someone else, and I was a reluctant observer who could not turn away.

I heard Megan cry out, heard the deep rumble of my father's voice. After that there was nothing save that relentless baying, the heat of my mother's breath in my mouth and the slickness of skin against skin as she wrapped her legs around me and drew me in.

I will not speak of what happened after that. From the revulsion written in your faces I suspect you do not want to hear it either. Believe me, the disgust you feel for me is as nothing compared to my own self-loathing. Believe me also when I tell you what happened that night was the work of the devil himself. For in those long hours between midnight and dawn we were seized by a kind of madness. And by *we* I mean everyone, the entire village.

That became apparent the following morning. When the rising sun woke me, I was alone in my bed. Raising myself up on one elbow, I could see my parents were asleep in theirs. Had I dreamt it all? The soreness between my legs told me otherwise, but surely we could not have slept so soundly if it had truly happened.

A cockerel crowed, and slowly the village stirred into life. The atmosphere in our hut was muted; none of us would look the others in the eye. We knew we had done a terrible wrong, so terrible we dared not speak of it. How could we, when we couldn't begin to understand why we had done it? My young mind could only suppose we had been possessed. Unable to bear it any longer, we made our way in gloomy silence to the hall to break fast with the villagers.

Although I was not hungry, I felt a desperate need to be with others, to be among those who had not shared my awful sin, but it was apparent on entering the hall that my family had not been alone.

No one spoke when we walked in. They were struggling with their own consciences and barely registered our presence. Gwyn, our *brehyrion*, looked as guilty as anyone in the room. His wife had died years ago and he had raised Arwel with the help of his mother, Bronwyn, a thin, harsh-voiced woman known to the children as Crow. She was a bad-tempered creature, too. I looked at her and then looked at Gwyn and had to swallow the bile in my throat.

Days passed. Whatever madness had overwhelmed us had passed, for there was no more wickedness. The dogs, or whatever they had been, were not heard again. A month went by and, as is often the way with such matters, the memories gradually grew less raw until village life returned to something like normal. But then the consequence of our accursed couplings became evident. One by one, eight of the women of the village, my mother and sister among them, discovered they were with child.

When I found out about Megan I ran from the hut and up the steep slope of the valley, not stopping until I reached the woods where she and I had... well. I stopped when I could run no further, and then I bent over and was violently sick. I collapsed to the ground and lay there, curled up in a ball of self-hatred and self-pity, until the sun set and the cooling air sent me home again.

I will spare you the mundane details. We endured a cold winter, but there was little joy when spring finally arrived, for we all knew the babies would arrive with it. Megan was the first to give birth, maybe because she was the youngest. Even now I can hear her screams from the midwife's hut when the child was delivered. Later I was to learn it had been born with mismatched eyes and six fingers and six toes.

I never saw it. Immediately when it was born they took it somewhere away from inquisitive eyes, a shepherd's hut away in the hills, fully expecting it to die. Against the odds it survived, as did the other seven born that spring. All were deformed in one way or another.

I was not privy to the fierce argument that raged in the hall when the time came to decide what to do with them. Word gets around, though. Some wanted to smother them. Others said they should not be made to pay for the sins of their parents. Agreement could not be reached. Then Bronwyn the Crow stepped forward and told the assembled villagers: "I will take them into the mountains and look after them. They will live or die as fate decrees."

Whatever had passed between her and Gwyn on the night of the barking dogs, she had borne no children, and she had never been well-disposed towards them anyway. So coming from her of all people, her offer immediately silenced the room. To cut to the chase, it was agreed that this was what should happen, and that Arwel, who would not become *brehyrion* after his father because he was too dim in the head, should stay with them. He could hunt for their food and protect them from the predators that stalked the high places.

And so it was that an expedition set out, taking the eight babies and their unlikely guardians into the mountains, to a valley where they could be hidden from the eyes of the world. They took with them basic comforts such as bedding and clothing, and weapons and tools for Arwel, who was good with his hands, to provide them with food and shelter. When the men who went with them returned after several days, a great weight seemed to lift from the village. The fruits of our sins were gone.

Life went back to how it used to be. When Megan went to the summer gathering and found a suitor I was not at all upset. When she married and moved to her husband's village, I was, quite frankly, relieved. Every time I saw her I was reminded of what we had done that August afternoon. After her wedding, I never saw her again. I suppose she's more than likely dead now.

All was well. To the surprise of all who knew me, I grew tall and strong. One autumn I went to the gathering with my parents and there I met the girl who would later become my wife. When we married, she came to live with me in the village. Soon afterwards she was pregnant, and in the spring of the following year, we had the first of our children.

Our eldest, a boy, had just turned ten when a girl around the same age went missing. A search was carried out, but the poor child was never found. It was assumed she had defied her parents, who had warned her never to leave the village alone, and had been taken by a wild animal. We had heard of such tragedies elsewhere, but for our village it was the first in living memory. The pain cut deep.

Several years passed, I forget exactly how many. It happened again. A little boy. Once more a search party set out. It returned in a hurry after finding mysterious tracks in the soft earth by the lake, heading north into the mountains. The men equipped themselves with provisions and weapons and set off in pursuit, Gwyn giving them his blessing but by now too old to travel with them.

They were never seen again. We could only assume they had fallen to their deaths in the treacherous mountains.

Our children grew up and raised families of their own. My wife died young and so the grandchildren were a welcome distraction. The missing children and the undiscovered fate of the search party gradually passed from memory. Gwyn went the way of all men and was returned to the earth, after which a new *brehyrion* was found. I got older but I kept my wits about me. People died, babies were born. The eternal cycle of life continued. Until the night the creatures came.

They must have been watching us for some time, because they knew what they wanted and where to get it. They waited until the early hours, when we were deep in sleep. Then they pounced, smashing down the doors of two huts, making off with two children.

You do not need me to tell you what happened that night. The terror that gripped the parents when they saw what foul things were stealing their children. The mad scramble for weapons as we tried in vain to stop them. The slaughter of those who stood in their way. By the time I had struggled up from bed and stumbled outside, bow primed in my trembling hands, they were already off and away with the young ones, leaving a trail of blood and broken bodies in their wake.

Men set off in pursuit, much as you have. They were gone all day. As the sun set we could hear screaming in the distance. The sound of it left us almost paralysed with fear. Fear of the unknown, fear of what might happen once darkness fell. No one slept that night, I can tell you. Fathers and older sons waited with swords and spears, pitchforks and scythes, anything they could lay their hands on.

The creatures did not return. The next morning it was decided to send a party of volunteers into the mountains, to find out what fate had befallen our men. They had no sooner climbed out of the valley than the volunteers found all six of them, emasculated, their eyes torn out, their bodies horribly mutilated, laid out ready to be discovered.

We spent the nights that followed in constant fear of attack. Weeks dragged by. People became sick with anxiety. The mother of one of the two stolen children died asleep in her bed; it was said she died of a broken heart. Again, though, once many months had passed without incident, we buried the memories of what had happened. It was easier than trying to live with them. We lowered our guard so gradually that I don't think we even realised we had done so. When, a year or so later, the creatures struck again, we were no more prepared than we had been the first time, and we had fewer warriors to protect us. Only now we offered no resistance. We let them take what they wanted.

We convinced ourselves it was better that way. They would take the children regardless and there would be no bloodshed if we did not try to stop them. They did not return for another five years, and when they did, again we made no attempt to stand in their way. We were doubly cursed; not just sinners, but cowards.

I cannot tell you what happened up in those cursed mountains after Crow and her idiot grandson were left to fend for themselves and the babies. But I can guess. I think they survived and the babies grew up and committed the same foul sin as their parents. Their offspring would have been born even more twisted than they. And as for *their* offspring... you've seen them with your own eyes. Less than human, more than wild beast. Ferocious, but clever with it.

The third time they raided us was to be the last. Who can say why they came when they did and why they stopped? Not I, not with any certainty. But there are villages beyond the mountains, beyond the valley where Crow raised them. I suspect they moved from place to place, plundering at random, letting time go by before they struck again, until there were no more children left to take.

That's what happened here. We lost six children all told, and after that, no more babies were born. It was not down to any conscious decision; it just happened that way. No woman wanted to live through the pain of losing a child, not to those monstrosities. I suspect one or two may have fallen pregnant;

no man can live without a woman's company, at least no normal man. But there are ways and means. None gave birth.

One by one the villagers died. Some of old age, some of illness; some of starvation, for our livestock sickened and died and there was no longer anything to hunt. There were those who preferred a sharp blade to living with the knowledge of what we had done. At times I thought I might do the same. I'd like to say I am still here out of some sense of defiance, a determination to outlast our bastard offspring. I'd like to claim that. But in truth I cannot. I was too afraid to take my own life, even if it would have been just another sin to add to a long list of sins.

I buried them when they died. I have been alone for so long I have forgotten how many years it has been since I spoke to a living soul. I have prayed for you to come this way, Dodinal, or someone like you. Someone with the courage to root out the evil and destroy it. Someone who is not afraid of the darkness that surrounds us all. That is why I keep the fires lit, you see; I am afraid of the dark and what dwells in it. Sometimes I hear them calling out to me: the tortured spirits of the children we let the creatures take, the restless souls of every man and woman who ever lived and died here.

Now I feel I am ready to join them. I will look after your friend until you come back. If you do not I will take him to your people, then return here. One night I will not light the fires. Instead, I will lay on my bed, and close my eyes for the last time.

Only with my passing will this village be rid of its shame.

TWENTY

Dodinal slept uneasily and was awake before dawn. Leaving the others to their snoring, farting slumber, he went outside and breathed deeply, to clear his lungs of the stale reek of so many men in such a confined space. He sat before one of the fires, now burned down to glowing embers but still giving off enough heat to hold back the early morning cold. Before settling down for the night, he had noticed a whetstone amongst the old man's weapons stash. Sitting by the fire, he now used it to put a keen edge on his sword, lost in reverie as he ran the stone along the blade, as he had done so many times before.

He knew he should hate the old man. As the last of his people, he must carry the blame for what they had done, the great sin they had committed. Yet he recalled, too, the old man's words. *It was as if it were happening to someone else, and I was a reluctant observer who could not turn away.* Dodinal understood. It was how he had felt all those years ago, when the rage had first overtaken him as he searched through the smouldering remains of his village, when he had hacked an injured and defenceless man to bloody shreds.

Incest. Murder. Different sides of the same coin.

He heard the creak of hinges and turned to see Hywel making his way carefully out of the hut, prodding the ground ahead of him with a spear, wary of obstructions. Dodinal got to his feet to help him. "What are you doing? You could trip and bang your thick head again. Then what would become of you?"

"Stop fussing," the tracker said, making his way steadily towards the fire. "I'm feeling better. I can even see you. Sort of."

For a moment Dodinal was silenced. It was not impossible. Head injuries were unpredictable. Even so, it sounded too good to be true, Hywel regaining his vision just as they were readying to leave. He raised a hand. "How many fingers am I holding up?"

Hywel waved away the question. "I said sort of, didn't I? You're a blur. To be honest, all I can see is the shape of you against the glow of the fire. But that's more than I could see yesterday."

"Not enough, though. Not to come with us."

"I know, I know," Hywel said, trying to sound unconcerned and not making a particularly convincing job of it. "My head still throbs. I think I'd better sit down before I fall down."

They sat together, not speaking, staring into the softly glowing embers as though they held some mysterious secret. Finally Hywel let out a long, hard sigh. "I'm not very good at goodbyes."

Dodinal kept his eyes on the fire. "Me neither."

"Then let's neither of us say it. I'm not going to ask to come with you. I'd get myself and the rest of you killed. No, I'll stay here with the old man. I'll pray for you and await your return. And if you don't, I'll accept his offer to take me home so I can tell Rhiannon and the rest what you did to try to help us; the sacrifices the two brothers made, too. Funny, I never really took to that pair when they were alive. Now they've gone I miss having them around."

Dodinal said nothing. Then he frowned as Hywel's words sunk in. "How did you know the old man said he would take you home?"

"Just because my eyes were closed didn't mean I was asleep. You'd be surprised how much you hear when people don't think you're listening." Hywel's tone grew serious. "Keep your wits about you, Dodinal. Find the boy and get away as quickly as you can. Don't try to be the hero and take them on. Better to live to fight another day."

"Getting away in one piece will be a task in itself. Even if there only eight of them, they still outnumber us two to one."

"You sound very calm. Aren't you afraid? I would be."

"Yes, I'm afraid." The fear was there, gnawing away at his guts. "Fear is healthy. Fear keeps you vigilant. When the time comes, I'll be ready."

"Not too ready, I hope. I know you, Dodinal. You creep through the forest like a ghost. Wherever they are, you can be in and back out with the boy before they even realise he's gone. Unless you're disturbed, there should be no reason for you to confront them. If you're tempted to avenge Idris and all those other poor bastards who died, just remember Owain will be relying on you for his life."

"I wouldn't be going after them if it wasn't for the boy. My first concern is getting him out in one piece. I won't even think about what else I should or should not do until he is safe."

"Forget anything else," said Hywel. "Just get back here so we can all go home together. I'd sooner walk through the forest with my victorious friends than that old man. He gives me the shivers. You heard that story of his. How can he live with the shame?"

"Don't be so hasty to pass judgement," Dodinal said, picking up his sword and resuming his slow, methodical sharpening. The scrape of metal on stone echoed around the narrow valley so that it sounded like a host of men preparing for battle. "Many people have secrets."

"Yourself too?"

Dodinal said nothing.

"Perhaps one day you'll tell me." Hywel stood, yawning as he stretched. "I'll go and wake the others. I don't suppose you'll be wanting to hang around here any longer than you have to."

Dodinal watched Hywel until he disappeared inside the hut, then finished sharpening the sword. Finally he held it straight out and plucked a hair from his beard, draping it across the blade. The hair split in two, the severed halves spiralling slowly to the ground. Satisfied, Dodinal sheathed the sword. Even the gargoyle creatures with their leathery hides would be no match for it.

The sky grew brighter. From inside the hut he could hear a chorus of coughing and raised voices, throaty with sleep and smoke. He made his way back in and was pleasantly surprised to find a pot set over the fire and a faint smell of food in the air. "It's not much," the old man said, squatting alongside the pot, stirring its contents. "But better to leave on a full stomach than an empty one."

He poured thick gruel into a variety of battered old dishes and beakers and handed them around. With no spoons to eat with, they waited until the gruel had cooled before scooping it into their mouths with their fingers. It tasted of nothing much and sat like a heavy stone in Dodinal's belly, but would keep hunger away for some time.

"Keep an eye out for goats," their host told them as they ate. "Tough little bastards, not afraid of anything. They'll trample and eat adders, or so it's said. But they make good eating."

Finally the time came for them to be on their way. They emptied their packs and sorted through their contents, taking only what they thought they would need, putting it into a single pack to lighten their load. They left their cloaks behind for the same reason.

They shook Hywel's hand one by one, each man vowing they would be back for him. The tracker somehow conjured a smile and told them he looked forward to that day, but it was plain to see he was desperate to go with them. Dodinal was the last to leave; he looked back just before he walked outside and saw the hunter slump to the ground, head down, looking lost and alone and defeated. For a moment he almost relented, but this was not the time to allow his heart to rule his head. He raised one hand in a half-hearted salute and set off after the others.

The old man waited for them, nodding towards the southern end of the valley. Now the sun had risen, banishing the shadows around them, Dodinal could see many of the trees had been felled, their stumps like broken teeth in the mouth of the coomb; fuel for the fires that kept the ghosts at bay.

"I'll take you as far as the lake and show you where you need to go from there. After that, you're on your own." The old man seemed almost pathetically eager to please, perhaps desperate to make amends in any way he could for what he and his people had done.

He led the way up the steep slope, setting a punishing pace that belied his advanced years and gaunt body. Gerwyn stayed close behind him, followed by Madoc and Gwythyr, all three of them gasping as they struggled to keep up. Dodinal saw no point in hurrying; they might as well conserve their strength. Emlyn must have felt the same way, for he walked at a steady gait alongside him. "Do you think he will be all right?" he suddenly asked.

Dodinal did not need to ask who. "He'll be fine."

"I wish I could be so sure." Emlyn tapped the side of his head. "That old man hasn't quite got a quiver full of arrows."

"Maybe not. He's harmless enough, though. He said he would look after Hywel, and I have no reason to doubt him. Mark my words, by the time we get back, Hywel will be too fat to do anything but waddle and we'll be delirious with hunger."

"You reckon we'll be back, then?"

"We'll be back," Dodinal assured him.

By the time they had struggled out of the valley, they were gasping for breath and sweating like pack horses. Dodinal stared around tensely. The lake was longer than it was wide, the forest crowding its left bank. Surrounding it was a solid wall of mountains, their bare steep flanks reflected in the water, so that it appeared there was an identical range of hills beneath the surface. At the far end of the lake was a single mighty peak, wide enough at its base to fill the landscape, narrowing as it rose impossibly high above them. Beyond it were more tall peaks, distance rendering them featureless.

"The valley lies beyond that mountain," the old man said.

"God help us," someone whispered.

The old man spat on the ground. "God won't. I will. I know what you're thinking. Might as well give up and go back."

"The thought had crossed my mind," Madoc growled.

"It looks bad, I'll grant you that. But there's always a way."

Emlyn sighed with frustration. "Then take us there."

The old man shook his head. "I gave you my word I would bring you here and I have; but no further. Too many memories. This is the first time I have stepped foot here since I heard my sister was with my father's child. I do not intend to stay a moment longer than I have to. Dodinal, you're the clever one. Step closer. I will tell you the way. Then I will leave you to find the valley without me."

They gathered around him, watching as he raised his spear to point to the mountain's left flank. "Continue to the head of the valley. You'll see an old track leading up. It's steep, but you'll manage. Once you get to the top you'll arrive at a narrow plateau. From there the going gets harder."

Dodinal listened while the old man continued to talk of cliffs and gullies, but did not really take it in. The words were meaningless. Gerwyn nodded as the old man spoke, hopefully to indicate his understanding rather than out of misguided sense of courtesy.

"Eventually you will have to cross a narrow ridge, between steep cliffs, high above the ground. Even once you have crossed it and are within reach of the summit, you will need to be wary. The going will not be easy underfoot and there are often rock falls. Big ones. I've heard them from the village."

"Sounds easy enough," Madoc said sourly.

The old man ignored him. "It's easy going once you get to the top. The descent into the valley is nowhere near as challenging."

"You've been there?" Dodinal asked.

"Me? Don't you listen? I told you, I haven't been even this far up since what happened to my sister. But the men who took Crow and Arwel and the young ones there, they talked about it for months. You'd swear they'd been on some brave quest rather than off to dump an old woman, a simpleton and a bunch of squawking infants in the middle of nowhere to fend for themselves."

"You sound as if you almost regret it," Dodinal observed.

"I regret what we did that night, nothing else. We did a great wrong and we tried to find a way to atone. We tried and we failed." He hawked and spat, then turned away. "You'd best be off. If you hurry, you should reach the valley this afternoon. A word of advice. Be well away from there by sunset, with or without the children you seek. Now go, and travel safely."

He turned and set off down the hill towards what remained of his village, raising an arm in farewell as he disappeared from view.

"Well, then," Gerwyn said after a moment. "You heard him. We need to be there and on our way back by sunset. Best to get moving."

He shrugged the pack until it hung comfortably from his shoulders and then took off towards the mountain without waiting for a response. The others hesitated, eyebrows raised. Dodinal gave them the nod and they set after him, with Dodinal following a short distance behind.

He could hear the murmur of their voices as they walked, but he was in no mood for idle talk, not when they were heading towards an uncertain fate. For all he knew they would be dead by nightfall. Now he almost regretted his decision to travel in their company. He had grown to like them, to see them as friends, even the near-silent Gwythyr. While death held no fear for him, he would prefer to die alone than take his companions with him.

The path the old man had indicated took them through the forest along the lake's western bank. The men became silent as they passed beneath the green-budded branches, perhaps remembering what had happened here that day all those years ago. Tramping along a woodland path, Dodinal found himself looking out for a tall cluster of ferns, but saw none. It had happened a long time ago. The boy had grown into a half-mad old man and the sister was far from here, perhaps dead. Only the spectre of unwanted memories remained.

Dodinal realised none of them had thought to ask the old man his name.

The forest felt suddenly oppressive and gloomy, bright wildflowers doing nothing to dispel a sense of foreboding that made his skin prickle. Again he had to remind himself why he was here. If it had not been for his feelings for Rhiannon and the boy, he would have gladly given up and gone home.

Home? Yes, home. Home to where she was waiting for him, for him and the boy and the others, not yet knowing that two of them would never come back and another was little better than blind.

He would get there yet, he told himself. Owain too. No matter what awaited them up in the mountains, he would find a way home.

It took them the best part of an hour to reach the head of the lake. When they emerged from the trees, the mountain suddenly reared up before them, impossibly high. Craning his neck to look up, Dodinal felt a tug of disquiet. He did not like heights; up in the high places, he would be a stranger in an unknown and dangerous realm. A man who fell in the forest could pick himself up, dust himself down and be on his way. A man who fell in the mountains would fall a very long way. And all they had to guide them were directions from someone who had not even walked this way before. It did not augur well.

The path petered out, and the ground became steeper and uneven. Some of the boulders were as tall as Dodinal, reminding him of a story his mother had once told him, about how warring giants had created the mountains, long ago in the time before memory, by hurling rocks at each other to settle their differences.

Soon they found the track, as the old man had said they would. It was overgrown and had not been walked on for many years, but the ground beneath the ankle-high grass was firm. It carved a crooked route up the face of the mountain, and they walked at a steady pace. When Gerwyn eventually called for a rest halt they turned back to face the valley, which spread out before them in miniature. They sat on the grass banks that edged the path on both sides, massaging cramping muscles and wiping the sweat from their brows. The sun, though strong, was still some way from its zenith. Dodinal nodded, satisfied with their progress.

They pushed on, their voices stilled. They needed all their breath for the ascent. The track became steeper the higher it took them: their lungs ached, their faces glowed, and their thighs and calves burned with the strain. When they reached the plateau the old man had spoken of, they dropped their weapons and packs where they stood and lay on their backs on the hard ground, chests heaving, until they could talk without gasping for air between words.

The first to recover, Dodinal sat up and looked down the path. It fell away from the plateau until it appeared no wider than the laces that tied his boots. It had taken them an hour to walk the length of the lake, but from here it looked to be about as long and as wide as his thumb. Instinctively he drew back from the plateau's edge. While there was no danger of falling, his stomach still gave an unpleasant lurch as he realised just how far up they had climbed. And the worst of it was, they still had a long way to go.

Reluctantly, he turned to look up at the tall peak ahead. This close it was no longer featureless: directly before him was a deep cleft in the rock, forming a ravine with cliffs rising up on either side. If there was a path, it was buried beneath a layer of stones and slabs that brought to mind the old man's talk of rock falls. Dodinal studied the cliffs. They were not sheer, but bellied out before curving up and levelling off far above his head. They appeared stable and, besides, the route between them was wide enough that they should be safe as long as they kept to the middle of the path.

He was so intent on studying the terrain ahead of them that he did not hear Gerwyn approach. "Have you considered what we'll do when we get there?"

"Not yet. When we get there, that's when I'll decide."

"Isn't that leaving it a little late?"

Dodinal sighed and looked at the younger man. "We have no idea of the lie of the land. It could be open ground, it could be forest. Why try to second guess? Better to wait until we're close enough to know what we're up against. Then we decide how to approach it."

"Fair enough. You know best, I'm sure." Gerwyn was silent for a moment. "You still don't trust me."

It was not a question.

Dodinal glanced across at the rest of their party. The men were still sprawled on their backs in the sunshine, knees drawn up, making the most of every moment of rest they had. They were talking in low voices as though afraid they might bring the mountain down on top of them if they spoke too loudly.

"You are here, that's all I care about," he answered. "Your motives for being here aren't important to me."

"I mean, trust me to be of use when we finally catch up with them." Gerwyn had taken off his sword belt before collapsing; now he reached out to pick it up and held it lightly in both hands, gazing down at it rather than at Dodinal. "I know what you think of me. What everyone thinks of me. I'm half the man my father was, lazy and feckless, more interested in going off hunting than helping when there's work to be done."

He broke off. Dodinal waited in silence for him to continue.

"I won't deny it. *Can't* deny it. But that was then. When he was still alive. My father, I mean. When I was growing up, there was never any point in trying to impress him. I knew all along he wanted my brother Elwyn to follow him as *brehyrion*. The way I saw it, I was never going to amount to anything, so why bother trying?"

"And after your brother died? You could have tried to impress your father then. He never spoke of it, but I think that was what he was waiting for. Hoping for, maybe."

Gerwyn put the sword back down and pinched his chin with one hand, the dark stubble rasping against his fingers. "It was too late for me by then. Some habits are hard to break. I was so used to being the second son, my father's second choice to succeed him, that when the chance finally came for me to prove myself I no longer cared."

"Until Idris died," Dodinal said.

"Yes, until he died. That woke me up more than Rhiannon's slap that night." Gerwyn smiled to himself, his fingers slipping from his chin to idly rub his cheek. "I deserved that. Deserved a lot more than that. I meant what I said to you, Dodinal. I want to find my brother's son and bring him home. Not for your sake or even Rhiannon's, but my own. I've been a failure all my life. This is my one chance of redemption."

"Even if it gets you killed?"

"You're as likely to die as I am, yet here you are. They're not even your family. And you say you have no feelings for Rhiannon?"

"She saved my life. I'm in her debt."

"No, she was in yours, for saving Owain." Gerwyn suddenly laughed, his reflective mood broken. "Go on. Admit it."

"Shut up," Dodinal growled at him, not unkindly. "You've been out in the sun for too long." He got to his feet, wincing as his knees creaked and his lower back began to complain. There was a long way to go yet. "Come on, you wastrels. Time we were moving."

Madoc said, "I grew up in a village in the hills. Not these hills; many miles to the south. The terrain there was less barren, but mountains are mountains. If it's all the same to you, Dodinal, I will lead the way here. I will find the quickest route to the summit."

"Go ahead," Dodinal answered gladly. He could track prey through the forest for days at a time, but up here he was helpless and could easily lead them far from where they wanted to be. He held back, Gerwyn at his side, until Madoc and the others were on their way, then the two of them followed behind, stepping out of the sunshine into the shadowy ravine.

Although it was not especially steep, the loose stones made the going far from easy, shifting under their boots as they scrambled upwards. The cliffs amplified their panting and cursing as they staggered and stumbled along, and the rattle of the stones underfoot. Dodinal found himself anxiously eyeing the towering cliffs overhead.

The walls began to close in, making him steadily more nervous. He almost called out to Madoc to stop for them to rest a while, but decided they would be better off getting through the ravine as quickly as they could.

He glanced up, sure he had glimpsed movement on the cliff top high to the right of them. It was nothing, he told himself. The shadow of a cloud passing across the sun. Yet there were no clouds to be seen in the violet sky. Dodinal looked at the cliff again as dust showered down, as though something had disturbed the rock face above. He slowed his pace as if tiring, allowing Gerwyn to pass him so he could keep a closer watch without causing undue alarm. He felt sure the experienced Madoc would have known if anything were amiss, but even so, he saw no harm in remaining vigilant.

A sound like thunder suddenly rumbled through the ravine.

Ahead of him, Madoc came to a halt and looked up sharply, eyes wide with terror and disbelief. Dodinal followed his gaze. For a moment he could not take in what he was seeing. It looked as though the entire cliff wall on their right was collapsing onto them. Boulders as big as a man plunged from the narrow band of sky far above. They struck the cliff wall with a deafening clatter, exploding into smaller chunks that spun wildly as they fell. Dodinal had no time to shout a warning. A slab of rock struck Madoc on the shoulder and he went down. Emlyn grabbed Gwythyr, who was frozen with shock, and tried to drag him away, but they were too slow. Dodinal's last glimpse was of them being bludgeoned to the ground, before a dense cloud of dust billowed up, filling the ravine, and they were gone from sight.

Then followed a roar that shook the ground, and a shrieking and splintering that pierced his head like a knife. He dropped the spear and clapped his hands to his ears in pain as part of the cliff wall shuddered and began to shear off; he turned to run, but the dust cloud swept over him, scouring his eyes and clogging his throat and lungs. He coughed and staggered, knowing he would be squashed like a fly in seconds unless he could somehow get away. It was hopeless. He couldn't breathe, couldn't see.

The cliff face toppled slowly towards him, ripping apart the dust cloud below it. Dodinal was disorientated, frozen in place. Then Gerwyn lurched towards him out of nowhere, arms outstretched, eyes bulging and his mouth moving as he screamed something that Dodinal could not hear.

Firm hands on his shoulders pushed him away and he staggered, lost his footing and crashed to earth hard enough to drive the air from his lungs. He tumbled down the ravine, sliding on the loose stones as the great slab of rock thumped the ground. It felt and sounded like the end of the world. Shards of rock exploded everywhere, striking the cliff walls and hurtling down the ravine towards where Dodinal lay helpless. He rolled onto his side and drew up his knees, curling into a ball with his arms wrapped around his head to protect it and to muffle his ears against the roar and crash of the rock fall.

It seemed to go on forever, the cataclysmic rumble bouncing off the ravine's narrow walls until he was sure it would shake the teeth loose from his gums and grind his bones to powder. With every beat of his heart, he was certain that he would die. It was surely only a matter of time before his luck ran out and a boulder rolled down the ravine towards where he lay, or a deadly shard of flying rock scythed into him.

Finally it was over, although it took him a moment to realise it, so tightly were his hands pressed to his ears. The ground gave one last violent shudder, and then all was still. The last few loose stones rattled and clattered as they fell into the dying echoes of the rockfall. Cautiously, Dodinal raised his head, shaking it to clear it, not quite believing he had somehow managed to survive.

He spent a few moments moving fingers and toes and running his hands over his body, searching for injuries, for he was numb and might not yet feel the pain if he had been wounded. Apart from his aching ribs, where his sword pommel had dug into his side when he fell, there was nothing. Not so much as a scratch. He shook his head. What were the chances?

Dodinal heard a low groan from nearby. It suddenly occurred to him it was not down to good fortune that he was still breathing. He owed his life to Gerwyn.

In the eerie oppressive silence, Dodinal could hear but not see him. White-grey dust obscured everything. The sky was indistinct. He coughed and spat to try to clear his throat of dust, but it was no use. Every time he breathed, he breathed in more.

He was loath to call out, for fear his voice would trigger another fall, so he got slowly to his feet and stood for a moment until the strength had returned to his legs. He headed up the ravine, step by careful step, each time testing the ground with his foot before putting his full weight down. It did not take him long to find Gerwyn, lying on his back with his arms loose at his side. He had dropped the pack but his bow was still slung over his shoulder, as was the quiver, which was empty, the arrows scattered around him. Dodinal knelt at Gerwyn's side and was relieved to hear him whisper, "Dodinal? Is that you?"

"Yes, it's me. Try not to move."

"My leg. I think it's broken." Even by the murky light, his face was pale and drawn.

"Are you hurting anywhere else?"

"Only the back of my head. I hit it when I fell."

Dodinal managed a grin and hoped Gerwyn could see it. "Then it's safe to assume no serious damage has been done."

Gerwyn's hand shot out and grabbed him by the sleeve. "What about Emlyn? And Madoc and Gwythyr?"

"I don't know yet. I haven't had chance to look."

"Then leave me here. I'm okay. Go and look for them."

Dodinal reached down and patted him on the shoulder, saying nothing. A faint whistling had him reaching for his sword, until he realised it was only a mountain breeze, gusting through the narrow passage, slowly dispersing the dust cloud until he could start to make out his surroundings. The path ahead was piled high with rocks and broken slabs. Nothing could have possibly survived that.

Not that he would rest until he was certain. Dodinal clambered up the rocks and looked around for any sign of life, but found none. As the breeze continued to blow away the dust and visibility improved he could see a ragged spray of blood on the cliff wall closest to him. He was, he realised, standing on top of a grave.

As he got to his knees to say a few last words for his friends, a dark figure dropped from above with barely a sound, landing catlike on all fours a few yards along the ravine and launching itself at him. Dodinal only just managed to throw himself to one side, leaving its claws to swish through empty air. Momentum carried the creature past him and he reached for his sword, drawing it as he scrambled to his feet. He realised the rock fall had not been an accident, and the world turned red. He bared his teeth in a grimace of fury.

The gargoyle creature spun around, talons scraping and scratching as it found purchase on the rocky ground, then it darted back towards him. Dodinal held the sword shoulder high and ran to meet it head on. With a roar of unbridled fury, he swung the blade out and down with murderous strength. The blow would have cleaved the beast in two were it not for its speed and agility; it ducked below the blade, then leapt onto the cliff face and clambered up it.

Dodinal recovered quickly and raced after the creature, hacking at its trailing leg, missing it by inches. Sparks flew as his blade clashed against granite.

Dust and debris showered down as the creature scaled the cliff. Dodinal reached for a stone the size of a man's fist, hurling it as he straightened and feeling a vicious satisfaction as it slammed into the creature's shoulder.

The screech of pain that echoed around the ravine spurred him on. He dropped the sword – it was useless now – and grabbed more stones, throwing them one after the other. He missed his target as often as not, but when he hit it, he hit it hard, until the creature's movements slowed and its blood fell through the air like red rain, making patterns in the dust on the ground.

Dodinal reached for more stones, scenting the kill. He drew back his hand to throw.

Before he could let fly, the creature coiled hard against the cliff and sprang across the ravine to the opposite wall, reaching out to grab a handhold in the rock. Dodinal shifted his balance to hurl the stone, and the creature coiled and pushed off again, hurtling through the air towards him. This time he was not fast enough. It crashed into him, slamming him against the cliff, and the back of his skull cracked against the rock. A burst of white light filled his head and he hit the ground.

His fury saved him, as it so often had, driving away the pain and clearing the ringing in his ears. Through streaming eyes, he saw the creature half-senseless, struggling to get to its feet, its body slick with blood from a dozen or more lacerations. Its mouth pulled back into a snarl as its malevolent eyes met Dodinal's.

The sword lay where Dodinal had dropped it, beyond his reach. Even in his fury, he knew he needed it. He clambered to his feet and threw two more stones at the creature as hard as he could, before crouching to grab more, intending to drive it back until he could get to the sword.

The beast took him by surprise, leaping forward despite the hail of stones that opened up yet more wounds in its flesh. Dodinal lunged desperately to one side and fought to keep his footing, but the uneven ground defeated him and he twisted and stumbled headlong, throwing out both hands to break his fall, the impact tearing skin from his palms.

He spun around on the ground to face the creature as it slowly advanced towards him. Dodinal bared his teeth. He did not need a sword. He would tear this abomination limb from limb with his bare hands.

The creature threw back its head and howled victoriously.

There was a rush of air overhead, and the howl was abruptly cut off as an arrow buried itself in the creature's throat. For a moment it did not move. Then its clawed hands flew up to its neck and it took a few staggering steps away as arterial blood began to pump around the shaft. Crimson froth bubbled up between its lips. Its fingers pulled weakly at the arrow but the barb was buried deep and the creature could not tear it out without ripping out its own throat.

Dodinal seized his moment, leaping to his feet and running to his sword, picking it up without breaking his stride. The creature's movements became frantic; black blood cascaded down its leathery neck as it tried to work the arrow free, hissing in agony.

Then Dodinal rammed the sword into its chest, hard enough for the point to scrape against its spine before punching out through its back. The creature went rigid, clutching the blade that skewered its body.

Dodinal shifted his grip on the sword, holding it in both hands, and drove it down with all his strength. The blade opened the creature from sternum to groin, slicing cleanly through skin and flesh.

Stinking viscera slithered out of its belly in a glistening mass that hit the ground with a slap. The creature writhed and screeched and batted at the sword, trying to pull itself free, but its feet became entangled in the slippery mass of its guts and it fell heavily to its knees before him.

Dodinal kicked it hard under the chin, snapping its head back. Then he yanked the sword loose, hoisted it, stepped away and swung. A flash of metal, a flutter of disturbed air and the body tumbled one way, the head another. The torso danced its death throes, feet drumming on the ground, then went still. The head bounced and spun and came to rest, the neck stump still gushing blood.

Dodinal stood for a moment, gasping for breath, waiting for the red mist to lift. It was only then that he noticed the broken arrow shaft that protruded from the creature's shoulder. He remembered Emlyn's shooting when they had been attacked in the forest. *Your aim was true, my friend*, he thought with a heaviness in his heart.

Once his head cleared he hurried back to Gerwyn, who was sitting up with his back against the cliff, one leg stretched out, the other bent. He had his bow in hand and a dazed grin on his face.

"Emlyn was not the only one with a good eye," he said. The grin faltered. "The others?"

Dodinal shook his head. "They're dead. I'm sorry. They were good men. They knew the dangers, knew they would probably never get through this alive, yet still they came. That takes a rare courage."

"Fuck,"[11] Gerwyn said, so softly it was little more than a breath.

"We were too quick to listen to the old man." Dodinal crouched and ran his hands gently along Gerwyn's leg, feeling for shattered bone. "We should have guessed they wouldn't leave us to pursue them unchallenged. We knew those things don't give up."

Gerwyn's body suddenly jerked and he moaned in pain.

"Try to keep still. It's broken, but it could have been worse."

"How?" Gerwyn gasped from behind his gritted teeth.

"The bone could be sticking out through your skin. Then you really would have something to cry about." Dodinal continued to probe the injured leg. Gerwyn squeezed his eyes shut; his body tensed and the tendons stood out in his neck. By the time Dodinal was done, his face was as white as chalk and his forehead glistened with sweat. "You'll live. But this is as far as you're going."

"To Hell with that. You cannot go after them alone. Not when we've come all this way. Not when..." He gestured towards the pile of rocks beneath which their companions were buried. "Not when our friends have died."

"You're in no fit state to travel with me." Dodinal got up and searched about until he found his spear. "And I cannot stay here with you." He took the spear across to the pile of rocks and used a heavy stone to smash off the blade. "Our

---

[11]"Goddes woundes," in the manuscript, which carried a great deal more weight in Middle English than it would today, hence the idiomatic translation.

friends are gone. We mourn their passing but we cannot bring them back." He put the shaft over his knee and broke it into two. "So I don't have a choice." He snapped each half in two until he was left with four roughly even lengths.

Then he returned to Gerwyn and rummaged through the pack, pulling out a handful of the cloth strips that Hywel had brought with him.

"This is going to hurt," Dodinal advised as he knelt alongside him. "Do you want something to bite down on?"

Gerwyn sighed heavily and lay flat on his back with the pack under his head, fists clenched. "Just get on with it."

For all his brave intent, he could not help but bellow his agony when Dodinal lifted the leg to straighten it. He jerked bolt upright at the waist, his eyes bulging and rolling back in his head. He fainted. Dodinal slipped one hand under his head and lowered it to the pack.

Working quickly, he wound the strips of cloth above and below the knee at intervals, then slid the wooden quarters between them before pulling the strips tight and knotting them.

He leant back to inspect his handiwork. It was rough and ready, and Rhiannon certainly had no fear of competition, but the leg was rigid, fixed in place. As long as Gerwyn was careful and patient, it should mend with enough rest. Unfortunately, a half-buried ravine midway up a mountain was not a good place to rest.

He could not see the sun in the narrow strip of sky between the cliffs, so he hurried back down to the plateau. It was gone midday. They had spent six hours getting this far and he had no idea how much longer it would take to get to the valley. Certainly he did not have time to help Gerwyn to the village. There was nothing else for it.

Gerwyn was still unconscious but he quickly came around when Dodinal slapped his face, lightly but persistently. "I don't know what you did to my leg," he said groggily, licking his lips. "But it feels worse than it did before."

"Are you a man or a baby? Come on. Sit up. You need to listen. Too much time has passed. If I don't leave soon, I may not get to the valley before sunset. And you heard what the old man said."

Gerwyn eased himself into a sitting position, shrugging off the hand Dodinal offered to help him. "I'm fine. Get going. I'll wait here. You can collect me on your way back. Then you can carry me down."

"It's not safe for you to stay here. You need to get back to the old man's village. It still gets cold at night and you have no cloak."

"You'll have returned for me by then."

"We both know that may not happen. There's no point pretending it will. I'll get you down as far as the plateau and then you'll have to manage on your own."

Dodinal bent to slip an arm beneath his shoulder and hoisted him from the ground. Gerwyn, sweating and swearing, stood on his good leg, bending the other at the hip to keep it elevated. It was ungainly, and without Dodinal to lean on, he would have fallen.

"And how do you suggest I get down the path?"

"Sit and slide down on your arse," Dodinal told him as he half-carried him down the uneven surface of the ravine, talking all the way to distract Gerwyn, who was clearly in discomfort. "It's not that steep. You should manage it in a couple of hours. Once you get down, start calling for help. The valley is narrow. Your voice will carry far. Even if the old man doesn't hear you, Hywel will."

They reached the plateau and Dodinal helped Gerwyn to the ground. Then he straightened. "This is where I leave you."

He dropped the pack. "There's a steel and flint in there, some kindling too. If you cannot reach the village by sunset you should at least have reached the lake. There'll be enough fallen wood in the forest to start a fire. You may not have a comfortable night but you at least you'll be warm."

Gerwyn reached out and pushed the pack towards Dodinal. "You take it. You have more need of it than I do."

"I have my sword and my shield. I need nothing else."

For a moment, Gerwyn was silent. Then he looked up at Dodinal, squinting against the sun, and held out his hand. "I wish it didn't have to be this way, but it does. I hope you return, Dodinal, for it will save me the trouble of having to tell your story to my sister-in-law and the rest of my people. I never was much of a storyteller."

Dodinal clasped his hand. "I'll do what I can. Not for your sake, but to spare Rhiannon your ceaseless prattle." He released Gerwyn. "I think your father would be pleased with you. Go home. Your people need their *brehyrion*. Farewell, then. Until the next time."

"Yes," Gerwyn said. "Until the next time."

Dodinal said nothing more. He nodded once, then turned and set off. The sunlight faded to shadow as the cleft in the rock swallowed him and the cliffs loomed over him again. His boots crunched and skittered on stone as he hurried along, anxious to make up for lost time. Even so, when he reached the rock fall, he paused to kneel and bowed his head with his eyes closed.

"Goodbye, Emlyn. You were a man of great courage and spirit. I know I will see you again. Goodbye, Madoc. You were a true leader of men. I will see you again too. And farewell, Gwythyr. You never got to avenge your son's death. At least now he is safe with you. I will avenge you both."

He got up and, with one last baleful look at the creature's blood-drenched, headless body, he continued on his way. The ravine grew steadily steeper and narrower until his shoulders almost brushed against the cliff walls. He kept his eyes on the ground, wary of any uneven stones that could cause him to lose his balance or twist an ankle. He was Owain's last hope. If anything happened to him, the child was lost; the girl Annwen, too. He refused to entertain the idea that they may be lost already, or else he might as well turn back and be done with it.

Time ceased to have any meaning well before he emerged from the ravine onto a wide rock shelf. His relief at seeing the light and feeling the warmth on his face when he finally left the shadows behind lasted only until he realised what awaited him.

Directly across from where he stood, the mountain face sloped up towards the empty sky. While imposing, it was hardly sheer, and its broken surface looked relatively easy to climb. The one drawback was that to reach it he would first have to cross the long, narrow ridge, which fell away vertiginously on both sides.

Dodinal leaned forward and looked down, wiped his palms on his shirt and stepped back. He did not like heights.

There was no point delaying the inevitable. He did not even consider attempting to walk across. The ridge was wide enough to stand on, but the surface was a mess of knobbly protrusions and wind-worn hollows; one wrong step, or a sudden gust of wind, would send him plunging to the ground far below. Instead he knelt at the edge of the ridge and began to crawl across it, keeping his eyes firmly ahead, feeling around with trembling fingers for handholds and pushing forward with his boots. It was undignified, but there was no one around to see him. Even if there had been, he would not have given a damn.

The sword banged against his leg each time he moved, and the shield strap dug into his shoulder, but he would not let go with either hand to deal with them. He was near the halfway point when he disturbed a loose rock, which shifted beneath his fingers, rolled to the edge and tumbled off into space. Seized by an irrational terror that the entire structure was about to collapse beneath him, Dodinal flattened his body against the rough surface and lay, eyes squeezed shut, pounding heart in mouth, for nearly a minute.

He set off again, but his hands were so slick with sweat that he began to worry they would simply slide off the ridge. The gentle breeze that ruffled his hair suddenly felt as powerful as a gale, threatening to tip him into the void. Chiding himself that the villagers had made this same dangerous crossing, burdened with an old woman, a simpleton and eight bawling children, did nothing to repel the panic. It was only when he thought of

Owain, stolen from his mother and no doubt terrified beyond comprehension as he was carried across this same ridge, that he became ashamed of his fear and summoned the strength to push on.

Finally he was across, reaching a rock wide enough for him to stand on, well away from the edge. Reluctant to give his muscles time to stiffen, he began to climb as soon as he had regained his composure. The going was easier than he could have hoped; the surface was broken, providing no shortage of handholds and footholds, and Dodinal climbed rapidly. Only once did he forget himself and look down. The sight of the ridge far below him, and the ground much further down than that, brought him out in a cold sweat. He reminded himself not to make the same mistake again.

It was steep at first, and his fingers became scraped and bloodied from gripping the sharp edges. When they started cramping he had to stop, balancing on his toes with his body pressed against the rock, flexing each hand in turn until the circulation flowed freely again.

After a while he found he was leaning forward as he climbed. The slope gradually levelled off until he reached a plateau; he was not yet at the summit but he sensed he was close. To the left of where he stood, taking deep breaths, was a narrow path, a goat track or some ancient trading route, winding up into the last stretch of mountain above him. He made his way across to it, relieved to feel firm ground beneath his feet again.

As he walked he looked up; the sun was approaching the horizon. The old man had said the route down into the valley was easier. Dodinal could but hope that was true. Time was slipping away.

He reached the summit without knowing it. Seen from the lake, the distant peak had seemed narrow, almost like an arrowhead, but in reality it was wide and round and flat. It was only when Dodinal became aware he was walking forward rather than up that realisation dawned. He stopped and stared, astounded by the view. Mountains stretched away in all directions, like pillars holding up the sky. The air was so clear he felt he could reach out and touch them. He smiled, thinking of his mother's story about giants. Up here on the roof of the world, he could almost believe that was how it had happened.

He walked the broad circle of the summit until he could see the valley, an elongated bowl carved out of the earth, surrounded on all sides by almost vertical hills, granite grey and patched with green. An ancient forest covered the valley floor. Even from a distance he could see the trees were dark and twisted with age.

From the rock wall at the head of the valley, a great waterfall tumbled into a narrow lake below, snaring a rainbow in its spray. Dodinal caught the glitter of water through the leafless branches; the lake extended the length of the valley.

This side of the mountain was nowhere near as steep or rugged as that which had brought him here. He sought out the way into the valley: another track, worn into the rock over the centuries by men or the beasts that dwelled in the high country, carving a serpentine trail across and down the face of the mountain.

The creatures were in there somewhere, in those aged trees. Even from a height he could hear them, strange cries and screeches that arose from the ancient woodland. There could be scores, maybe hundreds of them. He was one man alone, with nothing but his sword and his shield to protect him.

Dodinal grinned, daring fate. This was how it should be.

He set off down the track, striding with effortless grace, not once losing his footing on the rough surface. One hand rested lightly on his sword handle. Whatever awaited him, he was ready for it.

TWENTY-ONE

THE CACOPHONY GREW louder as Dodinal descended, his fate rushing to meet him. He had sought peace and had come to believe that death would be the price of finding it. Then he had met Rhiannon, and found the peace he longed for, and for a short while at least it seemed to have come without a cost. Then he had learned, not for the first time, that nothing in this life was free, and that a man had to pay for the consequences of his actions. He had come to care for these people, but had failed to protect them. Now he would bring the boy home or die trying. Either outcome would be a form of peace.

By the time he reached the ground, the sun was close to the mountaintops, rimming them with golden fire. Already the western side of the valley was deep in shadow. He would begin his search there, where he would be less likely to be seen.

It was like stepping back into the time before memory. Trees that had appeared small from the summit now towered over him, twisted and gnarled like surly old men. Exposed roots formed nests deep enough for a grown man to shelter in; the ivy that choked the trunks was as thick as a warrior's arm; skeletal branches sagged as though too weary to raise themselves towards the sun. Days of constant sunlight had left the undergrowth dry and brittle, crunching and snapping beneath Dodinal's boots as he made his way deeper into the forest. He was not unduly concerned. The hellish din the creatures were making masked all other sounds.

The ground rose and fell. He hid behind moss-covered boulders, searching the trees overhead, alert to any hint of movement. Again there was nothing. He pushed on, heading north, following the length of the valley. His throat was dry so he veered east, looking for the lake he had seen from on high.

It was closer than he had believed. The setting sun's reflection sent dazzling flashes of light through the spaces between the trees. Dodinal raised a hand to shade his eyes.

The forest reached right down to the water, crowding the shore on both sides. The bank was muddy and fell away sharply. He hesitated, despite his thirst, until he was satisfied there were no malformed tracks in the mud. Then he crouched at the edge, cupping his hands to scoop water into his mouth. It was cold and fresh, not brackish like he had expected.

The sun dipped behind the mountains, and the shadows thickened around him. The screeching chorus intensified; the creatures loved the night. Dodinal drank more water until his belly was full and the thirst had gone. His head felt clear. Not that there was much thinking to be done. He could not plan for the unknown.

As he had no idea where the creatures were, he decided to scour the western side of the lake first. He worked his way steadily towards the waterfall as the forest slowly succumbed to twilight.

The trees thinned as he reached the valley's westernmost edge. To his left, a cliff stretched away into the distance and up towards the darkling sky. It was sheer, its summit inaccessible. Dodinal peered into the gloom. Just ahead of him was the dark mouth of a cavern, taller than him. A boulder had fallen or been pushed across the entrance, blocking it. Dodinal ran a hand through his beard. The creatures must have pushed it into place.

What better place to hold the captured children? There would be no need for guards. No child, few men even, possessed the strength to roll such a heavy obstruction clear.

Dodinal drew his sword and eased towards the cavern, wary of a trap. The screeching was interminable, and louder than ever with the cliff to bounce it back. Had he believed in Hell this was what he would have imagined it to be like; a shadowy, grotesque place filled with the cries of the damned and the demented. Suddenly cold, he hastened to the cave and stood by the boulder with his back against the cliff, darting eyes scanning for any movement within the shadows.

The forest was still. As far as he could tell, he was alone. He sheathed the sword then leaned against the boulder and pushed. It did not move, and for a moment he wondered if the stone had been there untouched for so long it had sunk into place, held firm by earth and grass, but there were drag marks on the ground. He shifted position. Digging his boot heels into the ground, he pushed again, grunting with the effort, straining until the tendons stood out in his arms and neck and sweat ran down his brow into his eyes. The boulder trembled, and then gave, as if the earth's grip on it had been broken. It rolled away with a grating rumble until it was clear of the cave.

Sword and shield in his hands, Dodinal stepped cautiously inside. He waited just within the entrance while his eyes adjusted to the gloom, and thought he heard, above the feral din, a furtive rustle deep in the darkness. He held the shield steady and tightened his grip on the sword. There came another sound; a muffled sobbing.

Dodinal crept deeper into the cavern, booted feet scraping across the stone floor. The sobbing was immediately hushed.

"Owain?" he whispered, the word echoing in the close confines of the cave. "Don't be afraid. It's me, Dodinal."

There was no response, but as he looked around the cave it seemed the darkness was no longer absolute. The cave was small, no more than a modest hollow in the cliff, with a low ceiling that slowly dripped water. At the back, directly opposite the entrance, was a wooden pallet, the timber so cracked and dry it had partially collapsed.

Dodinal's eyes, however, were drawn to the small hunched form in the centre of the cave, its hands and feet bound, its clothes in tattered ruins. A rag had been tied around the child's eyes, and another used to gag its mouth.

Dodinal stepped forward and knelt, reaching with gentle hands to take hold of the trembling figure. Immediately the child cried out, the words lost behind the gag, and tried to struggle free of his grip.

"Don't be scared," he said, keeping his voice calm and friendly. "You know me. I have come to take you home."

Now he could see from the child's long hair it was Annwen he had found, not Owain. Dodinal reached around her head and undid the knot that held the blindfold, then removed the gag. "Hold still," he said. The girl, a few years older than Owain, looked at him with wide eyes as he used the sword to slice through the bindings. They fell away from her, and at once she clasped her hands together to massage them, whimpering as blood began flowing freely through her veins.

"Did they hurt you?"

The girl shook her head.

"Have you seen Owain?"

"Yes," she said, her voice a little-girl squeak. Dodinal was conscious of what she had been through. It must have been a horrific ordeal, and he would not have been surprised if she had been unable to talk at all. "They came and took him away."

"When?"

"I don't know. Not long ago. I'm sorry." Her voice hitched and she sounded close to tears, so Dodinal quickly patted her hand, not wanting to make an already perilous situation even more fraught.

"Don't get upset," he told her, his measured tone belying his nerves. How long did he have before the creatures returned for the girl? They could be approaching the cave even now. "I'll get you out of here. Then I'll come back for Owain."

That assumed the boy was still alive. This cave made him think of food being stored until it was needed.

"Can you stand?" In the dimness, he saw the girl nod her head. She got to her feet, struggling slightly, swaying for a second or two. Before Dodinal could reach out to steady her, she recovered her poise and stood with her arms folded across her chest. The gag and blindfold had been torn from her clothes. She would be freezing.

He looked across at the pallet, thinking perhaps that he might find an old blanket or cloth to wrap around her. When he saw what rested within the broken wood, he quickly placed his hand on the girl's shoulder and turned her so she faced the entrance.

"Wait just outside. If you see anything coming toward us, run back to me. Don't make a sound, though."

She nodded again and made to move off, but then hesitated. Dodinal was about to chivvy her on her way when the girl bent down and reached into the shadows. "Here," she said, holding out her hand. "This is Owain's. You should look after it. You're his friend."

Dodinal knew at once what it was. It was not much, not really; just a battered old leather pouch holding nothing of value to anyone, save a little boy who missed his father. To that boy it was priceless. Dodinal looked at it. The strap had snapped where Owain had torn it loose. He must have been desperate to keep it from the creatures, so they would not tarnish the memory of a father he would never get to know. Dodinal gripped it so tightly his fingers threatened to tear it apart. If they had harmed the boy, nothing – *nothing* – would save them from his wrath.

"Thank you," he said hoarsely. "Now, wait outside."

Annwen did as she was told, and Dodinal tied the pouch around his neck, so it rested against his chest, and crossed over to the pallet.

Resting on the tattered remains of a mattress, tufts of straw sticking out, were the remains of two people who had died many years ago. He knelt to study them closer.

There was nothing left but bones. The boy Arwel, and his grandmother Bronwyn, the one they had called Crow.

They had brought their village's twisted offspring here, had raised them and fed them and then had gone the way of all flesh. At first, Dodinal assumed they had been placed here out of respect, as a son or daughter might honour those who brought them into the world. Then, peering closer, he saw that neither skeleton was entirely intact after all. There was a cleft in the top of each skull, where they had been struck and killed.

There was also something unnerving about the precise way the skeletons had been placed, on their sides with the heads close enough to touch, their arms and legs intertwined. It was, Dodinal suddenly realised, intended as a mockery of lovemaking. However long the two had lived before the children turned on them, he assumed that grandmother and grandson had not wanted for intimacy. He spat on the ground in disgust. The old man had said the madness had gone away, and he had been right. The Crow and the *brehyrion*'s son had taken it with them.

"Can we go now?" the girl called quietly.

"Yes, of course." He joined her at the mouth of the cave and quickly looked around. Nothing to be seen. He crouched by the girl and looked at her intently. "I will take you out of the forest, to the mountain. There is a path you can follow. Once I know you are safe, I will return for Owain. But we have to hurry."

The girl shrunk away from him, fearful. "You can't leave me."

"You cannot stay here. It's too dangerous."

Her eyes welled up. "But I'm scared."

"I know. Owain gave chase when the creatures took you. He was very brave. Now you have to brave too. Once you get to the path, you will be fine. The creatures will not pursue you."

"You can't be certain of that."

"I'm certain," he assured her. "I found you and I got you out of the cave; now I'm asking you to trust me. Will you?"

She wiped her eyes and nodded.

"Good," he said, taking her hand in his. "Now, we go."

He led her through the forest, moving as quickly as he could, slowing whenever it became obvious she was struggling to keep up. The light was almost gone now, rendering the forest impenetrable to all but the keenest of eyes. When Annwen cried out and fell heavily to the ground, her hand tearing free from his, he picked her up and threw her over his shoulder, in much the same way as the creature had done when it stole her from her village. His progress was much swifter.

Finally they were out of the trees, the mountain's sheer mass dwarfing them. The sky was deep purple and the stars were out. A full moon was rising, its great round face peering over the rim of the hills and washing the valley with its cold silver light. Dodinal carried the girl as far as the start of the path and put her down.

"Follow the path. Go as fast as you can." He thought of her struggling to clamber down the rocks on the other side. After that, she would have to negotiate that fearsome ridge. He had barely made it across by daylight. If she tried it, she would almost certainly end up getting killed. "When you reach the summit, wait for me. I will come for you once I have found Owain."

"Do you promise?" Her voice sounded very small.

"I promise." Though it went against his nature to lie, it was better to give the child hope than admit the truth; he was almost certainly not coming back, and she might not survive the night without the means to keep warm. He had no intention of giving up, but if the worst happened, he hoped she would simply fall asleep and not wake again. "I thought you said you trusted me."

"I do," she said, throwing her arms around his waist and hugging him.

Dodinal cleared his throat, embarrassed, and gently pushed her away. "I have to go and find Owain now. Remember what I told you. As fast as you can. It will help to keep you warm."

He watched her go, her little legs carrying her away from him with surprising speed. Dodinal's heart ached with sympathy. She must have been terrified from the moment she was taken until the moment he found and released her. He had filled her with hope. He had promised to save her, knowing it was a promise he might not be able to keep. Well, he was not done yet. He was Dodinal; Sir Dodinal the Savage. Men feared him, and with good reason.

Now the creatures would learn to fear him too.

TWENTY-TWO

Dodinal raced through the forest, shield over his shoulder, sword in its sheath, running with barely a sound, even though the ancient trees' life-lights were too dim to guide him and the moon had created a realm of shadows whose secret paths would remain closed to those who lacked the art to find them. Not once did he stumble nor slow to search for the way. He was most at home in the forest. Any forest.

When the sun had set and the moon had risen, the cries of the creatures had become more subdued, spurring him on. There was an almost tangible feeling of anticipation in the air. Visions of murder, of ritual sacrifice, filled his head, and he had to quell the fury that burned inside him. Until he found the boy and established what he was up against, he had to keep his head clear.

The cave gaped at him like a toothless mouth as he sprinted past it. He had a feeling of time running out, and Owain's life with it. The screeching sounded like it was growing louder again, and for one heart-quickening moment he feared he was too late. Despair turned to hope when he realised it was louder because he was getting closer to them.

The ground sloped upwards, and Dodinal slowed to a fast walk. The cliff was to his left, the deep forest to his right. The trees around him thinned out, and he cut eastwards until the denser woods closed in, shielding him from any watchful eyes. He ran on, reaching the edge of a steep hill.

Beyond the rise was where he would find the boy, he was sure of it. The noise was piercing, almost unbearable, a calamity of howling and yelping and screaming, as if every lunatic that ever lived had somehow ended up in this place of lost souls. It disorientated him, made him feel vulnerable. He spun around, braced in readiness for the horde of creatures he imagined stealing up on him.

The forest was deserted all around him.

He leaned against a tree while his nerves steadied. Once, he would not have bothered. Once, he would have charged straight in, seeing the Saxons as nothing but meat for his sword. He had been younger then and faster with it. Even now – when his bones felt the cold like never before and his muscles grew stiff if he pushed his body too hard – even now, the rage gave him a strength and an animal ferocity that no man could hope to match. But he was not just there to kill. He was there to save a child's life or to surrender his own trying.

He ran at a crouch, stopping just short of the crest of the hill, where he got down on his belly and lay flat, using his elbows and knees to cover the last few yards. He edged forward until he could look down, the moonlight bright enough to leave nothing unseen.

The ground curved away on both sides of where he lay, sloping down to a deep, narrow bowl; he could have comfortably cast a spear to the opposite side. It might have been natural, a small lake whose waters had long ago run dry, or the hollowed-out remains of ancient stone workings. Forest debris littered the floor. Trees huddled around the lower edge of it, even more decrepit than those in the forest overlooking them. Their branches, bereft of green, seethed with a constant frenzy of motion; creatures, though nothing like as big as those that had attacked the village. These were as stunted as the trees they infested.

Scores of them crawled along or leapt between the branches. Two tumbled to the ground, where they rolled and thrashed about. But they were not fighting. No bigger than children, Dodinal thought, sickened, and already they were rutting.

Halfway across the depression from him was a squat slab of rock, pale as bone in the lunar glow, the cliff a solid wall behind it. Owain was bound to the rock, with vines tied tautly across his chest and waist and holding his arms and legs outstretched. At first, amidst the shifting shadows, Dodinal could not tell whether the boy was moving. While he watched, Owain lifted his head as though he could somehow see Dodinal hiding in the darkness.

He drew back carefully from the edge until the trees concealed him, dry, brittle undergrowth cracking under his weight as he moved. Once out of sight he sat with his back against an oak with his chin cupped in one hand. If he made a move for the boy, the creatures would see him. Assuming the young were anything like the adults, they would attack without hesitation. Dodinal was confident he could fight them off, but less certain he could keep the boy safe from harm as he did so. What he needed was a distraction.

He shifted position in a wasted attempt to get comfortable on the hard ground, and Owain's pouch bumped lightly against his chest. His hand closed around it. At once, his mind was back in the village, in Rhiannon's hut, that evening when Owain had proudly displayed his father's belongings for him to see. Dodinal lifted the pouch over his head, opened it, tipped its contents into his hand.

He grinned when he found what he was looking for. He would have his distraction.

He returned everything except the flint and steel, and their cushion of bark kindling, and tied the pack around his neck once more. That done, he ripped up a clump of bracken, screwed it into a small nest and placed the kindling inside it, then rested it against the base of the oak and worked flint and steel until the sparks brought forth a tiny flame.

Dodinal cupped his hands around the nest and gently blew until it ignited. Then he grabbed more handfuls of bracken and placed them carefully on the fledgling fire, anxious not to smother it. The bracken immediately started to burn, smoke rising from the flames. He nodded.

Using the trees for concealment, he worked his way around the edge of the depression. He had to get as close as he could to Owain before making his move. He smelled the smoke, and wondered how long it would be before the creatures smelled it too. Hopefully they would panic and flee.

The smoke was visible by the time he was close enough to look down directly onto the slab. It spiralled into the night sky, gusting across the moon. Yet the creatures seemed oblivious to it. Dodinal gnawed his lip. Surely they were not so distracted by their rutting and rollicking that it had escaped their attention.

Then it struck him. If the creatures were unaware of the smoke, with luck they would remain unaware of him if he went down to the slab. He could be there and back with Owain before they noticed the child was gone. It was risky, but he would have to act sooner or later anyway. Better now, when there were no adults around. Decision made, he did not waver. He drew his sword and ran at a crouch until he reached the edge and scrambled down it.

The slab was as high as Dodinal's waist. Owain twisted his head to watch him as he approached. The knight's boots kicked against fallen branches, and he glanced down, recoiling in disgust. Not branches. Bones. Skulls. Unmistakeable in the moonlight. The ground was littered with them. Despite his haste he crouched to take a closer look. All of them were small. Some were clearly human. Others were malformed. So the creatures killed and ate their own young as well as the children they stole. Outrage flared within him.

Whatever happened, he would not fail Owain, even if that meant taking his life painlessly before the creatures could snuff it out with cruel savagery.

The creatures had forced a cloth into the boy's mouth, unaware there would be no cries to smother. Dodinal did not waste time with words or reassurance. As soon as he was close enough he slashed through the vines around Owain's waist and chest, working as quickly as he could.

The blade parted the vines securing Owain's right arm and leg, and Dodinal hurried around the slab. The air was cool, but he was sweating hard. He wiped his hands on his tunic, and then went to cut the vine holding Owain's left arm fast.

A screech blasted out, louder and shriller than the rest, and the forest went silent.

Dodinal spun around.

The creatures were motionless, frozen in place, their heads all turned his way. He could see the moonlight reflected in their eyes as they watched him. Smoke drifted across his vision. They must finally have scented it and, looking for its source, had seen him. What he had intended as a distraction had given him away.

He raised the sword to cut through the last of the bindings. Owain might survive in the forest, or he might not, but at least he would have a chance, where he would have no chance at all trapped in the midst of a battle. They would tear him to pieces.

There was not enough time. As one, the creatures shrieked and leapt down from the trees, sweeping across the depression towards him.

"Try to undo the knots," he bellowed at Owain, then turned and faced the tide that was about to engulf him. He ran from the slab to lead them away from the boy, then stood his ground, sword raised. The red mist swam up, and his heart pounded with exhilaration. He could feel the blood rushing through his veins.

Clawed feet made a noise like rain on a roof as the child-creatures streamed across the depression. What they lacked in size they made up for in ferocity, mouths snarling and revealing rows of vicious teeth. Dodinal waded into them, slamming his shield into skulls and bodies, relishing the feel of bone crunching and breaking with every blow.

He wielded the sword wildly and to devastating effect, parting limbs from torsos and heads from necks until the ground was soaked with blood. More creatures surged towards him and he slammed them out of his way with the shield and skewered them with the blade. Though the size of children, they were anything but. He showed no mercy.

They came at him from every direction. Dodinal wheeled and struck, turned and struck again, bodies heaping at his feet. His boots crushed the twitching corpses as he drove forward. One of the creatures got close enough to leap at him and his sword met it in mid-air, cleaving it in two. The thing's entrails unravelled like a banner as its bloody halves fell to ground. Another slipped through his defences, crawling along until it could sink its claws into his ankle. Dodinal barely felt the pain. He rammed the sword down through the back of its deformed skull until the grip on his ankle went slack, and then stepped away and kicked it from him.

They grew wary and kept their distance. A few darted towards him, but fell back before he had the chance to turn the blade on them. They were trying to force him back into the bank, leaving him nowhere to go. If he turned around, he would find more of them at the top of the bowl, waiting to swoop down on him the moment he was trapped. He bared his teeth. Let them try.

He went on the offensive, suddenly lunging forward as two of the creatures came at him, swinging the sword with such brutal force that the blade sliced clean through them both. The rest turned tail and fled, regrouping half a dozen strides away, crouching on all fours, hissing and spitting in fury.

A sudden weight on his back nearly knocked him off balance, and he felt sharp claws digging into his shoulders. Shifting the sword to his left hand, he reached back with his right and grabbed the creature by the throat, squeezing hard. It thrashed wildly, fangs piercing his skin, and he squeezed harder until he had crushed its windpipe. The creature went limp, and Dodinal hurled its lifeless body into the trees.

He strode relentlessly towards the horde, blind anger giving him strength, the stink of their blood driving him on. There was no room in his head for conscious thought, or in his heart for compassion. Maybe half of them were dead, but he wanted them *all* dead, would not stop until he had cut the life from every last one of them.

They cowered and backed away, sensing his righteous fury, looking around urgently as though seeking a means of escape. One tried to rally the rest by letting out a howl and throwing itself at him, and he spun on his heel and slammed the flat of his shield into its face. It took a few faltering steps back, and Dodinal thrust the sword deep into its eye. The creature went stiff as he pulled the blade free, dead before it hit the ground.

And then the earth shook.

Dodinal felt it tremble under his boots.

It shook again, as if struck a massive blow.

None of the creatures moved. They were no longer looking at him. Their heads were turned, gazing intensely up the bank towards the unknowable dark of the forest. Dodinal swallowed hard.

Another percussive blow, which rattled his teeth and shook his bones, followed by a great splintering, tearing and crashing. It sounded like the trees were being torn up by their roots.

Something was coming. Dodinal edged towards Owain. He had no idea what it was. Surely there was no creature on earth capable of making the earth shake in such a way. Whatever it was, he wanted the child out of the way before it got any closer.

The ground convulsed. Trees swayed and groaned.

Dodinal cut through the vine that held the boy's foot.

A dark, monstrous shape emerged from the forest with a great clattering of branches, and came to a shuddering halt at the depression's edge. He saw it well enough in the moonlight to know it was bigger than any living thing he had ever set eyes on before. He cast out his senses and immediately recoiled. What they had touched was ancient and cold, not malevolent but uncaring, like nature itself. Dodinal had sensed it before. It had unnerved him then. Now, when it was almost close enough to spit on, its presence was like fuel on the flames of his anger.

It was unnatural, an abomination, just like the creatures. This was what must have sent them out to steal the children. Judging from the bones on the ground, it had an insatiable taste for human young.

Now the adults swooped into sight, dropping from the trees near the beast and scurrying down the bank ahead of it. There were eight of them, one was badly burned. Another was much smaller, presumably drawn from the ranks of the young to make up for the absence of the adult he and Gerwyn had slain.

They could not have missed Dodinal, his back to the slab only yards from them, yet they paid him no attention. Instead, they waited behind the cowering young, their heads bowed. The forest was as silent as the church where Dodinal had often sought peace.

He frowned. A church...

Understanding struck him like a physical blow.

Whatever it was, these twisted creatures worshipped it.

It was their god. And they had brought it sacrifices.

The monstrous shape juddered; Dodinal saw movement in the darkness around it and had the impression of a long thin neck raised skywards so the beast could peer down at him and the boy. Then, moving slowly and carefully, it lowered itself into the depression, earth and rock cascading as the bank gave way under its weight. With each thunderous step, the very world seemed to tremble. Visions of giants filled Dodinal's head again, but he shook them off. This was no giant, no mythical beast out of a child's story.

Whatever it was, it was real.

It stepped beyond the shadow of the forest, into the moonlight.

Dodinal saw it clearly, but he did not believe what he saw.

Its body was that of a leopard, the haunches those of a lion, and the feet a hart's. It had a serpent's neck and head, which swayed in time with its leonine tail as it lumbered across the ground, passing the assembled throng of creatures watching its every move. Dodinal stepped cautiously away as it came to a juddering halt before him, his mind struggling to comprehend what he saw. It beggared belief. It challenged everything he had ever known. There was man and there was nature, nothing else. Yet here, standing within touching distance, was living proof that there *was* something else.

Sir Palomides, the Saracen, had often spoken of such a creature. The Questing Beast,[12] he had named it, and dedicated his life to hunting it down. Camelot's knights, Dodinal amongst them, had humoured him and wished him well, but between themselves had dismissed it as a fool's errand. Such a chimera could be found nowhere but the realm of myth. If it existed, they argued, why had it not been found?

The beast lowered its sinuous neck and thrust it towards him, its mouth opened wide and its forked tongue flicked out. A sound like the baying of three score hounds poured forth from its belly. Dodinal flinched, remembering the old man's story. The baying of hounds that long-ago summer had been the harbinger of disaster.

He continued to step away, moving slowly, until he felt the hard edge of the slab press into his back. There he stood, raised to his full height. He held the sword with both hands at chest height, the blade raised to the stars. To reach the child the beast would first have to get past him, and he would cut its head from its body.

The Questing Beast roared again but did not move. What was it waiting for? Dodinal was torn by indecision. Part of him wanted to stand his ground. Another felt compelled to attack.

The adults moved before he could, fanning out around the young, yelping and barking in what Dodinal now recognised was a feeble attempt to emulate the voice of their god, trying to herd the child-creatures across to where Dodinal waited. The young shuffled and whined and cast anxious glances at each other, and at their siblings lying broken and bleeding on the ground.

Without warning, one of the adults broke away from the rest and loped towards the slab. The Questing Beast opened its mouth and again came that hideous baying. The gargoyle

[12]First appearing in *Perlesvaus*, the Questing Beast is the most famous monster of Arthurian legend. The name refers to the sound the creature makes; in Middle English, the barking of hunting dogs was sometimes known as *questing*. The Beast is commonly used as a symbol of incest and the breakdown of society, appearing to Arthur the morning after he slept with his half-sister, Morgause, and fathered his murderous bastard son, Mordred.

creature stumbled and looked around as though uncertain of its actions, then seemed to shrug off any misgivings and continued its headlong rush. At the last second it coiled and leapt over Dodinal, landing on the farthest edge of the slab. Dodinal spun around to face it, the Questing Beast and its horde of worshippers forgotten.

The creature turned to face its kin, and then bent and thrust a hand towards Owain's chest.

Dodinal twisted and hurled the shield, clipping the thing's skull and stunning it. Then he lashed out with the sword and took its arm off above the elbow. The creature howled and flung itself away from him, losing its footing and falling from the slab's edge.

A furious shrieking filled the air as Dodinal slashed through the last of the bindings and lifted Owain away from the rock. The boy wrapped his arms so tightly around his neck that the knight could scarcely breathe. He tried to put him down and push him towards the bank, but Owain refused to let go.

Dodinal spun around. The Questing Beast had still not moved, but the creatures were closing in on him, the adults now leading the way, the young following tremulously behind them.

He could not fight them all.

Dodinal lifted the blade and rested the metal against Owain's throat. It would be kinder this way, a mercy killing. The boy must have known what was going to happen, but didn't flinch. He was brave, no doubt about that. His mother was right to be proud of him.

The creatures were almost within reach. Dodinal smelled their foul carrion breath as they yelped and howled.

He shook his head. He could not do it. Could not take an innocent life even if it was for the best. Very well, he would take out as many of them as he could and go down fighting. At least neither he nor the boy would die alone.

The creatures stumbled to a standstill and fell silent.

Their eyes, Dodinal saw, no longer reflected the moonlight, but swum with a rich amber glow.

Tall shadows danced on the cliff face as orange light bathed the bowl, casting the stunted trees into sharp relief. Now the creatures had ceased their shrieking and hollering, he could hear the rush of the wind through the branches. Smoke, dense and choking, gusted over him, over them all.

Dodinal turned his head. The trees were now pillars of fire, and the flames were spreading. Burning tendrils reached out across the dark spaces of the forest.

Dodinal could barely draw breath, between the smoke and the child around his neck, but laughed all the same.

He had wanted a distraction. Now he had one.

The creatures immediately turned away from him and Owain, scattering, running and leaping away from the flames, making for the trees and scrambling up into the branches. They vanished into the wood, the clamour of their panic-stricken flight carrying back after they had disappeared from sight, leaving man and boy alone. The Questing Beast was gone too. Dodinal frowned, confused. It could shake the earth with each step and yet he had not heard it leave.

He felt a sharp pain as Owain pulled hard on his beard and pointed over Dodinal's shoulder. The knight turned to look and saw that the fire had almost completed a full circle of the closest trees surrounding them. If they did not move now they would be trapped and would suffocate, or burn to death.

Neither was any way to die.

Dodinal left the shield where he had thrown it and sheathed the sword. Holding Owain with both hands, he fled across the clearing, only just outrunning the flames as they closed the circle. Earth flew up under his boots as he scrambled up the bank and raced into the forest, neither knowing nor caring which way he was heading, as long as it was away from the fire. Blistering heat toasted his neck as the trees around him were engulfed. The sound of it snapped at his heels, crackling and roaring. Even the air his hungry lungs gulped down felt hot.

Dodinal looked sharply to his left and right as he ran. Everything was alight, from the undergrowth to the crowns of the trees. He had no choice but to keep pushing blindly forward. Ahead of him, a tree burst into flame as though struck by lighting and started to lean across his path. Holding Owain tightly, Dodinal drove himself on, sprinting under the tree at the very moment it crashed to the ground, a searing blast of air washing up his back. He stumbled, but managed to stay on his feet, letting go of Owain with one hand long enough to swipe embers from his hair before they could singe his scalp.

Smoke closed his throat. He began to cough, great hacking barks, and could not stop. His eyes swam with tears. He had no sense of direction, careering blindly towards the darkness, like a narrowing passage through the turbulent light. Sparks and burning debris landed and stung his face and hands.

Then he was tumbling into space. Owain slipped from his grasp, and Dodinal tensed, bracing for impact. Instead of hard ground, he felt the shock of cold water as the lake closed around him. A roaring filled his ears. Dodinal flailed around, swallowing water, not knowing which way was up and which was down.

Then his feet touched the bottom and he pushed hard. His head broke the surface, and he gasped and coughed and threw up water. Smoke swirled and boiled around him. The fire was a fierce glow, which had spread all along this side of the lake and was now encroaching on the other.

As he watched, still spitting out water, the tinder-dry forest succumbed to the inferno, the wind harrying the flames on their way. He imagined he saw movement within the trees, pictured the creatures trying in vain to escape as death closed around them.

"Owain," he shouted, throat raw. He thought hard, trying to remember if he had still had hold of the boy when he hit the water. If not, he could still be on the bank. "Owain, where are you?"

The water was deep even a few yards out, rising to the top of his chest. He waded back towards the lakeside, calling all the way, straining for an answer, cursing himself for a fool when it occurred to him he would not get one even if Owain had heard.

A ball of fire burst out of the forest and hurtled towards the lake, wailing like something possessed. It hit the water with a hissing plume of steam. Before Dodinal could reach for his sword a head burst up through the surface right before him, its gargoyle face rendered uglier by fire. Most of the skin had been burned away, so it was little more than a skull. It lunged at Dodinal, mouth agape; he grabbed its jaws and wrenched them apart until they snapped, then broke its neck and tossed the body aside.

Something grabbed his arm. Dodinal spun around, hand raised to strike, staying the blow when he saw with relief it was Owain. The boy was struggling to tread water and shaking badly, from fear or cold or both. Dodinal lifted him up.

The fire had leapt from tree to tree, spreading not just around the edges of the lake but rampaging through the forest until the entire valley was ablaze, turning the walls of the mountains around it into a cauldron of shifting light and shadow. The searing brightness turned the night sky to dawn, driving back the moon and stars. The roar of the fire was a thousand times louder than that of the Questing Beast.

The choking smoke was bad enough, but there were other dangers. Windblown debris rained down around them, sizzling as it plunged into the water. It was cold, too. They would not survive in the lake for long, but neither could they climb out of it with the fire raging so close to the water's edge. The safest course of action would be to strike out for the centre of the lake where there was less chance of being struck and where the air might be clearer.

But Dodinal was not a strong swimmer, and he suspected the boy was not either. They would drown before they froze to death. Then again they would suffocate or be roasted alive if they stayed here. The heat was almost unbearable. He had to take his chance in deep water. He turned his back on the forest and forced his way out into the lake, by now so cold that he could barely feel anything.

Owain's fingers dug into his arm with surprising strength, and Dodinal looked back sharply. A tree, ablaze from root to crown, slowly toppled towards them, flames fanning behind it as it fell. There was no time to move out of its way. Holding his breath and clutching the boy as tightly as he could with numb fingers, he dived and kicked hard until he was flat on the lake's weed-infested bed.

There was a flash of orange light, instantly snuffed out, and a percussive blow that sent him tumbling helplessly through the churning water. Somehow he managed to keep hold of Owain, and when the turbulence subsided, he pushed his feet hard against the bed. His head broke the surface and he lifted the boy clear, and they held each other while the fire raged around them and the lake glowed like molten copper.

He felt a bump against his shoulder: the remains of the tree, blackened but soaked through. It was too thin for them to sit on, but they could use it to get away from the fire without fear of drowning. "Here," he said, lifting Owain towards it. "Hold on with both hands. When I tell you, start kicking."

They made for the centre of the lake, Dodinal warming from the exertion. The eddying wind blew the smoke from the surface, and he and the boy could breathe easier. He decided they might just as well head south now, towards the mountain path, rather than wait for the fire to burn out.

They passed countless bodies on the way, bobbing facedown in the water around them. It seemed the creatures had never learned to swim. Dodinal watched the corpses float by with grim satisfaction.

The inferno took little time to consume itself. Old and dry, the trees burned fiercely and were soon spent. As the firelight dimmed, flickered and was extinguished, the wind dispersed the remaining smoke overhead and the moon and stars reappeared. Dodinal squinted towards the shore: even by moonlight, he could see that almost nothing of the forest remained.

He steered them shoreward. They waded out onto dry land, staying close to the waterline, warmed by the charred ruins as they walked. Embers peered like glowing eyes in the darkness. The smoke was fairly thick here, the acrid stench of it filling their nostrils. Dodinal cast wary glances around. It was almost beyond belief that anything could have survived, but not impossible. He and the boy were proof of that.

They reached the path without incident. He was both surprised and gladdened to find the girl Annwen waiting there. Owain seemed as pleased to see her as she was to see him. When asked, she admitted she had been too scared to try to escape the valley alone.

"I walked halfway up the path and then I hid behind a rock," she said as the three of them sat close to the smouldering forest, making the most of its fading heat. "I was cold. When I saw the fire I hurried back down; I was worried about you, about both of you. When there was no sign of you, I was certain you had both perished. And then I saw you walking out of the smoke. It was like a miracle."

Miracle. Not long ago Dodinal would immediately have dismissed such an idea as nonsense. Now he was not so certain.

It was certainly a stroke of good fortune that Owain's little pouch of memories had included his father's flint and steel, for Dodinal had carried nothing with him with which to start a fire. It was strange, he thought, how the world could turn on such small matters. If Owain had not wandered off into the snowbound forest in the first place, Dodinal would not have had to save him from the wolves, and he would never have encountered Rhiannon or her people, several of whom he had come to regard as friends.

"You're sure no creature came by here?" he asked, for the third or fourth time. He had to be certain.

Annwen rolled her eyes and sighed theatrically. "I said no and I meant no. Do you think I would not have seen them?"

Dodinal raised a hand in apology.

They remained there for the night. Eventually the children slept, huddled together for warmth, and Dodinal stayed awake to watch over them. When the sky began to brighten, he stood and surveyed the valley. Where the forest had been was now a jumble of blackened stumps and twisted wood. Nothing moved. The lake was calm, its waters black and oily, dotted with scores of small shapes. Was it too much to hope the creatures had all perished, either by fire or by water? The pass was the only way in or out of the valley. Annwen had been insistent nothing had passed her.

A miracle? Perhaps.

The sun nudged over the mountains.

Dodinal gently shook the children awake.

"Come on," he said. "It's time we were heading home."

EPILOGUE

THE FIRE CRACKLED in its hearth. The smell of roast meat still hung in the air. While they were gone, the old man had hunted and brought down a goat, and on their return he had roasted a haunch in their honour. Like Hywel, he had been desperate to know what had happened in the hills, but they had been too tired to talk, other than to confirm what the absence of their friends implied.

Now, with his belly full and his aching legs rested, Dodinal told them the story from beginning to end, leaving out nothing. They were astonished by his description of the Questing Beast. Truth be told, he was still having trouble believing it himself.

"You are certain they all perished?" Gerwyn asked. He had made it no further than the bottom of the mountain before night fell, and had done as Dodinal had advised, setting a fire from fallen branches to keep him warm until dawn. He had slept late while his bruised and battered body recovered, and had not made much progress along the lake by the time Dodinal and the children caught up with him. He had seemed genuinely overwhelmed to see his nephew unharmed, and had held him, wordlessly, for quite some time.

Dodinal had snapped off two forked branches and fashioned him a pair of makeshift but sturdy crutches. The two men and their charges were back in the old village by mid afternoon.

"I'm certain. You didn't see it. The fire… nothing could have lived through that. It was a miracle we survived," Dodinal added.

Hywel said nothing. The bruise on his head was already fading and his vision, though blurred, was slowly returning. But he had been grief-stricken to hear of the death of his close friend Emlyn.

"This strange beast of which you spoke," Gerwyn continued. "The Questing Beast."

"Yes. It killed the children they brought it?"

Dodinal shook his head. He had considered this same question while they had made their way out of the valley. When the creature had jumped on the slab and stretched its hand out to Owain, Dodinal had naturally assumed it meant to kill him. Having thought it over, he realised the creature was trying to encourage the young. The message in the gesture was clear. *Here is your prey. Take it. It's yours.* The adults brought the children there, but it was the young that tore them apart. It was not about worship, or at least not worship alone. It was about jealousy, revenge and hatred. The knowledge of what they were, the memory of who had made them, had been passed down from generation to generation. "No, the creatures did that."

The old man spoke. "From what you said of the noise it made, the baying of many hounds, it must have been the same beast we heard all those years ago. The sound of it drove us insane, made us commit a great sin. Were it not for the Questing Beast, none of this would have happened. Now it is dead, I have perhaps been forgiven. And for that, Dodinal, you have my eternal gratitude."

Dodinal nodded in acknowledgement but said nothing. He was not convinced the old man was right. Yes, it would have been the Questing Beast the villagers had heard. What was not so certain was whether it was the beast that had made father sleep with daughter and mother with son. In a village this remote there must have been temptation, especially when a fierce winter had rendered it more isolated than usual. Perhaps it was the villagers' unnatural lust that had drawn the beast to them. If so, then the incestuous rutting of the creatures they spawned would have drawn it back to the valley.

It could have been a reluctant god, its roar a cry of torment.

Perhaps. Perhaps not. Dodinal would never know.

Neither could he say the beast was dead. It had appeared out of nowhere and had gone the same way. He would be sure to tell the Saracen, when next he saw him. Palomides may be fated never to find it, but this was as good a place as any to start looking.

They made small talk for a while until exhaustion overcame them. They were asleep before sunset and woke before dawn.

"Are you sure you won't come with us?" Hywel asked the old man, as they readied to leave. The hunter had perked up a little. It must have been the imminent prospect of returning home. "We would not speak of what happened here. You would be made welcome."

The old man shook his head. "Thank you, but you and your friends have done enough for me already. I don't know how much time I have left, but what I do have I would prefer to spend here in my home, now that the ghosts of the past no longer haunt me."

They said their farewells and left him.

Gerwyn needed help climbing out of the valley, but was otherwise surprisingly adept with the crutches. They made good progress, even allowing for the children, and reached the edge of the forest by noon. They halted in the shade of the trees and ate cold meat which the old man had given them. Lost in thought, Dodinal stared at the mountains while he chewed. Eventually, Gerwyn suggested it was time they continued their journey, and Hywel helped him to his feet.

"Wait," Dodinal told them.

Gerwyn raised an eyebrow. "The longer we sit around here, the longer it will take us to get home. I'd rather push on."

"I have something to tell you." He hesitated.

Then he took a moment to tell them who he was. Where he'd come from.

Both men looked thunderstruck. Then Hywel shrugged. "I knew there was something different about you. A traveller who fought as well as you... I should have guessed. Anything else you'd like to share with us, *Sir* Dodinal?"

"Yes. I'm not coming with you."

He raised a hand to silence their immediate cries of protest. "As much as I want to, I cannot."

"Why not?" Gerwyn demanded. "You promised Rhiannon."

"I promised her I would return. And I will. But not today."

"When, then? And what am I supposed to tell her?"

"Tell her…" He considered his words for a moment. "Tell her I have healed a great wound. But there are other wounds in this world that need healing. She knows what I am, as do you. I am a knight of Camelot. I swore the King's Oath.[13] I have to uphold it."

"Have to or want to?" Gerwyn fired back bitterly.

"Not long ago, you wanted me gone," Dodinal said with a smile. "Now you don't want me to leave. I wish you'd make up your mind!"

"He'll get used to the idea once he's had enough time," Hywel said. He reached out and held Dodinal in a tight embrace. Then he let go and stepped back. "It has been an honour to know you. You say you will return to our village; I look forward to that day."

"As do I," Dodinal said. He looked at Gerwyn and put one hand on his shoulder. "You have done your father proud. You will make a great *brehyrion*, especially with Hywel around to guide you. Look after Rhiannon for me."

Gerwyn nodded, unable to speak.

The children were hovering nearby, and Dodinal crouched by them. "You were very brave," he said to Annwen. "I am glad I was able to save you. Now go and wait with the others."

The girl hugged him briefly, then skipped off towards the two men, leaving Dodinal alone with the boy. "Walk with me a moment," the knight said, and led him away. Once they were

---

[13]The Penecostal Oath, which Arthur insists his knights swear when he first forms the Round Table, in Book I of the *Morte*. The Oath does not explicitly require the knights to seek out injustices, although it enjoins them "to give mercy unto him that asketh mercy," and to "always to do ladies, damosels, and gentlewomen succour." Dodinal is far from the only knight to interpret this by actively questing for opportunities to do both.

out of earshot, he stopped and knelt at Owain's side. "I know you talk to your mother. Tell her that I love her and I will see her again one day soon. Tell her I hope she understands what it is I have to do."

Owain stared at him with unblinking eyes. He nodded.

"Good. Thank you." Dodinal hesitated, aware that Gerwyn and Hywel were watching him intently. Perhaps they were wondering what he was saying, that he couldn't say in their hearing. "Now, before you return to the others and head off home, there is something I want to ask you. Something I have to know."

The boy watched him without expression.

"I've been thinking," Dodinal said, not sure how to frame the question without sounding like a fool. "I've been thinking about the way everything happened. About how everything worked out."

He struggled, lost for words. The idea had come to him on the trek out of the mountains. At first he had shrugged it off as ridiculous, but the more he thought about it the more convinced he became.

That Dodinal had tracked down the creatures and slain them was not down to chance. There had been an influencing force guiding his every thought and deed. That force had not been fate or fortune, but an eight-year-old boy. It was Owain who had wandered into the forest and, later, gone in pursuit of Annwen. He had deliberately exposed himself to danger, trusting in Dodinal to save him.

Owain had been aware of the presence of Ellis and of the scouting creature, before anyone else, even before the dogs.

Then, as the creatures were taking him from the cave, he had torn the pouch from around his neck and left it for Dodinal. Were it not for the flint and steel, the knight could not have started the fire.

No, there were too many coincidences for Dodinal's liking.

Rhiannon's mother had been a seer. Rhiannon was not. Could it be the gift had been passed on to her son instead?

Owain leant in close to put his mouth by Dodinal's ear.

"Yes," he whispered. He smiled and put a finger to his lips. Then he turned and ran towards the forest.

Dodinal laughed and followed after him. He would say farewell to his friends, and then he would be on his way. If he headed west, he could be at the coast before nightfall. A change of scenery would do him good. He had spent too much time in the forest, and he would be a happy man if he never had to climb a mountain again.

He sensed the wildlife returning. In the sky above the forest a hawk soared, and fell like a stone as it sighted prey.

There would be other battles to fight, he felt certain. Perhaps it was too much to hope that a man such as he would ever find peace.

But he was at peace with himself. And that would do for now.

Here endeth the worthie Tale of

Sir Dodinale the savage Knyght

and the Questing Beeste...

ABOUT THE TRANSLATOR

PAUL LEWIS has written hundreds of comedy sketches for UK network TV, including *Spitting Image*, as well as radio sitcoms and plays. Paul co-edited the *Cold Cuts* horror anthology and is co-author of the novels *The Ragchild* and *The Quarry*, several novellas and numerous short stories, including a *Doctor Who* contribution for BBC Books. Paul works as a journalist and lives with his wife and son in a village near Swansea, Wales.

APPENDIX I

The Salisbury Manuscript
and the Hereford Fragment

UNCOVERED IN JUNE 2006 in the vestry of the nine-hundred-year-old parish church of St. Barbara and St. Christopher in Salisbury, the Salisbury Manuscript (British Library MS Add. 1138) was one of the most explosive documents to hit the generally quiet world of medieval literature in decades.

More than seven hundred published academic papers have been dedicated to the Salisbury, discussing its age, provenance and authority, the symbolism and themes in the texts, its influences, and its place in the Arthurian canon. Careers have started, or ended, over the text and its implications.

Arthur Drake, canon at St. Barbara and St. Christopher, has been pleased by the attention the church has been receiving since the manuscript's discovery, although it has caused a certain amount of disruption.

"The manuscript itself is in the British Library now, of course," says Drake, "but we receive visitors every day, interested in seeing where it was found, and asking about the history of the building. They even study the stained-glass windows, looking for clues as to the manuscript's history, although I try and tell them that the windows are Victorian.

"I've heard from someone at the Council about having a small museum annex built on the church grounds. Last I heard, they were talking to the Bishop, although with budget cuts I suppose it may end up being cancelled."

Purporting to be "The Seconde Boke of kyng Arthur and also His noble Knyghts, as writen by Sir Tomas Malorye before hys deth," the manuscript appears genuine: written on fifteenth-century paper stock, it bears marks suggesting it was in Caxton's workshop around the time *Le Morte D'Arthur* was printed.

Unlike the *Morte*, which weaves dozens of stories into a more-or-less continuous narrative, the *Second Book* is more disjointed, consisting of stand-alone stories, loosely – and erratically – organised into chronological order, with no clear connections between most of the stories.

The second story, "The worthie Tale of Sir Dodinale the savage Knyght and the Questing Beeste," is of particular interest to medieval scholars, in that it appears to draw a connection between the *Second Book* and an obscure piece of Arthuriana from Hereford.

The Hereford Fragment

THE HEREFORD FRAGMENT (Hereford Cathedral Library MS 1701.E) is an incomplete manuscript consisting of forty-seven leaves of seventeenth-century vellum, originally found bound into the back of an eighteenth-century volume of the New Testament in the home of a wool-merchant in Hereford. Removed from the scriptural volume and rebound in sheepskin sometime in the early nineteenth century, it has been kept in Hereford Cathedral's library ever since.

Written in Welsh, the fragment consists of seven disconnected narratives. Known as the *Lesser Dodinal*, the *Lesser Bors*, the *Lesser Pellinore* and so on, the narratives deal with the upbringings and childhood adventures of seven of the members of the Round Table, and the events that led to them taking up arms as knights and entering Arthur's service.

Prior to the discovery of the *Second Book*, the Hereford Fragment was largely disregarded by Arthurian scholarship. Welsh texts were not often studied in the nineteenth century, the fragment was assumed to have been written late – certainly no earlier than the second half of the seventeenth century – and the stories themselves were deemed ideosyncratic, even frivolous.

"The fragment was brought before the worthies at Cambridge in 1836 or 1837," writes Dr Nadine Holmes, author of *Children's Tales: The Hereford Fragment* (Nottingham University Press, 2009), "and summarily dismissed. From the surviving correspondence, it seems that the good men of the University not only thought it 'of questionable provenance' and 'assuredly recent heritage,' but felt that 'the generally bucolic and frequently domestic subject matter suggests that it may have been composed by an aristocratic woman, possibly the wife of an English knight living on the border, presumably to practice writing in Welsh, and was never intended for public consumption.'"

Holmes criticises this view, "although why the text would have any less value or relevance if it *were* true is unclear." The hand and various marks suggest a professional scribe, possibly a church clerk, she argues; and the language and spelling – particularly the use of the letter *k*, which disappeared from written Welsh in the sixteenth century – suggest that the source material is older than the fragment. "Whoever wrote it, the original source of the fragment is not only ancient, but was considered important enough, in the late seventeenth century, to be copied, preserved, and bound."

And the discovery of the *Second Book* in 2006 has changed everything. In particular, one detail of "The worthie Tale of Sir Dodinale the savage Knyght."

"We were working on the second story in the *Second Book*," remembers Becker Balisovitch of the University of Southern

California, "and trying to interpret the phrase '*flamys of the trees liffes.*' The 'flames of the trees' lives'? What the hell does he mean by that? There was nothing like it in any of Malory's other works.

"I was talking to my brother Jared and he reminded me of an old book our mother used to have, *Children of Camelot* (Oxford University Press, 1929). It's got the story of when Dodinal was a child in it, and he could see these 'life-lights,' from any animal or plant in the wild."

The *Lesser Dodinal* was brought back into the light, and closely compared with the *Second Book*. Although written in different languages and telling largely different tales, the argument that there is some kind of common origin for the texts is compelling.

"Put simply," says Balisovitch, "these two documents are the only places where Dodinal's ability to sense wild creatures can be found. On top of that, Dodinal appears to reminisce about events – the slaughter of his parents' village, for instance – that only appear in the *Lesser Dodinal*. It's uncertain whether Malory had access to the *Lesser Dodinal*, or the author of the *Dodinal* had the *Second Book*, or both books were influenced by a common source, but there's a strong possibility of some sort of connection."

One way or the other, Abaddon Books' translator Paul Lewis chose, in his adaptation of "The worthie Tale," to incorporate the majority of the *Lesser Dodinal* (specifically, lines 4-187, 192-403, 443-688 and 727-802) into his translation, as four "flashback" sequences in the story, arguing that it serves – and may once have been intended – as a narrative whole.

APPENDIX II

The Savage Knight

*"Inceste ond mourdre are i'faith like
the two faces of but ane coine."*

WHAT IS SAVAGERY? What is wildness? First introduced to the
Arthurian canon in Chrétien de Troyes' *Erec and Enide* in
the twelfth century, Sir Dodinal (or Dedinet, or Dondanix, or
Oddinello, or any of a dozen other names) is more or less a cipher
for the question of what civilisation means, to the medieval
mindset, and what it means to be wild. Called *le Sauvage* ("the
Wild" or "the Fierce"), he is generally described as having a love
of hunting, or as living in the wilderness; in Ulrich's *Lanzelet*,
he lives near the fearsome Shrieking Marsh. And certainly, to
the medieval mind, the wilderness was a terrible thing: wolves
and bears haunted the countryside, even in the British Isles, and
brigands and thieves preyed with impunity, rarely challenged or
pursued from one lord's demesne to the next.

And yet, the tales told of his deeds do not suggest a particularly
fearsome man. In *Le Morte D'Arthur* and the *Prose Tristan*, he
is humiliated by Tristan and Morhalt. In the Vulgate *Merlin* and
Lancelot, his adventures generally involve him being rescued
from imprisonment – variously, in Dolorous Guard, the Castle

Langree, the Forbidden Hill and Meleagant's castle – by the more famous and heroic Lancelot. A minor knight, the incestuous son of King Belinant and his niece, Dodinal serves the King and the Round Table, quests, fights, and dies, either falling in Arthur's final battle against Mordred or killed by Sir Gaheris.

Enter the *Lesser Dodinal*. In this utterly remarkable and criminally under-recognised Welsh work, we encounter a very different Dodinal. He has gone from royalty to the son of a commoner, raised in a village in a wood. Not merely at home in the wild, he is now mystically tied to the forests he calls home, moving like a ghost amidst the trees, able to sense his fellow beasts and track them without error.

And he has become fearsome. Gone is the pompous knight made to look a fool by the great and good; gone is the hapless adventurer needing rescue by his betters. Driven by vengeance against his family's murderers, he is subject to an ungovernable rage, in which he cannot even distinguish friend from foe. It is this rage, and not his honour or his courage, that impresses King Arthur and earns him an invitation to the Round Table. Savage indeed.

PERHAPS MOST EXTRAORDINARILY, Dodinal is an atheist. Not merely a pagan or Saracen, like Sir Palomedes, to be converted to the Christian faith, but a true nominalist, denying even the existence of the supernatural, believing that "everie deth, everie tragedie or mishap in the Worlde was the caus of heedlesse Natoure or of cruell Man."

How exactly to interpret Dodinal's beliefs is a matter of fierce debate. "[The *Second Book*] was written three hundred years before the Enlightenment," argues Prof Brubaker (Inst. Stud.). "There was literally no such thing as an atheist; there wasn't even a framework to question God's existence. Malory wouldn't have had the mental tools to understand what an atheist *was*.

"Dodinal's faithlessness is intended as a satire on the nominalism of Occam, of the philosophers and early scientists of Malory's time. People who professed not to believe in the existence of the supernatural in a world which, to Malory and his contemporaries, was still full of wonder."

Dr Katherin Ann Lee (Laesi Fortes, Aevum), however, argues that "skepticism was rife by the fifteenth century. The ontological proof was already four hundred years old; why produce a proof of the existence of God if there's no question of it? Malory himself was dubious about the authority of the Church – consider the prevalence of wise hermits and holy ladies in the *Morte*, as opposed to priests and ministers, and the corrupt, sinister power of Rome in Book II – and may have been questioning the whole Christian mindset. Sir Dodinal's outlook on the world, and the tension between his materialism and the existence of creatures like the Questing Beast, arose from Malory exploring his own ideas about faith and the world."

MORE THAN ANYTHING, though, in both the *Lesser Dodinal* and the *Second Book*, Dodinal is an *outsider*. Among knights of royal lineage, he was born a peasant; among the ceaseless tourneys and banquets, he is most at home in the trackless wild; among those who quest for glory or honour, he seeks only to quench his boundless rage; and among Christians, he is and steadfastly remains a heathen.

And being an outsider, he is ideally placed to observe and pass comment on his world. As a young man, he watches Arthur's men as "they slitt the throtes of theer enemies and gave mercie unto theer allyen." With a slight change of emphasis – casually murdering their enemies, giving mercy to their allies – he emphasises the blandly awful nature of medieval warfare, undermining Arthur's chivalry at their first meeting.

As his comrades and peers still seek to make their names as heroes, he reflects that they're all growing older, and should be grateful that they do not have to face the Saxon menace again. And even when confronted with proof of the supernatural in the form of the Questing Beast, he questions whether it should be regarded as the cause of the nameless village's downfall, or as an excuse. Did the Beast inspire the villagers' incest, or was it drawn to it? In many ways, this is the major question of the story: are all our beliefs about ourselves and the world merely excuses for our conduct?

WHICH BRINGS US back around to civilisation, and savagery. Ultimately, "The worthie Tale of Sir Dodinale the savage Knyght" is a story about crime: specifically, murder and incest, two of the worst crimes one can commit, and the antithesis of civilisation.

For all that he was motivated by revenge, and fought for the King, Dodinal sees himself – in his fury and violence – as a murderer, and unfit for the sanctity of Camelot. He drives himself through the wild, punishing himself, looking for a just death. The villagers in the hills, in turn, have committed incest, and are punished by their own progeny, and allow themselves to pass into history.

And Dodinal finds he cannot judge them. Incest and murder are reflections of one another, he believes, and the uncontrollable lust they felt on the night they condemned themselves feels too like the blinding hate that comes upon him in battle.

But Dodinal, who judges the world around him so impartially, cannot truly see himself. His rage is terrible, of course, but he exercises constant restraint, and not once in the story lays hand on anyone who does not merit it. The outsider, the heathen, the humble peasant turned knight, more at home in the wild and in the company of beasts, proves to be the true champion of civilisation.

Also available in this series

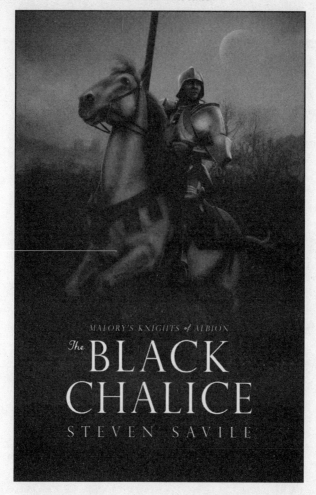

MALORY'S KNIGHTS of ALBION

The BLACK CHALICE

STEVEN SAVILE

UK ISBN: 978 1 907519 66 6 • US ISBN: 978 1 907519 67 3 • £7.99/$9.99

Son of a knight and aspirant to the Round Table, Alymere yearns to take his place in the world, and for a quest to prove his worth. He comes across the foul Devil's Bible – said to have been written in one night by an insane hermit – which leads and drives him, by turns, to seek the unholy Black Chalice. On his quest he will face, and overcome, dire obstacles and cunning enemies, becoming a knight of renown; but the ultimate threat is to his very soul.

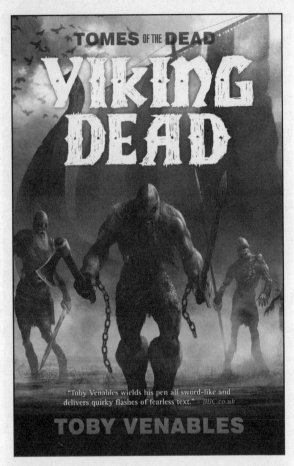

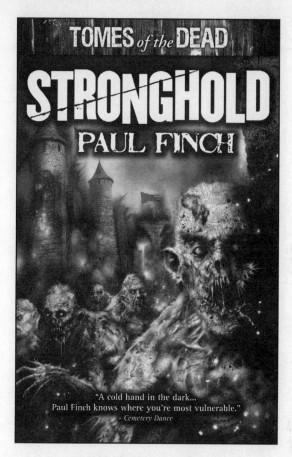

TOMES *of the* DEAD

STRONGHOLD
PAUL FINCH

"A cold hand in the dark...
Paul Finch knows where you're most vulnerable."
- *Cemetery Dance*

ISBN: 978 1 907519 10 9 • £7.99/$9.99

Ranulf, a young English knight sent to recapture Grogen Castle from Welsh rebels, comes into conflict with his leaders over their brutal methods. Unbeknownst to any of them, the native druids are planning a devastating counterattack, using an ancient artifact to summon an army that even the castle's superstitious medieval defenders could never have imagined.

Grogen Castle, seemingly impregnable to assault — armed with fiendish devices to slaughter would-be attackers in their multitudes — is besieged by countless, tireless soldiers forged from bone and raddled flesh. As lives are held in the balance, Ranulf must defy his masters and rescue the daughter of his enemy, but hope lasts only so long as the stronghold holds out against the legions of the angry dead...

WWW.ABADDONBOOKS.COM
Follow us on Twitter! www.twitter.com/abaddonbooks